Dilly's Girls

Dilly's Girls

A BLETCHLEY PARK MUSICAL

David Dell

First published in Great Britain in 2021

Editing, Design, typesetting and publishing by UK Book Publishing
www.ukbookpublishing.com

ISBN: 978-1-914195-58-7

Contents

Preface

BLETCHLEY PARK WAS THE HOME of Britain's codebreakers during the Second World War.

My story centres around the leading codebreaker at Bletchley Park, a man called Dillwyn Knox, known to everyone as 'Dilly', and his team of ladies who did much of their work in the cottage by the Bletchley Mansion.

Hollywood has ensured that the name associated with the codebreaking activities at Bletchley Park will forevermore be that of Alan Turing. But Knox had been breaking codes at the Admiralty during the First World War, was Chief Codebreaker at Bletchley, and was one of the few to successfully transfer from the manual ciphers of The Great War to the mechanical ciphers of World War Two.

I first encountered 'Dilly' while watching a play about the maths genius Alan Turing. It was a student production of 'Breaking the Code', and my son (also a gifted mathematician) was the director. The play presented an interpretation of Turing's story but also featured a character based on Knox.

Whether accidental or researched, the young man portraying Dilly did a first-class job, and I was intrigued by this tall, gangly, and highly eccentric character as he hobbled around the stage with his stick and pipe.

A family day out to Bletchley Park followed, which included a highly informative tour, and I was hooked.

The more I researched Bletchley, the more Dilly's name stood out. Perhaps what struck me more than anything was the love and affection those that worked in his section had for him.

Dilly was a brilliant mathematician in his youth, but ultimately went on to study Classics at Cambridge.

He grew up the second oldest of four brothers, all highly intelligent and gifted. From an early age he had a passion for puzzles and logic. He loved the 'chopped logic' of Lewis Carroll. He wrote poetry, inventing new types of poem and rhyme. Dilly and his brothers were devoted Punch readers – a weekly satire magazine – and they once wrote to Arthur Conan Doyle pointing out all the plot errors in his Sherlock Holmes stories.

During the First World War, Dilly worked at the Admiralty as a codebreaker in what became known as 'Room 40', later to become Section 25 of Naval Intelligence Division (ID25).

At the end of the Great War, Dilly and his good friend and fellow codebreaker Frank Birch wrote a skit about ID25 based on Alice's Adventures in Wonderland. It was performed by the codebreakers in pantomime style during a concert held to celebrate the end of the First World War in 1918. Frank wrote the story and Dilly wrote the poems. They called it 'Alice in ID25'.

Concerts were also staged by the codebreakers at Bletchley Park during the Second World War. Various events were held in the old dining hall in the mansion, there were dances in Elmer's School hall (the school was right next to Bletchley Park and was being used by the codebreakers during the war), and many musical performances and plays were put on in the nearby and recently constructed Assembly Hall which boasted a 'proper' stage.

These shows were often of a high quality with expert writing, musicianship and acting due to the varied backgrounds of many of the staff working at the Park, which included professionals from all these fields.

DILLY'S GIRLS tells the true story of Dilly and his team of codebreaking ladies as a fictional show, put on in the Assembly Hall to celebrate the end of the war and to recognise one of Bletchley's most beloved characters.

All the references to Knox in this production are true and many come directly from the ladies that worked with him. He really did put a sandwich in his pipe and once mistook a cupboard for the cottage door!

Preface

Although all historical references are true, they are not all depicted in chronological order. For example, Jean did not join the team until ISK was up and running and she did not turn up at Bletchley carrying a suitcase, though many did. Dilly in fact drove to her house for her interview since she lived nearby. But it is true that her interview consisted of just a single question.

Above all, the aim of this book is to highlight the fact that more than three quarters of the staff at Bletchley during the Second World War were women. Knox insisted that only ladies could work on his team and he was always pushing for their recognition via promotion and equal pay. He respected and valued his staff and when he was awarded the CMG medal just before his death, he immediately had it sent to Bletchley to be hung in the cottage saying that the award had been earned by the girls.

Knox was genuinely adored by the ladies who worked for him.

All of the 'songs' in this book were written with melodies in mind, but sadly I lack the musical skills to be able to share with you what I hear when I read the words. I hope that as you read the lines you might imagine the tunes and see yourself sat in the Assembly Hall watching all the codebreakers perform.

Who knows, someone with the musical knowhow might one day stumble across my efforts and be inspired to turn my lyrics into actual music!

But even if you just read the 'songs' as a form of poetry you will still very much be in Dilly's world, because he loved to write poems and verse throughout his life. So, it is fitting in a way that large sections of this book about Dilly and his team of ladies are given over to rhyme.

This book first recounts the fictional events of the evening in the Assembly Hall as the show is staged, with all the scripted passages shown indented and in a different font. It is a musical script within a story. The second half of the book is then given over to more detail about the historical context of the events portrayed in this fictional codebreaker's production.

Those that lived through the Second World War really were our 'Greatest Generation'. Many men and women made the ultimate sacrifice so that we can enjoy the freedoms we do today. This is also touched on as the story of two sailors who died while retrieving crucial German codebooks is told during the song 'Atlantic Convoy'.

I never imagined that I would ever attempt to write a book, but as Dilly so often told the girls in the cottage, 'nothing is impossible'.

For my sons who both love musical theatre.

PART ONE

Dilly's Girls

ACT I

Prologue

FRANK BIRCH TOOK A MOMENT to peek out through the curtains at the side of the stage into the Assembly Hall.

The hall was certainly the most wonderful facility and the codebreakers of Bletchley Park had made full use of it during the war, staging various shows from Shakespeare plays to their own self-penned revues.

It boasted a full stage with wings where steps led down on each side to either a door out into the main hall, or if you turned in the opposite direction, to a backstage area that included several rooms and even a kitchen.

The main hall area was large and could easily seat several hundred people. The core centre block was a little wider than the stage and ran back under a large gabled roof. The side walls dropped down from the roof and then the roof spanned out to give half as much floor space again on either side. Tonight, every single bit of this space would be used, since it seemed that almost everyone that worked at Bletchley had wanted to be there.

A balcony ran across the back wall of the hall. Up on the balcony there was a whole collection of lights of all shapes and sizes, all of which had been craftily procured from various army and service stores by the Bletchley Dramatic Society during the war years.

Frank felt a slight pain of regret as he took in the pre-show excitement all around. He had not taken part in any of the productions at Bletchley during the war and had only just begun to realise how much he had missed life in the theatre.

Opening night was always so special, whether in the West End or in an amateur production just like this one. That special feeling was always the same. There was nothing quite like it. He smiled as he watched the members of the band who were seated just in front of the stage busily tuning up. Many of them were professional musicians before the war and Frank had marvelled at the quality of their playing during rehearsals. Behind the band, guests were now filling the hall and taking their seats. The hall was buzzing with the sound of excited chatter.

Frank Birch was a professional actor and had appeared in the West End between the wars. He had also been a theatrical producer and director, staging several productions at the Cambridge Festival Theatre.

He had, however, worked as a codebreaker during the Great War of 1914-1918 and it was because of this background that he had found himself back at the Government Code & Cipher School – or GC&CS – and part of the Bletchley scene when war had broken out again in 1939.

Frank had been very much a key part of that scene, in fact, as he had headed up the Naval Section in Hut 4, which had played a big part in the effort to break Enigma, the electro-mechanical cipher machine that had been used by the Germans and which had been the nemesis of so many at Bletchley. But being so focused on the codebreaking job in hand meant that he had completely missed out on the various theatrical activities at Bletchley during the war.

'Hello Frank, you look miles away.'

Frank quickly turned and immediately broke out into a broad smile.

'Oh, my dear Mavis, how wonderful you look.'

Mavis Batey was a Bletchley codebreaking legend but performing on stage was something she had never tried before. Frank had not doubted for one moment that she would be anything but dazzling, and from the very first rehearsal he knew that she would excel on the boards just as she did at everything else she turned her hand to.

Mavis gave Frank a quick playful curtsy and twirl.

'I never dreamt I'd end up doing anything like this; what have you got me into, Mr Birch?'

'My dear, if I only had a shilling for every time I've heard someone say that to me this evening I wouldn't have to work again!'

Prologue

Frank and Mavis laughed and embraced.

'That said, this was all your idea, you know, so you've only yourself to blame, my dear.'

This was true. When word got out that there was to be one final Bletchley Park revue to celebrate the end of the war, Mavis had thrown her suggestion into the hat along with all the others, and it had been her idea that had been chosen for this final show.

Mavis had wanted Bletchley to recognise the contribution of her old boss Dillwyn Knox, known to everyone as Dilly, who just like Frank had worked as a cryptographer during both world wars.

She had also put Frank's name forward to write and produce it, since not only had Frank and Dilly been very good friends, but the two of them had written their own show to celebrate the end of the First World War. It seemed to her the perfect way to mark the end of codebreaking here at Bletchley too.

Frank had met Dilly whilst studying history at Cambridge, and they soon became firm friends. Both men ended up working for the Admiralty in Naval Intelligence during the first war in a department known originally as Room-40 and then later as ID25, or Section 25 of Naval Intelligence Division.

Frank and Dilly were both admirers of Lewis Carroll, and their 1918 skit at the end of the war had been based on Carroll's book 'Alice's Adventures in Wonderland'. In their version, Alice found herself in Whitehall before suddenly sliding down a chute and dropping into a wire basket in one of the offices of ID25. Frank had written the story and Dilly had written all the poems.

'You've done such a wonderful job, Frank. I just know that Dilly would have approved had he been here.'

'Ah, thank you, Mavis, you're too kind. I did have lots of help, mind you, especially with the music. Who would have possibly guessed that one of the young ladies working in Hut 6 had been thinking up such wonderful melodies and tunes all this time while poring over those Enigma messages for hours on end? I am so glad she came to see me. Jo has really brought my words and lyrics to life.'

'Oh yes, I'm particularly fond of the song Keith and I sing. Joanna is such a talent.'

Frank could hear Jo giving her musicians some final instructions out front. She had been thrilled when he had asked her to take charge of the music for the show and conduct their little orchestra.

'There are some seriously talented people here at Bletchley,' Frank pondered out loud. 'Speaking of which, Mavis, how is your new husband coping with his first foray into the world of theatre?'

Mavis laughed.

'He is absolutely terrified, bless him, but he had no choice in the matter! I've just left him out by the side door pacing up and down, muttering his lines over and over.'

'Keith will be fine. I have no doubt whatsoever that anyone who can capture the heart of the famous Mavis Lever will have no problem with a bit of acting.'

'I think it's the singing that is worrying him the most!'

'Did I hear someone mention my name?'

Mavis's husband Keith appeared with a lady on his arm.

'Now look who I just found outside chatting to Denniston,' Keith announced.

'Hello, Keith,' said Frank. 'Ah, Olive, my dear, you made it! How wonderful it is to see you again. How are you?'

Olive was Dilly's wife and had known Frank since the days back at ID25. She had worked as Dilly's secretary at ID25 and then after the war she and Dilly had married and had shared a house for a while with the Birches in London. She had also become good friends with Mavis over the last few years.

'Oh, I'm fine, thank you, Frank. And thank you so much for the invite. I wouldn't have missed tonight for the world.' Olive turned to Mavis. 'Hello, Mavis.'

'Hello, Olive, it's so lovely to see you. I hope my husband has been looking after you.'

'Keith is the perfect gentleman; you are such a lucky girl, Mavis.'

'You haven't heard me trying to sing yet, Mrs Knox,' Keith chipped in. 'You may well change your mind by the end of the evening!'

Mavis reached out and held her husband's hand. She was so proud of him. She knew that he was only doing this show for her. Keith was such a reserved man, and it had been such a struggle sometimes to even get him to dance with her at the various Bletchley social events.

'I'm sure I won't, Keith.' Olive smiled at the young couple and then turned back to Frank. 'Dilly would have been so touched by all of this, thank you so much, Frank. You always produced a magical change in Dilly when you and he got together, and the boys always looked forward to your visits. Christopher once told me that he thought that you were the jolliest and most amusing man he had ever met.'

Mavis laughed. 'I'm not sure Hut 4 would agree with that, the Frank Birch we know and love at Bletchley has a bit of a reputation for being very strict indeed.'

'Well, Mavis, you should have seen his Widow Twankey in Aladdin; Dilly took us all down to London to see him at the Lyric Hammersmith. Frank got us front row seats and we all had a wonderful time. Now when was that, Frank, 1934 was it?'

Frank smiled. He had enjoyed his time on the stage between the wars and had even been on the big screen a few times having landed parts in several films.

'So, who is playing my husband tonight?' Olive asked. 'I am dying to know.'

'Ah! That would be The Dormouse!' Frank teased.

Olive looked puzzled for a moment and then burst out laughing.

'Oh, you mean Nigel! Nigel de Grey. I'm not sure what Dilly would have made of this news!'

Nigel de Grey had also been one of the original World War One cryptographers at the Admiralty. Working together it had been he and Dilly who broke the famous Zimmerman telegram that had finally brought America into the conflict. Nigel, therefore, had of course featured in Dilly and Frank's Alice in ID25 skit, and in it had been cast as the Dormouse.

'Actually, Olive, Nigel has been fantastic in rehearsals,' Mavis offered. 'He also played a big role persuading many of the others to take part.'

'Mavis is right; it did all work out rather well, didn't it? Nigel has been a big part of the amateur dramatic scene here at Bletchley and so he did not take much persuading, to be honest, and jumped at the chance of one of the lead roles. Of course, he knew Dilly well and being the Deputy Commander here at Bletchley he was able to twist some arms.

I mean, who would have believed that anyone could have talked Alan into appearing in something like this.'

'You mean Alan Turing?' Olive looked really surprised. 'Oh, bless him. He is such a shy man as I remember. Dilly was extremely fond of Alan. I remember him coming out to stay with us at Courns Wood just before the war.'

'Turns out he's not just a genius mathematician and a first-class athlete, but he can hold a tune as well,' sighed Keith.

'Yes, we have pretty much roped in everyone, Olive. We hope you approve of the lady that we have chosen to play you,' Frank teased.

Olive laughed and hugged Frank. 'I'm sure I will, Frank, but what about you? Surely you have a part too?'

'He's our Churchill, Olive,' Mavis offered. 'Seriously; if you close your eyes, you'd think it was actually the Prime Minister up there on the stage when Frank is doing his bit.'

'Oh, how wonderful! Christopher and Oliver used to love your impressions, Frank. I look forward to seeing you up on the stage again. Dilly always used to say that you were a born actor and quite a brilliant talker too.'

'Mr Birch! Mr Birch!'

'Oh, excuse me, Olive. Yes, Jean, what is it, dear?'

'It's almost time, Mr Birch!'

'Thank you, Jean.' Frank could not help but smile at Jean's obvious excitement. Jean was another of Dilly's team from the cottage and her enthusiasm throughout all the rehearsals had endeared her to everyone. He turned back to Olive. 'Olive, you must excuse me, things to attend to. Keith, would you mind making sure Olive gets to her seat please? She has one reserved down at the front next to Alistair and his wife. I hope you enjoy the show, Olive, and that Dilly would approve of what we've done.'

'I'm sure he would, Frank, good luck!'

Frank and Olive embraced once more. Frank looked round to Mavis and Jean, 'Right, come along, ladies, we have a show to put on!'

Keith and Olive turned to head down the steps at the edge of the stage while Frank, Mavis and Jean walked back across the stage behind the curtains.

Prologue

Frank could see Bill Marchant – the deputy head of Hut 3 – and his wife across the stage talking to Barbara Abernethy, who would be the first character seen by the audience when the show began.

The Marchants were widely respected amongst the Bletchley theatrical fraternity and had produced all the big revues in the Assembly Hall throughout the war. They seemed to Frank to have raised the bar even higher than normal for this final production, and just walking back across the stage Frank could not take his eyes off the magnificent painted backdrop and the stunning scenery that lay in wait to astonish the audience. He wondered if there had ever before been such a varied collection of highly talented and skilled people brought together to work towards a common cause as there had been at Bletchley these last few years.

The set was beautifully simple in appearance but fiendishly clever behind the scenes. An office in the mansion had been recreated stage-right. There was a side wall with a door that ran down the side of the stage and then a back wall which protruded out at a right angle for about three yards, but it had been cleverly done in such a way that it could be quickly folded away or completely detached if needed.

This design was mirrored stage-left, but here made to replicate a room in the cottage where Dilly and his girls had worked. Both back walls were currently folded-back ready for the opening scene.

Centre-stage was free of props allowing full view of the backdrop, which was a wonderful painting of the Bletchley mansion. Frank made a mental note to find out just who it was that had done the painting: a talent like that should be working in the West End.

Just as Frank and the girls quickly made their way down the steps that led backstage, the house lights dropped and the excited chatter of the audience suddenly fell silent.

Frank touched both girls on the shoulder and whispered, 'Let's just watch the opening scene from out front. We can sneak back round the back when the overture starts. I want to see everyone's reaction.'

Both girls smiled, and Frank, Mavis and Jean quietly made their way out through the door by the side of the stage and into the audience, standing in the dark over to the side of the hall.

A hushed air of anticipation had descended around the hall. Everyone's eyes were glued to the stage which was still covered by the broad velvet drapes.

There was a loud clunk as a projector was switched on at the back of the hall and the following words suddenly appeared on the curtains:

This is a true story.

Everyone in the Assembly Hall cheered!

Another clunk from the projector saw a photograph of the Bletchley Park mansion appear.

The audience cheered again.

'Barbara took that picture,' whispered Frank, 'on the day Dilly and the others first came here.'

Barbara's Photograph

Captain Ridley's Shooting Party

THE SHOW WAS NOW UNDERWAY. A lady appeared on the left side of the stage in front of the curtain. She was dressed smartly in a typical late-1930s skirt-suit. Her jacket had squared shoulders and a narrow waist, and the matching tailored skirt fell to just below the knee. A pair of brogues, laced, flat-heeled Oxford style shoes completed her outfit, which was the same outfit that she had been wearing on the day she took the photograph that was still being projected onto the curtains. It was Barbara Abernethy, and she was carrying her large black Kodak camera.

The audience were now cheering again, and some were whistling too. Barbara smiled and could not resist a quick look out into the audience, though she could not see much because of the bright light from the projector. She opened her camera case, causing the lens to pop out and extend forward, and then pretended to set up the shot. As Barbara acted out the taking of the picture the projector clicked off and the curtains swung back, and the audience could now see some of the cast posed – as per the photograph – in front of the painting of the Bletchley mansion at the back of the stage.

The band was quiet. All that could be heard was a countryside soundscape: tweeting birds, wind in the trees, and the cries of a peacock.

Frank smiled. 'Someone in special effects is doing a grand job,' he thought to himself.

Barbara walked upstage and joined the group immediately in front of the mansion.

Two men were stood together downstage and to the right. One was Oliver Strachey and the other the highly eccentric Alfred Dillwyn 'Dilly' Knox, who was, as he always was, puffing on his pipe.

Dilly & Oliver

Strachey: You have to hand it to Sinclair, Dilly; this really is the perfect place.

Dilly: Hmmm.

Strachey: Absolutely perfect. Can you believe that the train station is literally at the end of the lane?

The journey up here this morning from London could not have been easier.

Dilly continued to puff on his pipe.

Strachey: Not only that but turns out Bletchley is a key rail junction too, North-South and East-West. The so-called Varsity Line will certainly help Denniston's plan of recruiting academics from Oxford and Cambridge.

Dilly murmured in agreement again.

Strachey: Did you know that the Ministry would not give Sinclair a penny toward relocating us and so he bought this place out of his own pocket?

Dilly nodded, sucked on his pipe, and muttered in agreement once more.

Strachey: He saw what the bombing did in Spain and knew he had to get us out of London with war imminent. Away from the Jerry spies too. But this place is perfect. Isn't the house great?

Dilly was now busily scraping the inside of his pipe.

Strachey: Which room have you claimed, Dilly, old boy? Denniston has chosen Lady Leon's morning room. You know; the one to the left of the main entrance? As the Commander I suppose he is entitled to first dibs. Old 'Nobby' Clarke has picked the library for his naval section. Tiltman's bagged the dining room and Cooper has got his air section in the drawing room. So which room have you selected for your team, Dilly? I didn't see you in the house with the others earlier.

Dilly was still fiddling with his pipe and was now packing it with some more tobacco.

Dilly: My section is going to be in the cottage, Oliver.
Strachey: The cottage? What cottage? You don't mean that old groom's cottage in the stable yard? What, with all the pigeons?
Dilly: Indeed.

Strachey laughed and slapped his old friend on the back.

Strachey: Good for you, old man! Good for you!

As Dilly and Oliver turned and smiled at one another the rest of the cast began to walk down-stage toward the two intrepid codebreakers.

Ridley: Excellent! Excellent! That should do us for our first visit. We will start to get things a bit more organised tomorrow. Now where are those cars, they should have been here by now. I have arranged for a welcome lunch back at the Bridge Hotel in Bedford.

Two women ATS drivers appeared on the stage.

Ridley: Ah, Excellent! You must be here for us?
Driver: Yes, sir. I believe so. I have been told to collect Captain Ridley's Shooting Party.

Some of the others laughed at this reference to a 'Shooting Party' as they turned and left the stage. Dilly, however, hung back and stood alone on stage for a few moments. He turned to look back at the mansion as he struck a match and cupped his pipe with his hands, trying to light it. Strachey reappeared.

Strachey: Come on, Dilly old man. We are all hungry you know!

Dilly managed to relight his pipe, took a couple of puffs, and paused for a moment.

`Dilly: Yes, Oliver, you are right. It is perfect.`

The two men walked offstage. The lights went down as the curtains closed once more and the band began to play the overture. Meanwhile, back in the auditorium, Frank moved to usher Mavis and Jean back toward the door by the stage.

'Come on, you two,' Frank urged, 'we need to get you backstage now. Bill will be wondering where his leading ladies have got to!'

Jean's Arrival

FRANK WAS RIGHT.

'Oh, my dear, Jean, there you are! Quick, quick, you should be on the other side of the stage already. Oh, my word, I thought we had lost you.'

'Sorry, Bill old boy. It was my fault entirely,' Frank explained. 'I dragged the girls out front to see the opening scene.'

'Not to worry, Frank. All is well now. Here's your bag, Jean, oh and your hat.'

Jean smiled. 'Thank you, Bill,' and then gave him a huge hug. 'Thank you for everything. You and Mrs Marchant have been so kind to me through all the rehearsals.'

'You have a wonderful talent, Jean, such a lovely voice. Now hurry!'

Jean hugged Bill once more and then turned and hugged Mavis too.

'Go knock them for six, Jean,' Mavis told her friend. 'The rest of us will see you on stage shortly.'

The girls hugged again, and Jean set off across the stage behind the curtain.

The overture sounded amazing, and Jean could not resist a twirl as she skipped across the stage.

'Careful, miss!'

She had almost hit one of the stagehands with her bag. Two men were busy positioning a sentry gatepost set piece in the middle of the stage. Both men grinned and one gave Jean a cheeky wink.

'Sorry,' Jean mouthed as she ran over to the far side of the stage where Mrs Marchant was waiting.

'This is it, Jean. Just sing like you did in all the rehearsals.'

'I will.' Jean smiled. 'Thank you so much, Mrs Marchant.'

Jean stood in the wing clutching her bag and waiting for her cue. She had been totally surprised when she was selected to play the lead role, well one of the main roles at least. Margaret and Mavis had insisted that all the girls audition and she had thoroughly enjoyed the whole experience.

The orchestra was quietening down: just a piano and a violin playing now. This was it. Mrs Marchant touched her shoulder and smiled. Jean grinned back; her heart was thumping wildly but she could not wait to get started.

The curtains partially swung back, revealing the sentry-post and two soldiers stood beside it. The soldiers were puffing on cigarettes and quietly acting out yet another boring sentry duty guarding the entrance to Bletchley.

Jean stepped out onto the stage just in front of the curtain, and the audience cheered once more. She looked down at Jo for her cue, and then began to sing.

Jean: *I'm here for a job*
Oh, my name is Jean
I hope they don't tell me I'm too young,
you see, I'm just seventeen.

The Wrens told me 'No'
Said I was too young
But I'm good at Maths, so applied to work here,
it had to be done.

I'm so willing to work.
Will make sure that I do it right.
So want to be able to help,
Be part of my country's fight.

Though I really don't understand Bletchley
and what it all means...

So full of hope
I know that I can.
I'm so not a joke.
I'm as good as a man.
I'm so full of hope.

The last note hung for several seconds until Jo swung her arm and the band cut. The hall erupted in cheering and applause. The show was well and truly on its way now.

Jean approached the guards by the sentry-post at the Bletchley Park entrance; one was a sergeant and the other a private.

Arrival

Jean's Arrival

Sergeant: Hello there, Miss. Can I see your papers please?
Jean: Yes of course.

Jean reached inside her bag for her papers and then held them out toward the Sergeant.

Jean: Here you are, sir. My name is Jean Orme and I am here for a job interview. I am here to see a Mr Knox.
Sergeant: Old Dilly, eh? So, you're going to be one of Dilly's Girls, are you?
Jean: Excuse me?
Private: Dillwyn Knox, Miss. He only allows ladies in his section. Dilly's Fillies! Reckons you ladies have what it takes.
Sergeant: You are to see him in the main house, Miss. I will escort you. It's this way.
Jean: "Dilly's Fillies"? Really, sergeant, are you serious?
Sergeant: Sorry, ma'am, we really don't mean any harm. But Professor Knox will only work with ladies. Only ladies are allowed on his team.
Jean: Ah, so he's a bit of a ladies man, is he?

Jean's question made the sergeant roar with laughter.

Sergeant: Oh no, ma'am! Not at all! You wait 'till you meet him. You will see. Reckon he just thinks you ladies have a greater aptitude for the work required, that is all. The nimbleness of a lady's mind, I suppose. He probably thinks you all have far more attention for detail than a lot of us blokes have, and he is probably right!

The sergeant laughed again.

```
Sergeant: Welcome to the biggest lunatic asylum in
   Britain, Miss. The main house is just up here.
Jean: Is that where his team works?
Sergeant: Oh no, Miss. Dilly's ladies all work in the
   Cottage.
```

The band started up for the next song of the show and the curtains opened fully to reveal the stage now with the mansion office stage-right and the room in the cottage stage-left. Two stagehands quickly ran on and removed the sentry barrier.

Jean and the sergeant walked back toward the huge painting of the mansion which was still showing at the back of the stage. As they turned to their left to disappear from sight behind the back of the mansion office, Jean could not resist a quick look over her right shoulder and across the stage where she knew her friends would be waiting ready to come on. All six were smiling and waving at her. Jean grinned back giving them a disguised wave, trying her best to keep her arm against her coat so that hopefully nobody in the audience would notice.

Jean knew that her defining memory of her time at Bletchley during the war would be of the friendship and the camaraderie that had existed between all the girls in the cottage. Jean was in total awe of the likes of Margaret and Mavis, and while she didn't fully understand the maths and logic behind many of the jobs she had learned to do, she had become rather good at using the techniques she had been taught, particularly Dilly's 'rods'. The cottage had been such a lovely place to work, and Dilly had been the most wonderful of bosses. Jean was so proud to have been one of Dilly's Girls.

Dilly's Girls – Part I

THE INTRODUCTION TO the second song was now well underway and the audience were all clapping along to the upbeat tempo.

Claire Harding caught the attention of the other five ladies, Margaret, Mavis, Joyce, Elizabeth – more familiarly known as Betty – and Flo.

'Right, that's it. Come on, we had better get going; we are on in a second. Let's show them what Dilly's Girls are made of!'

The others all smiled, and they made their way around the back of the wooden set of the cottage readying themselves behind its door on the side of the stage out of view of the audience.

Bill Marchant was there waiting for them.

'Now, off you go,' he whispered.

'Good luck, girls.' Frank was there too, and he and Claire exchanged smiles.

Claire opened the cottage door and strode out onto the stage followed by the rest of the girls.

They were all greeted by yet another huge cheer from the crowd – the biggest yet – and Claire began to sing.

Claire: *You will find us in the cottage*
by the mansion.

Always busy working focused on our jobs.
We're working on Italian Enigma.
And we're breaking it by using Dilly's Rods!

Margaret: *Knox's Rodding's a linguistic*
type of method.
An idea that was developed by our man.
We've used it to decrypt Italian signals.
But the trick is not to tell them that we can!

Mavis: *The Rods – or "Sticks" –*
are issued in three colours,
They come in either red or blue or green.
Each stick is marked with every single letter,
One of the neatest little systems that you've seen!

ALL: *They call us Dilly's Girls*
Or Dilly's Fillies!
Betty: *Only ladies are permitted on our crew.*
ALL: *Do we mind?*
Don't be silly!
Margaret: *Solving the Enigma's what we do!*

ALL: *We're Dilly's Girls*
Dilly's Fillies!
Joyce: *You've always got to think*
outside the box.
ALL: *Clues to find!*
Count on Dilly!
Flo: *So proud to be the team of Dillwyn Knox!*

As Flo sang that final line of the first chorus, the door of the mansion office across the stage opened and Dilly Knox appeared. It was, of course, Nigel de Grey playing the part of Dilly, but he was certainly most convincing. The girls had teased Nigel endlessly during rehearsals about the fact that

Dilly's Girls

he was too short and had far too much hair to be Dilly. But despite these obvious differences Nigel was otherwise very precise in his tribute to his old friend. He was limping and using Dilly's old walking stick as he manoeuvred around the table in the office. After crashing his motorcycle between the wars and badly smashing his leg, Dilly had walked with a bad limp and required the trusted assistance of his walking stick to get by. Dilly was trying to find his glasses and watching Nigel act this out reminded Claire that she had spent endless hours over the last few years searching through piles of paper and messages looking for her boss' spectacles. If it were not his glasses that had gone missing it would have been his pipe.

Along with Joyce and Betty, Claire had been one of the first girls to join Dilly's section in the cottage after it was set up in August 1939. Claire and Betty's fathers had been members of Commander Denniston's Ashtead Golf Club and this was how they had ended up at Bletchley. That was the way it had worked in those early days, with workers being selected through word of mouth.

Claire was a little older than the other ladies and had been 27 when she had joined. Dilly had very quickly recognised her organisational skills and she was soon appointed as the Office Manager in the cottage.

This scene had been choreographed by Bill and Frank such that Dilly would appear busy in his office and not aware of any of the ladies dancing and singing around him. Nigel had been frustratingly good at totally ignoring all the commotion around him during rehearsals, but the girls were determined to try and get a reaction on opening night.

Claire: *Alfred Dillwyn "Dilly" Knox*
grew up in Kibworth
Flo: *To Eton was the place he headed next*
Mavis: *And finally to the college*
King's in Cambridge
Margaret: *A Classics scholar in the joys*
of ancient texts!

Mavis: *So the first code Dilly faced*
was not Enigma
Margaret: *But instead an ancient scroll that*
someone found
Betty: *At a dig about one hundred miles*
from Cairo
Joyce: *For 2000 years lay buried in the ground!*

Betty: *In World War I recruited by the Navy.*
Claire: *Now here's a fact if you promise*
not to laugh
Mavis: *He joined their crypto-logical research team*
Flo: *Where they say he did his best*
work in the bath!

The girls had secretly asked Frank if he thought it would be possible to have Flo pushed onto the stage in an old bath when she sang this line and he had jumped at the idea. A suitable old bathtub had been found and one of the set builders had fitted some wheels. All of this had been arranged without Nigel knowing. Claire had been watching Nigel as Flo appeared on stage sat in the bath, but despite the audience laughing and cheering he had not flinched from his concentrated performance and Claire made a mental note to congratulate him afterward.

ALL: *They call us Dilly's Girls*
Or Dilly's Fillies!
Betty: *Only ladies are permitted on our crew.*
ALL: *Do we mind?*
Don't be silly!
Margaret: *Solving the Enigma's what we do!*

ALL: *We're Dilly's Girls*
Dilly's Fillies!
Joyce: *You've always got to think*
outside the box.
ALL: *Clues to find!*
Count on Dilly!
Mavis: *So proud to be the team of Dillwyn Knox!*

Joyce: *Between the wars he continued*
his code breaking.
Betty: *And then did something really rather cool.*
Claire: *With the help of those around him*
he created
Mavis: *The Government Code and Cipher School!*

Mavis: *Soon after that he purchased an Enigma*
And even though it was against all odds
With a method using coloured strips of cardboard
He worked out how to break it with his Rods!

Margaret: *A new German one upgraded with a Stecker*
How the keyboard mapped he really
should have guessed

When he found out from his Polish
friends near Warsaw
Dilly's methods once again could do the rest!

ALL: *They call us Dilly's Girls*
Or Dilly's Fillies!
Betty: *Only ladies are permitted on our crew.*
ALL: *Do we mind?*
Don't be silly!
Margaret: *Solving the Enigma's what we do!*

ALL: *We're Dilly's Girls*
Dilly's Fillies!
Joyce: *You've always got to think*
outside the box.
ALL: *Clues to find!*
Count on Dilly!
Mavis: *So proud to be the team of Dillwyn Knox!*

Claire: *Although our Dilly's only in his 50s*
Joyce: *He's looking so much older than his days*
Claire: *The pressure he is under is enormous*
Flo: *But I doubt we'll ever make him*
change his ways.

Margaret: *Lately he's been looking really poorly*
Mavis: *Working so much harder than he should*
Flo: *He only stops to eat when we remind him*
Betty: *We've told him without rest he'll be no good.*

Claire: *And now he's such a key man here*
at Bletchley.
So dear to us and we all love him so.
He built his team of ladies and we adore him,
Breaking codes at Bletchley here we go!

Dilly's Girls – Part I

ALL: *They call us Dilly's Girls*
Or Dilly's Fillies!
Betty: *Only ladies are permitted on our crew.*
ALL: *Do we mind?*
Don't be silly!
Margaret: *Solving the Enigma's what we do!*

ALL: *We're Dilly's Girls*
Dilly's Fillies!
Joyce: *You've always got to think outside the box.*
ALL: *Clues to find!*
Count on Dilly!
Flo: *So proud to be the team of Dillwyn Knox!*

ALL: *We're so proud to be the team of Dillwyn Knox!*

Throughout this last song Keith Batey had been stood waiting behind the cottage door. He had instantly regretted agreeing to be part of the production, but he had realised just how much this meant to his new wife and he did not want to disappoint her. Besides, he doubted that he would have had much of a choice anyway since Mavis was a force to be reckoned with.

He and Mavis had started dating when he had joined Dilly's ISK section, but they had known one another for about a year before that.

He had been a mass of nerves all day worrying about tonight's show, but for the last five minutes Keith had stood in the stage wing on the back side of the wooden set wall listening to his beloved Mavis and the other girls singing with such gusto and joy, and he had just felt so relaxed and happy.

Hearing the girls singing put Keith in mind of his very first day at Bletchley when he had to sit through a talk about Enigma being given by Hugh Alexander in the mansion. Alexander was one of the leading experts on Enigma at Bletchley. It had not been the most riveting of presentations. The Enigma machine had in fact been broken and this had really flustered Alexander who had struggled to make anything like a coherent talk. Keith had fortunately been sat by a window and he now chuckled to himself as he remembered spending most of that hour looking outside watching all the young ladies busy going about their business in the park and thinking how much he was going to love working here at Bletchley.

Keith had heard about Mavis Lever before they even met, since she was already somewhat of a Bletchley star. Keith was not sure about love at first sight, but Mavis had certainly caught his eye the night they first met when she appeared in Hut 3 with a message that needed attention, and now they were husband and wife.

'Are you alright, Keith?'

It was Frank.

'I'm fine, thank you, Frank, in fact more than fine.' Keith grinned. 'I never thanked you for writing the song for Mavis and me. I cannot begin to tell you how much it means to us. Thank you, Frank.'

Frank beamed back at his friend.

'Go knock 'em dead, my boy!'

The girls had finished their song and the hall was filled with applause, whistles and yet more cheering.

Keith waited for the noise to settle down, smiled again at Frank, took a deep breath, and knocked loudly on the cottage door. The door swung open, and Keith was momentarily taken aback by the bright lights illuminating the cottage. It had been quite dark stood in the wing. It really did feel as if he were about to step into some other strange world.

`Flo: Oh hello, Mr Batey! Do come in.`

Keith stepped through the door into the bright light and onto the stage, joining the girls in the cottage. His direction had been to act a little awkward, as if in awe of the girls, especially Mavis who – the script had stressed much to his young wife's amusement – he was sweet on.

Keith had known before he stepped through the door that little acting would be needed on his part because he found the whole experience of being up on the stage in front of everyone terrifying, and that had been just in rehearsal. He immediately caught his wife's eye. Mavis was doing a wonderful job of acting coy and somewhat embarrassed to see him. Keith could feel his cheeks beginning to flush. Now, just get that first line out, it is only three words.

Keith: Thank you, Flo.
Margaret: Hello, Keith. Have you come to see Mavis?
Keith: Ah, hello. Good morning, Miss Rock. Ladies, Miss Lever...

Keith caught himself and corrected the formality he had used to address his wife.

Keith: Hello, Mavis.
Mavis: Good morning, Keith.
Keith: Ah, I am looking for Dilly. Is he about?
Betty: He is over at the mansion this morning.
Keith: Ah, right. How are you today, Mavis?

Mavis was sitting at the cottage table sorting some papers.

Mavis: I am fine, thank you, Keith. As busy as ever, well you know.
Keith: Yes of course. Right, I will be off over to the main house then. Good morning, ladies.
Claire: Cheerio, Keith. Be aware that Dilly might not be free right now. He is interviewing a new girl for the team this morning.
Keith: Ah, right, thank you, Claire. Good morning, ladies.
ALL: Morning, Keith!
Mavis: Will I see you for lunch, Keith?
Keith: Oh yes! That would be lovely. Shall we say the usual time?
Mavis: All being well.

Keith nervously stepped back through the cottage door, exhaled a huge sigh of relief, and decided that despite all his worries he had quite enjoyed that after all.

Meanwhile on stage the girls were all laughing and had begun to tease Mavis.

Betty: So, come on then, Mavis, when is he going to ask you out?

Flo: Dilly says you do not want to be dating a mathematician as mathematicians are far too dull.

Joyce: Dull as dishwater I would say.

Betty: Dullest of the dull!

Mavis: Well, mine isn't!

Mavis stood up from the table and turned to face the audience. She quickly looked down and nodded at Jo who waved her arm and the band struck up the introduction to Mavis's special song. Breaking Enigma was a piece of cake compared to this, she thought, and she took in a deep breath.

Quod Erat Demonstrandum

Mavis: *Oh, why would you date a mathematician?*
That's all I ever hear them say.
Geeky, dull and dreary
So intense and never cheery
But I know you're really not at all that way.

But if theorems fill your books
Whether Euler's, Swan's or Cook's
Euclid's, Riemann's, Cox or Bell I just don't mind
Fermat's, Bertrand's, Wilkes, Lotz-Nagell
Pythagoras, Brooks or Abel
All that matters is you're courteous
and kind

You must know that I like you
And I'm sure that you like me

Our equation is resolved
Q.E.D.

Dilly's Girls

Did you ever? No not never!
Men so odd, but oh so clever!
Brought together for the war at Bletchley Park

A little freaky? Yes, completely!
Genii, but oh so geeky!
Oxbridge boffins all so keen to make their mark.

Oh why would you date a mathematician?
When is he going to ask me out?
I've flirted, posed and smiled
Oh why is this such a trial?
We'd be so good together I've no doubt.

And if numbers are your line
Transcendental, Real or Prime
Complex, Perfect, Base or Pi I just don't care
Transfinite or Trinomial
Natural, Rational, Binomial
All that matters is you're honourable and fair

You must know that I like you
And I'm sure that you like me

Our equation is resolved
Q.E.D.

A mathematics band of brothers
But you're so not like the others
I could see you were so different from
the start

But I have to ask you why
It is that you're so shy
Don't you realise you already have my heart?

Quod Erat Demonstrandum

Oh why would you date a mathematician?
Oh why can't I make him notice me?
He's so busy with his sums
What is there to be done?
But I know how happy we could be.

If trigonometry's your scene
Isosceles, Scalene
Equilateral, Obtuse, It's up to you.
Find the secant and the sine,
or the tangent works just fine?
All that matters is I know that you'll
be true.

You must know that I like you
And I'm sure that you like me

Our equation is resolved
Q.E.D.

Can't you see my raw elation?
You will solve my love equation
Simultaneously our love could then unfurl.

Quadratic, Linear,
Differential would concur,
The answer is that I must be your girl.

You must know that I like you
And I'm sure that you like me

Our equation is resolved
Q.E.D.

Mavis was by now standing right at the front of the stage. There had been a nervous crack in her voice right at the start of the song but now she was completely relaxed and was thoroughly enjoying the moment. The audience were quiet and totally captivated by Mavis's voice, Frank's lyrics, and Jo's music.

Mavis turned toward the back of the stage and was just a little relieved to see that Keith had walked out from behind the cottage perfectly on his cue. She knew just how worried he had been about tonight and when she saw him smile at her, and take a breath ready to sing his verse, she felt an overwhelming sense of love and admiration for her man.

Keith began to sing.

Keith: *Oh why would she want a mathematician?*
That's all I ever hear them say.
They say we're dull and dreary
So intense and never cheery
But I promise you I'm really not that way.

I so want to have her hear me
I would love to hold her near me
What are the chances if I asked her she'd say yes?
I could leave it with the Gods
But no, I'll calculate the odds
Maths will always be much better than a guess.

Mavis had walked over toward her husband while he was singing and they were now standing side by side, holding hands as they sang the final few lines together.

Mavis & Keith: *You must know that*
I like you
And I'm sure that you like me

Our equation is resolved
Q.E.D.

The hall erupted with applause.

'Well done, darling,' Mavis whispered to her husband. 'I so love you.'

Keith looked down at his pretty young wife. 'Piece of cake,' he smiled. 'I love you too.'

Mavis felt him lightly squeeze her hand and she watched as he turned away and continued across the stage behind the mansion. Mavis followed suit and headed back to the cottage where the rest of the girls had been watching her and Keith.

The lights went down on the cottage and came up on the office in the mansion.

Dillwyn Knox was back in the office sat at his desk. As usual, he was looking for something buried amongst all the papers piled up in front of him. This time it was his tobacco tin. There was a knock on the office door.

Dilly: Yes?

Secretary: Mr Knox, there is a Miss Orme here to see you, sir.

Dilly: Ah yes, thank you, Barbara. Please do come in, Miss Orme.

Jean nervously walked into the office and stood in front of the desk.

Dilly: Please sit down, my dear.

Jean sat down across the table from Nigel, who she noticed was still totally engrossed in his portrayal of her old boss. She could not help but smile. Suddenly the whole scene seemed to her as bizarre as she remembered that actual first meeting with Dilly had been. It had not been at Bletchley when Jean first met Dilly. Instead, Dilly had driven over to her house for the interview. Her father knew someone who knew someone, and her name had been put forward. The next thing she knew this odd man called Dillwyn Knox had arrived to interview her for a job which would be at some top-secret place that she knew nothing about. She had been feeling unwell that day and was in bed when his car pulled up outside.

She had quickly dressed and headed downstairs to be introduced. Jean remembered her first impression of Dilly had been of just how ill the poor man had looked. What a pair they had made that day.

Jean: Thank you, sir.
Dilly: Please, call me Dilly, everyone else here does.
Jean: Thank you, sir.
Dilly: So, you would like to join my team?
Jean: Yes please, sir.
Dilly: Do you speak any German?

Jean hesitated.

Jean: No, sir.
Dilly: Ah, that is a shame. It might have been helpful if you had a few words. Never mind, not to worry. Welcome aboard, Miss Orme. May I call you Jean?
Jean: Of course, sir. Is that it, sir?
Dilly: Ah, well I must warn you that my team is made up entirely of ladies. They are a lovely bunch, and I am sure you will fit in fine. They can be a little eccentric, mind you: one in particular is a very nice person but a little odd. She likes to wear trousers and a bowtie, and she smokes a pipe, you know.

Jean smiled again. She remembered an evening she had spent with Frank and Mavis in the Eight Bells pub discussing her interview with Dilly. Frank had written this first part of the scene almost word for word as Jean had remembered that first meeting at her parents' house. It had been such a strange affair. These were the only questions that Dilly had actually asked her. From this point on though Frank was now using artistic licence since Enigma would never have been mentioned outside of Bletchley.

Dilly: Now have you got any questions, Jean?
Jean: What exactly will I be doing, sir?

Jean remembered how Dilly had always loved to talk about Enigma. His eyes would light up at any chance to discuss this fiendishly clever encryption device. Nigel continued to mimic his old friend perfectly and Jean thought his reaction to her question was just as Dilly's would have been.

Dilly: Ah! Your job will be to help us to break the Italian Naval Enigma codes.
Jean: Enigma? What is Enigma, sir?

Suddenly, the lights cut out over the mansion office and the centre of the stage lit up. A disgruntled looking man wearing a white scientific laboratory overcoat marched on from the other side of the stage carrying a wooden box, which the audience immediately recognised as being an Enigma machine.

Scherbius: Enigma! Enigma! You do not know what Enigma is? Let me tell you about my beautiful Enigma.

The man was Arthur Scherbius, the inventor of the Enigma machine, or rather this was a senior cryptologist called Josh Cooper who was playing the part of Arthur Scherbius.

Frank Birch had wanted his Arthur Scherbius to be portrayed as the stereotypical mad professor and he had known from the off just who he had wanted to play the part. There was absolutely no evidence whatsoever that Scherbius had in any way been this sort of crazy professor character, but Frank wanted a comedic break in his production, and this song about the Enigma machine was going to be it.

Some years ago, Frank had seen a photograph of Scherbius and he had immediately noted a striking likeness between the German inventor and one of Bletchley's senior codebreakers, Josh Cooper. Both men had combed over hair, bushy eyebrows, round rimmed glasses, a well-defined nose, and a large bushy moustache. Not only this, but if his old friend Dilly Knox was widely recognised as the most eccentric of all the Bletchley cryptologists, then there was no doubt that Cooper was a close second and would be perfect to play Birch's eccentric scientist.

Josh Cooper was renowned at Bletchley for moments of complete madness, and more often than not these episodes appeared hilarious to those who witnessed them. Co-workers had seen him dissolve into a frenzied panic when a fire extinguisher accidentally went off in his hut. On another occasion, his instinct had caused him to jump to his feet and return a Nazi salute to a Luftwaffe officer at the start of what was to be a cross-examination. Realising his mistake, he had quickly gone to sit back down only to miss the chair completely and slide down under the table. Often, he would also suddenly shout out when an idea hit him causing those around him to jump; and his famous thinking pose was to stand with his right arm wrapped around the back of his head scratching his left ear.

Cooper was no stranger to the Bletchley theatrical scene. He had previously appeared in several of the revues where he had once been on stage dressed in desert fatigues. Having served in Palestine in the 1920s, his old uniform had seemed to him to be the perfect costume irrespective of how it had fitted into the scene in hand.

When Frank had approached Josh about playing Scherbius, he had jumped at the chance.

Cooper was followed onto the stage by six other characters. Three of the ladies from his German Air Force section were dressed in traditional Bavarian costume and three men appeared as German soldiers, all dressed in full Nazi Stormtrooper regalia.

Frank looked on from the stage wing and was very pleased with how it was all going so far. The audience loved the appearance on stage of all these odd Germanic characters, and the song had not even started yet. Cheers were mixed in with friendly jeers and boos, but laughter was the overriding reaction.

The cottage table had been discreetly moved to the centre of the stage and this is where Scherbius placed the Enigma machine.

Then as Dilly and Jean silently acted out the remainder of the interview in the background, Scherbius opened the Enigma machine and turned to address the audience with the Stormtroopers on one side of him and the Bavarian ladies on the other.

The band struck up the introduction to his song and Cooper began to sing.

My Beautiful Enigma

Scherbius: *My name is Arthur Scherbius,*
I'm a German engineer,
Inventor of machinery and a cipher pioneer.
I am always very busy, but 1918 was the year
When I invented my beautiful Enigma
[When he invented his beautiful Enigma!]

I founded my new company of Scherbius and Ritter,
What is that you claim? Don't like the name?
Entschuldigen Sie bitte!
I had to work long hours, use all my powers,
but I've never been a quitter
When I invented my beautiful Enigma
[When he invented his beautiful Enigma!]

I registered a patent for a ciphering machine.
A revolution in design, within it nothing is routine.
Based on rotors that can move and that are
wired along the seam
And I'd invented my beautiful Enigma
[And he'd invented his beautiful Enigma!]

My first one it was too big,
and it gave us all a fright!
My next one was much smaller,
but there's something still not right.
Then finally I had a small one with the
letters lit by lights
And I'd invented my beautiful Enigma
[And he'd invented his beautiful Enigma!]

I showed it to the Navy, but the Admiral said,
'No thanks!'
So I took it out to businesses and
sold it to the banks
But then the Nazis come to power and
they took it in their ranks
And now they're using my beautiful Enigma
[And now they are using his beautiful Enigma!]

Jo looked out over her band of musicians, nodding as she adjusted the movements of her baton in line with the changing tempo of the song.

It has a keyboard and a plug-board and
connects to battery.
Press a key it turns a rotor, this is 'stepping'
there you see.
Scrambled words and cipher text,
What will I think of next?
No one will ever be able to beat my Enigma!
[No one will ever be able to beat his Enigma!]

Plug and patch it, trip a ratchet,
it's spring loaded via a beam.
Pseudo-random substitution based on
wiring of machine.
Spring loaded with its spindles,

Read all about it on your Kindles!
No one will ever be able to beat my Enigma!
[No one will ever be able to beat his Enigma!]

Plug connections pair the letters via the
Steckerbrett at the front.
Each letter on the plug-board has two jacks
to cause a 'jump'
Encryption at a pace
The German Army thinks it's ace!
No one will ever be able to beat my Enigma!
[No one will ever be able to beat his Enigma!]

Decode the wiring – it's so tiring – via coils and
through the rings
Cause connections – it's perfection! –
using German-made brass pins
With reflectors and three rotors
Who needs electric motors?!
No one will ever be able to beat my Enigma!
[No one will ever be able to beat his Enigma!]

Jo swung her arms to temporarily stop the orchestra: the next line was to be sung by Cooper a cappella.

No doubt that some will try

But three rotors! Eins zwie drie!
No one will ever be able to beat my Enigma!
[No one will ever be able to beat his Enigma!]

Just you see!
[No one will ever be able to beat his Enigma!]

All down to me!
[No one will ever be able to beat his Enigma!]

The audience greeted the end of the Enigma song with a huge cheer and a thunderous round of applause. As the Bavarian lady and Nazi Stormtrooper ensemble had sung out that nobody would ever be able to solve Enigma, a section of the crowd had started to shout back 'Oh yes we will!' until by the final few verses everyone was joining in with this impromptu response. The hall was still full of laughter as Scherbius and his Bavarian ladies and soldiers left the stage, leaving behind the Enigma machine on the table.

Frank was there to greet Cooper as he walked off the stage. 'Well done, old man. That was splendid!'

'It did go rather well, didn't it?' Cooper responded, instinctively wrapping his right arm around the back of his head and scratching his left ear. 'You don't think that I overdid it a little, do you?'

Frank laughed. 'Josh, you could never overdo anything!'

Meanwhile out in the hall the audience's attention had switched back to the end of Jean's interview as the mansion office was lit up once more.

Dilly stood and led Jean over to the table where the Enigma machine sat waiting.

Dilly: So here it is, Jean, the Enigma machine. It is a truly remarkable piece of engineering. Enigma allows an operator to type in a message, which it then scrambles by using three of five notched wheels, or rotors, which display different letters of the alphabet. Now, the last rotor is a reflector, which ensures that Enigma is self-reciprocal meaning that encryption is the same as decryption. However, this reflector also gives Enigma the property that no letter ever encrypts to itself. This is a severe conceptual flaw, Jean and a cryptological mistake that we aim to exploit here at Bletchley! The receiver needs to know the exact settings of these rotors in order to reconstitute the coded text. Over the years the basic machine has become more complicated as German code experts added plugs with electronic circuits, here you see, at the front.

Nigel leant forward and swapped two of the plug cables over on the front panel of the Enigma.

```
Dilly: Breaking Enigma is not easy, Jean. Combining
    three rotors from a set of five, the rotor settings
    with 26 positions, and the plug-board with ten pairs
    of letters connected, the military Enigma has 159
    quintillion different possible settings!
Jean: Gosh, sir.
```

Keith and Frank were stood together in the wings opposite the mansion office watching the scene unfold. Keith nudged Frank's arm and leant in toward him.

'I remember once having to explain how an Enigma machine worked to a new recruit to the cottage not long after I joined Dilly's ISK section. The poor girl was a trembling wreck by the time I'd finished, and we never saw her again after that,' Keith whispered.

'Just imagine how she would have coped with Dilly!' Frank replied, grinning.

```
Dilly: That is enough of all that for now, Jean. Welcome
    aboard! Claire, Miss Harding, my Office Manager, will
    get you sorted now with all the paperwork. There are a
    few things you will need to sign, but then we must get
    you over to the cottage to meet the rest of the team.
Jean: Thank you so much, sir.
```

Dilly and Jean moved back over into the office and left the stage through the office door.

The main lights on the stage dimmed as stagehands rushed on to quickly move the table and Enigma machine back into the cottage.

The introduction to the next song was now well underway and the hall was filled with an up-beat melody.

'I do like this one,' Keith said to Frank. 'It's a real foot tapper!'

On the Team!

THERE WAS NO NEED for whispering now as the music was loud and jovial.

The stage was full of cast members acting out the parts of Bletchley workers all going about their business in the park in front of the mansion. The girls had also come back through the cottage door and were busying themselves around the table in the cottage.

Bletchley was a hive of activity.

Jean is on the team!

On the Team!

Finally, as the music reached the end of the introduction, Jean skipped out onto the stage from behind the mansion, swinging her bag, and began to sing.

Jean:

I did it
I've run it
I can't believe I've done it
I've only gone and made the Team!

So happy
Delighted
Nervous but excited
Working here will be my dream!

Just look around.
Oh what delight.
The sun is dancing on the lake, now that's a sight!

The birds in song.
Up in the trees.
It's hard to tell that Britain's on her knees!

So I'm here at Bletchley.
No fear at Bletchley.
I want to play my part!
Team play at Bletchley.
Each day at Bletchley.
Breaking codes at Bletchley Park!

So I'm here at Bletchley.
No fear at Bletchley.
I want to play my part!
Team play at Bletchley.
Each day at Bletchley.
Breaking codes at Bletchley Park!

Be careful.
Don't say it.
Take care never to betray it.
Make sure I never say it true.

Top secret!
Protected!
And now that I'm selected,
Can't tell anybody what I do.

At this point in the song Jean had come face to face with a soldier who was checking the workers' passes.

Oh here's a guard.
It's my first test.
Take a breath and crack a smile,
I'll do my best.
Show him my pass.
Nothing to say.
He just smiled at me and sent
me on my way!

So I'm here at Bletchley.
No fear at Bletchley.
I want to play my part!
Team play at Bletchley.
Each day at Bletchley.
Breaking codes at Bletchley Park!

So I'm here at Bletchley.
No fear at Bletchley.
I want to play my part!
Team play at Bletchley.
Each day at Bletchley.
Breaking codes at Bletchley Park!

On the Team!

Now Jean found herself by the cottage and she stopped for a moment, watching the girls who were busy at their codebreaking work.

Oh, Heavens!
Just strike me!
Will the others like me?
I guess I'll have to wait and see.
Dress up?
Wear make-up?
Give my clothes a shake-up?
The thing to do is just be me!

The six girls then left the stage through the cottage door and headed around the set in the wing to reappear upstage from behind the cottage. Jean turned back to the audience and continued to sing.

Here come the girls.
They're on their way.
They look so clever, so esteemed, what do I say?

All of Dilly's Girls gathered around Jean, smiling, and looked so pleased to see her.

Oh, they're so nice.
So friendly too.
Now I know we're going to see this conflict through!

Finally, all seven of the ladies burst into a final rendition of the chorus, all singing and dancing together.

ALL: *So we're here at Bletchley.*
No fear at Bletchley.
We want to play our part!
Team play at Bletchley.
Each day at Bletchley.
Breaking codes at Bletchley Park!

So we're here at Bletchley.
No fear at Bletchley.
We want to play our part!
Team play at Bletchley.
Each day at Bletchley.
Breaking codes at Bletchley Park!

So we're here at Bletchley.
No fear at Bletchley.
We want to play our part!
Team play at Bletchley.
Each day at Bletchley.
Breaking codes at Bletchley Park!

As the audience applause rang around the hall, the girls all fussed around Jean, eventually leading her around the back of the cottage and off the stage.

Jean meets the girls from the cottage.

Welcome to The Cottage!

THE COTTAGE DOOR BURST OPEN, and all the girls walked through and back onto the stage.

Claire: Come on in, Jean. Welcome to the cottage!

Jean: So how is it that you all work in here, in the cottage?

Once again the band struck up and Claire began to sing the next song.

Claire: *Well that's all down to Dilly,*
We know it's really silly,
But he's a loner and so likes to work alone.
Mavis: *So the cottage was ideal,*
As it really made him feel
He had a special place, almost a home from home.

Margaret: *As far as code breaking goes,*
He's the number one, you know
A total genius, no one will disagree.
Flo: *He broke the German telegram,*

That brought in Uncle Sam
To the last war and ensured our victory!

Joyce: *Next up Enigma was the test,*
And that saw Dilly at his best
Breaking codes, from Spain and Italy.
Betty: *But he didn't want to dwell*
So broke the German one as well
Quite remarkably our man had cracked all three!

Mavis: *But then the Germans they got mean,*
And upgraded their machines
And by 1940 we were all back to square one.
Claire: *Though Dilly was quite sure*
He could break the codes once more
He didn't count on our Commander Denniston!

Margaret: *He took Enigma*
Away from Dilly
Gave it to Turing and Welchman instead
Closed down the cottage
Transferred his staff away
And moved Dilly's office into Bletchley's old plum shed!

Claire: *Despite him being*
Head codebreaker
Dilly found himself now cast aside
Decided it was
Time to resign
Even code breaking geniuses have pride.

Jean: Oh, my goodness no! What happened? What did he do?

Claire: *Well Dilly's letter was refused,*
They knew that Dilly must be used

And reopened the cottage with him back in charge
Of solving all the codes and clues,
That no one else would do
All Dilly needed now was an entourage.

Girls: And that is where we all come in!

All the girls laughed together.

Jean: But why all ladies?

At this point in the song Dilly once again appeared over on the other side of the stage in the office and began to act out all the things that the girls then went on to sing about him in the next few verses of the song.

Mavis: *I don't believe that there's a man,*
Who can begin to understand
our Dilly and what it is that makes him tick.
Flo: *Wildly eccentric in his ways,*
He will ponder things for days
And then a mad-cap idea will
spring up and do the trick!

Betty: *Poor Dilly's tall, thin and bald,*
All his clothes look really old
All his trousers and his jackets are way too short.
Joyce: *Without his glasses he is blind*
Absent minded all the time,
But all it takes is just another crazy thought.

Margaret: *He's put his sandwich in his pipe,*
Oh there's nothing not to like
As he stuffs his glasses in his tobacco pouch!
Claire: *Mistook the cupboard for the door,*
Oh Jean, there's so much more!

But through all this we've never
ever heard him grouch.

Flo: *Dilly trusts us*
And respects us
Told the commander he didn't want any men.
Betty: *He wasn't bothered*
Where we came from
Whether 'Lower', 'Middle', 'Upper', WAAF or Wren!
(Betty) (Flo) (Mavis) (Joyce) (Claire) (Margaret)

Claire: *All that mattered*
All: *Is our ability*
He's even fought hard to get us equal pay!
Mavis: *And we adore our*
Brilliant Dilly
Just years ahead of his time in every way!

Jean: So who's who? What is it that you all do?

Mavis: *Let's get off the starting block,*
This is Margaret, she's his rock
Betty: *In more ways than one since*
that's her name!
Mavis: *A maths wizard you will find*
Margaret: *Oh, Mavis, you're too kind*
Mavis: *Not many better at this war*
code breaking game

Margaret: *Well, this is Mavis, Mavis Lever*
And you better had believe her!
Since in German she can fluently converse.
Claire: *I once heard Dilly taking stock,*
"Give me a Lever and a Rock"
"And together we can move the Universe!"

Welcome to The Cottage!

Joyce: *Right, Jean, next to meet is Claire*
And we're so glad that she is there
She's so organised and keeps us
all in trim.
Betty: *She's an admin work machine,*
Flo: *Office Manager supreme!*
Claire: *When I'm not looking for Dilly's*
glasses or his tin!

Claire: *And here's Betty, Joyce and Flo,*
Joyce is a speech therapist, you know
Betty & Flo: *And we were actresses before*
the Bletchley 'road'.
Jean: *Wow actresses! Crikey!*
Now that seems so unlikely?
Margaret: *Ah, but Dilly thinks their training*
helps spot rhythms in the code!

Finally, all the girls joined in to sing the last part of the song together.

ALL: *So welcome*
To the team, Jean
It's really great to have you on board
It's long hours
And often dull work
But breaking Nazi codes is our reward!

So welcome
To the team, Jean
It's really great to have you on board
It's long hours
And often dull work
But breaking Nazi codes is our reward!

But breaking Nazi codes

Of which there's always loads!

But breaking Nazi codes is our reward!

The audience erupted once more in vigorous applause and cheering and on the stage there was much laughter from all the girls as they congratulated themselves with hugs and smiles all round.

Claire: Well, Jean, you are one of Dilly's Girls now. Welcome to The Cottage!

Mavis: Hey, Claire, isn't it time you took 'The Prof' his lunch? You know he will stop working at exactly twelve thirty and will be looking out for you.

Jean: 'The Prof'?

The other girls all laughed once more.

Betty: Oh, that's Alan, Alan Turing.

Margaret: Alan was working with Dilly on Enigma before we all arrived here at the cottage, Jean. He is a mathematician from Cambridge and quite brilliant.

Joyce: And very odd. He cycled past me the other day wearing his gas mask!

Claire: Oh, that is to help him with the pollen.

All the girls laughed again.

Mavis: As soon as Alan arrived here at the cottage he wanted to tackle Naval Enigma which Dilly had put to one side. We were all waiting and hoping to get some sort of 'pinch' on their daily settings to get us started.

Margaret: Well, that suited Alan down to the ground. He likes to work by himself and he felt that the naval Enigma problem was something he could really get his teeth into.

Mavis: He is also working on a mechanical solution to cryptography. Dilly told him what he had seen the Poles doing out in Warsaw. They had built an electro-mechanical device based on the replica Enigma machine they had made. Alan is convinced that this is the way to go. He is quite the engineer too, you know, as well as a maths genius.

Margaret: And he is an even bigger loner than Dilly! It wasn't long before he took himself off and disappeared into the loft above the stable in the yard so he could work on his problems undisturbed.

Joyce: Just the Prof and his pigeons.

Betty: He really does keep himself to himself. He won't go over to the Mansion for coffee breaks, meals or anything, so Claire and I have to take him his drinks and his lunch.

Claire: And he won't even come down for those. We have had to rig up a pulley and we send his sandwiches and drinks up to him in a basket!

Jean: A pulley?

Joyce: Welcome to Bletchley, Jean!

Claire: Come on, Jean, we will show you around and introduce you to Alan.

Jean: Well, I hope you don't expect me to get into the basket!

All the girls laughed together once more as the stage lights faded on the scene.

A Letter to Churchill

ONCE ALL THE CLAPPING in the hall had faded, the lights came back up on the stage, this time focused back on the office.

Dilly was sat at his desk, but he was not alone. Four other men were there with him.

Alan Turing was standing just behind Dilly, Hugh Alexander was casually sitting on the edge of the table, Gordon Welchman was wedged back into the corner of the office nervously playing with his pipe, and Keith was there too standing a little way back from the others.

Keith had tried to dissuade Frank from including this next song in his show. His reasoning had nothing to do with the actual song, which Keith thought was nice enough – in fact the tune was another catchy little gem by Jo – but it was because the scene was recreating the event that had caused a massive change in the structure of Bletchley and one which had ultimately cost the original commander of the park his job.

Dilly and Denniston had had their moments, make no mistake, but at the end of the day they were old friends from way back and Dilly would have hated seeing Denniston ousted in the way that he had been.

This seismic change had been triggered by a letter to Winston Churchill, which had been written by Turing, Welchman, Alexander and another senior codebreaker called Stuart Milner-Barry.

Dilly and Keith had had nothing to do with it, which as far as Keith was concerned was good enough reason alone for not including it here.

However, Keith could not deny the reason for writing the letter, which was a plea for more urgently needed resources at Bletchley. It was just too ridiculous to consider that battles might be lost because intelligence was missing simply due to a lack of some extra typists in one of the Huts, for example.

There was also no denying either the effectiveness of the letter which prompted an immediate response from the Prime Minister. However, Keith felt it was a shame that it all could not have been handled without the need to go behind the commander's back. But it was the fact that neither Dilly, nor any of the girls, had been involved, which was Keith's biggest gripe.

'Nonsense!' Frank had retorted. 'It was Dilly who put Turing onto the idea of a mechanical solution to Enigma when he came back from Warsaw, and we can't have a show around Bletchley without including Turing's Bombes now, can we, old man?'

So, Frank had twisted the reason behind the letter to Churchill as being a plea for funds to build Turing's electro-mechanical Enigma breaking machines – which were known as Bombes – even though history would show that these funds had long since been approved and the machines were already being built when the letter had been sent.

To be honest, Keith reckoned Frank had written this song just because he had wanted to ham it up on stage as Winston Churchill.

Then there was the question of why involve him, since Keith had been in no way connected to any of this.

'Ah, but this is another chance to play on your and Mavis' love story, my boy,' Frank had explained, 'and besides, Milner-Barry has refused outright to be involved and there had to be four of you and you did used to work for Welchman!'

Milner-Barry had flat out refused because he didn't like Dilly, and that was that; no one was ever going to be able to persuade him otherwise. It was well known that Welchman did not like Dilly much either and it had amazed everyone to see him in rehearsals.

Gordon Welchman was the head of Hut 6 and one of the key players at Bletchley. He had started out life at Bletchley working for Dilly in the cottage, but it had all gone sour when he had been asked to move out and work from Elmers School, which was next to the Park and which had been taken over by the Bletchley codebreakers at the beginning of the war. The reason for his move had been quite logical. Welchman had been tasked with planning the expansion of Bletchley Park, which he ended up doing quite brilliantly, but it was felt that there was just no room to do this in the cramped confines of the cottage. However, the old school would suit the job perfectly, with plenty of room and ample table space to spread out all the plans and drawings. Welchman, however, took this decision as a personal slur and assumed that it was because Dilly did not like him.

Keith had been told years later that Dilly had been totally baffled when someone explained this to him.

'But why would he think that?' Dilly had exclaimed. 'I have never said anything to him.'

'That's part of the problem,' had been the wry response.

Thus, Keith and many of the other performers had been really surprised when Gordon had agreed to take part. Keith surmised that it was probably because Welchman felt he could monitor Frank's telling of the story more closely from the inside by being part of the cast. No one knew for sure, but he had been a massive help on the organisational side of things and so everyone involved was glad to have had him on board.

Hugh Alexander was respected by everyone and totally adored by all the ladies. He was a chess champion and had been out competing in Argentina when the war broke out. He was another of the Cambridge maths graduates and between the wars had been teaching mathematics at Winchester. He was intelligent, witty, tall and handsome, and on joining Bletchley had gone to work with Welchman in Hut 6. He soon transferred to Hut 8 to work with Turing on the naval Enigma problem, eventually taking overall charge there. Keith had always got on well with Hugh, and with Turing for that matter.

Alan Turing was Frank's biggest coup of all, and no one could quite believe it when Frank had said that Alan had agreed to take part in this final show at Bletchley.

Just like Hugh, Alan was also very intelligent, tall, and handsome, but unlike Hugh, Turing was deeply shy and reserved. Despite the best efforts of many of the young ladies at Bletchley to catch his eye, Alan would shuffle awkwardly around the park and huts with his eyes always looking away so as never to make eye contact with anyone. It really was true that the girls in the cottage used to take him his lunch and send it up to him via a pulley when he was working in the old barn loft in the stable yard. He was very athletic too and most people that saw him run were convinced that he might one day even represent his country, maybe even at the Olympic Games. Everyone liked Alan and found his eccentric ways most endearing.

Keith knew that Dilly had liked him too and had recognised his abilities from very early on. Keith had noticed how Olive's eyes had lit up when she had heard that Alan was in this evening's production. When Keith escorted her to her seat earlier that evening, she had enthusiastically told Keith how Alan had come to stay with them at Courn's Wood right at the start of the war and how well they had all got on.

But it was once again time to concentrate. The sight of Turing, Welchman and Alexander on the stage when the lights came up had caused the most enormous cheer in the hall and it was now time to focus on remembering lines again. It was Welchman who set the next scene into motion.

Welchman: Alan's design is sound, Dilly, and his new machine could potentially speed up our breaking the daily Enigma settings by, well, a huge amount.

Turing: As you know, Dilly, it is based on the concept originally developed in Poland where they linked several Enigma machines together.

Dilly: So, your design does not actually use any Enigma machines?

Turing: No, it doesn't, Dilly. It will make use of over one hundred rotating drums all with electrical connections to replicate the action of many Enigma machines at once. Each drum will represent a different Enigma wheel.

Welchman: Multiple Enigma machines at once, Dilly, imagine that!

Dilly: This machine of yours will be pretty big then, Alan?

Turing: According to my latest designs over six feet high, seven feet wide and over two foot deep.

Welchman: The problem is, Dilly, building it will not be cheap.

Dilly: What does Denniston think?

Keith: He is all for it, Dilly, but all his efforts to get more funding for Bletchley just fall on deaf ears in Whitehall. Poor old Denniston is just seen by Whitehall as the head of some obscure Foreign Office department that cannot possibly be allowed to compete with the actual armed forces fighting the war.

Alexander: It is not just the Bombes either. Bletchley needs more staff, equipment and resources generally to deal with all the traffic we are now getting from operations in North Africa, the Balkans and on the Eastern Front.

There was a loud firm knock on the office door. Keith smiled to himself. He knew it was his wife and Jean who were waiting to come out onto the stage just the other side.

Dilly: Yes?

Jean: Excuse me, sir; we have those documents you asked for.

Dilly: Ah, yes. Please come in, ladies. Jean, let me introduce you to Alan, Gordon, Hugh, and Keith.

Jean: We have already met, sir.

Turing: It is nice to see you again, Jean.

Welchman: I hope you are not taking any nonsense from old Dilly, eh?

Keith: Hello, Mavis.

Mavis: Hello, Keith.

Keith was beaming as he and his new wife locked eyes.

Alexander: Ah, Miss Lever, may I say how lovely you are looking this evening?
Mavis: Why thank you, Hugh.
Alexander: You know, I would ask you out to dinner right this instant if I did not know that your affections may already lay elsewhere.
Mavis: You are such a cad, Hugh!

Keith could feel himself colouring up.

Dilly: Ah, excellent, well ladies, Alan here has designs for a machine which might just help us crack the new plug board Enigmas, but we are short of a hundred thousand pounds or so. I don't suppose you two have some money you can lend us?
Jean: No, sir!

Jean laughed.

Jean: But excuse me, sir, Betty said to tell you that Churchill is making an important speech right now and it is live on the radio. Would you like me to tune it in for you?
Dilly: Ah, excellent! Yes please, Jean.

Jean lifted a rather old and battered radio set which had been placed on the floor in the corner of the office up onto the table and switched it on. Lots of static and crackling gave way to a very familiar voice.

Keith could not help but smile. Frank was clearly in his element now!

The main stage light swung away from the office and back across to the cottage, which while the others had all been talking had been transformed by the stagehands into what was an attempt to look like the main chamber of the House of Commons.

Frank was there of course, standing at the desk on which there was now a replica of the famous dispatch box.

He was wearing an oversized black suit which had been suitably padded out. A neat gold chain looped from his button to his waistcoat pocket, a large white handkerchief protruded from his top jacket pocket, and a black and white spotted bowtie completed the outfit. He was also wearing a pair of black framed round spectacles which were balanced on the end of his nose, and he was holding the most enormous cigar.

Keith smiled and shook his head. Now he was certain he was right as to why Frank had insisted on keeping this song in the show!

Frank was surrounded by other suitably dressed members of Parliament who were waving sheets of paper in the air and baying loudly as Mr Speaker shouted for order.

Mr Speaker: Order! Order! Orrrr-der! Continue, Prime Minister.

Churchill:

... Even though large tracts of Europe and
many old and famous States have fallen or may
fall into the grip of the Gestapo and all the
odious apparatus of Nazi rule, we shall not
flag or fail.
We shall go on to the end,
We shall fight in France,
We shall fight on the seas and oceans,
We shall fight with growing confidence and
growing strength in the air,
We shall defend our Island, whatever the
cost may be.
We shall fight on the beaches; we shall fight
on the landing grounds,
We shall fight in the fields and in the streets,
We shall fight in the hills.
We shall never surrender!

Now it was not just the members of Parliament that were cheering, the entire hall was in uproar and it took a good few minutes before things settled back down again.

Keith caught his wife's eye and gave her a wink.

```
Mavis: Well Winston certainly gave the impression that
    he understands the value of what we do here when he
    visited Bletchley last month.
Keith: He certainly did. He called Bletchley the 'Goose
    that lays the Golden Egg'!
```

Keith found himself struggling not to laugh. Frank's Churchillian performance had certainly been one he would never forget.

```
Jean: Sir, why don't you cut out the 'middle-men' and
    write directly to Prime Minister Churchill and ask
    him for the money?
Dilly: Jean, that might not be such a bad idea! Please,
    would you mind staying and taking this down for me?
Jean: Of course not, sir.
Dilly: Right, let me see.
```

Dilly coughed to clear his throat.

```
Dilly: Dear Prime Minister Churchill.
        Money needed to build Turing's electro-mechanical
    machine which we believe will allow us to identify
    latest Enigma settings.
        Please send £100,000 urgently.
        Very best regards,
        Knox, Turing, Welchman, Alexander and Batey
        Bletchley, Government Code and Cipher School etc etc

Dilly: How was that, chaps?
Turing: Oh, first rate, Dilly, old boy.
```

Welchman: Straight to the point, my man.

Dilly: Jean, Mavis? What do you two think?

Jean: Well, forgive me, sir, but maybe you could be just a little more lyrical in your request?

Dilly: Goodness me, Jean, whatever do you mean?

Mavis: Well, Dilly, I think what Jean means is that Churchill is a great orator; take what he has just said on the radio as an example. Go on to the end, never surrender, fighting on the beaches and so on. You should make your request stand out and hit him with sentiments that will really resonate with him.

Alexander: She has got a point there, Dilly, old man.

Dilly: What would you say, Jean? How would you word it?

Jean: Well, sir, perhaps something like this.

Jean looked down at Jo and the band, and Jo smiled back. Jean heard Jo do a quick count and the band struck up once more. Jean began to sing.

Jean: *Dear Mr Churchill*
We're writing with a plea.
It's not just guns, but brains and sums,
That leads to Victory.

Dear Mr Churchill
We hope that you can see,
We're sure we know, the way to go,
That leads to Victory.

Mavis joined in.

Mavis & Jean: *Unless we crack Enigma,*
those Nazi flags will rise.
Those German ranks, their subs and tanks,
Will take us by surprise.

A Letter to Churchill

Dear Mr Churchill
We know it's lots to ask,
Without this spend, war may not end
Please trust us with this task.

Dilly had got to his feet and was now standing between Jean and Mavis, and he now took over the singing for the small bridge section of the song.

Dilly: *Enigma code is hard to break,*
Loads have tried and lost.
But there's this thing, we want to make,
But doing it's going to cost.

Now Jean, Mavis and Dilly all sang together.

Jean, Mavis & Dilly: *Dear Mr Churchill*
You said we'll fight in France.
Let's make our mark, at Bletchley Park
Please let us have this chance.

Now it was Turing's turn to interject and sing the next bridge piece alone.

Turing: *A million billion routes to try,*
Just can't be done by hand.
So my machine, you have to buy
We hope you understand.

Jean, Mavis, Dilly and Alan all continued together.

Jean, Mavis, Dilly & Alan:
Dear Mr Churchill
To win on air and sea,
Let's break this code, then hit the road,
That leads to Victory.

Unless we crack Enigma, those Nazi flags will rise.
Those German ranks, their subs and tanks,
Will take us by surprise.

Dear Mr Churchill
We're writing with a plea.
It's not just guns, but brains and sums,
That leads to Victory.

Dear Mr Churchill
Our Island to defend.
But all's not lost, there's just the cost,
To get us to the end.

Next, Gordon Welchman joined in and took charge of the following few lines, which were sung at a much slower pace.

Welchman: *So there it is, you have our plan,*
Ambitious though it sounds,
We just need you, to say we can,
And one hundred, thousand, pounds!

Finally, all seven were singing at full gusto for the final part of the song.

ALL: *Dear Mr Churchill*
We're writing with a plea.
It's not just guns, but brains and sums,
That leads to Victory.

Dear Mr Churchill
We hope that you'll agree,
That Bletchley Park, can light the spark,
That leads to Victory.

A Letter to Churchill

Unless we crack Enigma, those Nazi flags will rise.
Those German ranks, their subs and tanks,
Will take us by surprise.

Dear Mr Churchill
On keeping Britain free:
We'll use our math, beat Nazi wrath,
It's all cryptology!

Dear Mr Churchill
So inspiring with your speeches.
We need to fight, with mental might,
As well as on the beaches.

Unless we crack Enigma, those Nazi flags will rise.
Those German ranks, their subs and tanks,
Will take us by surprise.

Dear Mr Churchill
You're Britain's great defender,
Release our chains; we'll use our brains,
We never need surrender.

Dear Mr Churchill
We hope that you now see,
We're sure we know, the way to go,
That leads to Victory.

That leads to Victory!

The audience had begun to clap immediately the music stopped, but soon fell quiet again very quickly as the stage light swung back over onto Frank as Winston Churchill in the cottage where he was holding the letter and was reading it out loud.

Churchill: 'Our reason for writing to you direct is that for months we have done everything we possibly can through the normal channels and that we despair of any early improvement without your intervention.'

Churchill: Mary! Mary! Take down a minute for me and attach this letter! To General Ismay, Chief Military Assistant. Make sure they have all they want EXTREME PRIORITY and report to me that this has been done. ACTION THIS DAY!

On this instruction from the Prime Minister, Jo brought the music back in once more for the final line of the song.

ALL: *That leads to Victory!*

As the audience showed their appreciation with yet more thunderous applause, Keith took his wife's hand.

'Just look at Frank, darling.'

Mavis looked across the stage at Frank, who was thoroughly enjoying himself. Still in full Churchill mode he was bowing and waving the letter and his cigar, and totally milking the audience's reaction.

'Anyone would think he had just sung the song,' laughed Mavis.

Endless Hours

WHEN THE CLAPPING EVENTUALLY died down the lights were cut, and several stagehands ran on and began some sizable alterations to the set.

The back walls of both the office and the cottage were unlatched from their respective side panels, swung around, and then brought together at the back-centre of the stage. The reverse side of each of these back walls had been decorated and fitted out to look like the back wall of one of the code-breaking huts. The office and cottage tables were also pushed together and so suddenly everyone in the hall was looking inside 'Hut 6'.

Several Bletchley ladies appeared on the stage and sat down at the tables and were soon hard at work on their daily code breaking tasks. Other Bletchley workers were busy in the hut too, coming and going, delivering messages which were being continuously loaded into and taken out of the wire-trays on the tables. The work was piling up and seemed endless.

Mair Russell-Jones was one of the ladies now sat at a table. She had worked in the real Hut 6 during the war. Not only that, but she had written the song with Joanna that she was about to sing in front of everyone.

Mair had never dreamt that she would find herself back at Bletchley again. Toward the end of the war she had fallen very ill with pneumonia, and after a lengthy stay in hospital where she had nearly died, Mair had been sent back to her home in Wales to complete her recovery. Then in May, not long after VE day, she had received her discharge letter from Bletchley, and that, she had thought, was that.

Mair's time at Bletchley had begun in August 1941, but it had not started well when she had been billeted with the most dreadful couple in the most awful house. Unable to get any proper sleep back at her digs after the long hard days working in Hut 6, and also not having any decent food to eat, Mair very quickly found herself drained and exhausted and soon fell ill with a heavy flu. After collapsing during an evening shift she was sent back to Wales for six weeks to recover.

But in October she was back at Bletchley, and on returning she was introduced to Joanna, who had also just arrived at Bletchley. The two girls quickly hit it off and decided to look for new digs together.

Both girls had a passion for music, and both had been studying music at university before the war. Mair was an accomplished pianist and Joanna excelled at the violin. The family they found to stay with had an old piano in the front parlour and encouraged the girls to practise and play in their spare time.

It had been Joanna who had written to Mair to tell her all about Frank's end of war production, and to ask her to come back to Bletchley to take part. Jo had told Frank all about her friend, and how she and Mair had come up with many of the melodies and had written several songs together during their time at the Park.

Mair had jumped at the chance to see her old friend again and had hoped to be part of the band and play the piano, but Frank was having none of that.

'This is your song, and you should sing it,' he had exclaimed. 'Besides, you have the loveliest voice, Mair, and it would be a crime not to use it.'

So Mair had found herself part of the cast and with her own song, and here she was on stage now just minutes away from her big moment.

Mair tried to catch Jo's eye, but her seat was just in the wrong place to be able to see down to where her friend was standing in front of the band. Never mind, she just knew that Jo would be willing her on.

Mair was just a little startled when the main stage lights came up. She had not expected it to be quite this bright.

'Bright, isn't it? Don't worry, you'll quickly get used to it. It took me by surprise too.'

It was Keith, who was already on the stage with the other workers, and he had leant across Mair to put some documents in the wire tray on the table next to her.

'Good luck with your song, Mair,' he whispered, 'you'll be amazing.'

Mair smiled back nervously, as Keith moved around the table and sat down.

With the stage once again fully lit, Mavis, Jean, Betty and Joyce reappeared.

Keith was in charge of the hut today, and he jumped up when he saw Mavis and the others arrive.

Keith: Mavis!

Keith noticed several of the workers look up at his informal exclamation and felt a little embarrassed by this public display of excitement. He corrected himself and continued.

Keith: Ah, Miss Lever, it is lovely to see you.

Mavis: Hello, Keith, you too. Claire said you needed some help over here in Hut 6 today. I believe you were expecting us?

Keith: Yes, that's right. Please come through, this way.

Mavis reached out and touched his arm, causing Keith to stop and turn back toward her:

Mavis: Keith, we heard about Miss Fletcher. It is so sad, I am so sorry, Keith. It was pneumonia, wasn't it?

Keith: Yes, yes it was. When you think about pneumonia you think about older people, not younger men and women in their twenties and thirties dying of it. We have three other ladies off sick with it at the moment too. It is such a worry. She was such a bright young thing. She always had a smile. We are expecting some

new recruits later this week but are sinking under the current volume of traffic, and that's why Gordon spoke to Dilly about getting some help.
Mavis: We are all so sorry, Keith.

Mavis and Keith paused for a moment. They locked eyes and smiled warmly at one another. She was still holding his arm and wondered whether to give him a hug. She decided against it.

Mavis: Well hopefully Jean, Betty and Joyce will be able to help out for a few days. Right, I best get back to the cottage now.
Keith: Thank you, Ma... er Miss Lever.

Mavis turned to leave.

Keith: Oh, Mavis!
Mavis: Yes Keith?
Keith: I was wondering, I hope this isn't inappropriate, but I just wanted to ask you about next Friday.
Mavis: Yes, Keith?

One of the Hut 6 workers suddenly shouted out.

Worker: Mr Batey! Mr Batey! I think you had better come and look at this!
Keith: Oh, I will be right there, Joan! Please excuse me, Mavis. Jean, Betty, Joyce, this is Mair; she will explain what we would like you to help with. I must go, please excuse me.

Mavis sighed.

Jean: I bet he was going to ask you accompany him to the dance at Woburn next week.

Mavis: Well, Jean, knowing Mr Batey we will probably never know. I will see you down by the lake later. Good luck!

Mavis walked back off the stage, on her way back to the cottage. Meanwhile, Mair had stood up from the table and had walked over to stand with the other girls.

Mair meets the girls.

Mair: Hello, I'm Mair.
Jean: Hello, Mair, my name is Jean, and this is Betty and Joyce.
Mair: It is lovely to meet you all. Welcome to Hut 6.
Betty: Oh, it is so gloomy in here. I am never going to complain about working in the cottage again!

Mair: Yes, it is, isn't it? All the windows are blocked by those heavy blackout curtains so there is no natural light at all and these strip lights they have suspended from the ceiling just give out this eerie light. It's not ideal.

Joyce: It reminds me of the light given out by the old gas lamps we used to have back at home.

Jean: It makes everyone look so ill and deathly. Oh, I am sorry! I didn't mean to—

Mair: Please, don't worry, it's alright. We have girls falling ill quite regularly, though Jenny was the first one that has actually died. She was a lovely girl and a really hard worker. Her billet was awful, Jean, and that didn't help. She told me once that she had to sleep on a board which she had to fit on the bath every night. Her landlady would not let her lock the door either in case someone needed to use the toilet during the night. Can you imagine? I don't think she was getting any decent sleep or food there, and what with the conditions here in the hut, well she never stood a chance really.

Mair paused.

Joyce: Oh, Mair, that is terrible. My place sounds like heaven compared to what Jenny had to put up with.

Mair: Whereabouts have they put you?

Joyce: I am over at Gayhurst Manor. Sir Walter and Lady Carlisle are still living there, and they look after us pretty well. Lady Carlisle is a strange one. She always has an old sack tied around her waist for some reason.

Mair: A sack?

Joyce: I know, bizarre, isn't it? But the only thing we have to put up with is the RAF continually flying low over the house. Sir Walter is always on to them about it, but he does not realise that it is all down to my sister who likes to sunbathe naked on the roof when the weather's nice!

The girls all laughed, but a loud chesty cough from one of the hut workers caused them to stop.

Betty: Oh dear! That sounds bad.

Mair: There is always someone coughing or with a chest condition of some sort. Those sorts of respiratory problems are common in here, you know, a general sort of 'wheeziness'. We call it the 'Bletchley Park Rattle'.

Jean: I am so sorry, Mair.

Betty: And gosh what is that awful smell?

Joyce: Oh yes, it smells like sulphur!

Mair: Oh, that will be the boiler. We are convinced the heaters in here are slowly poisoning us with their toxic fumes. If the boilers don't get us the tobacco will. Pretty much everyone smokes in here. There is always someone puffing on a pipe or cigarette. I hate it. My clothes always smell so bad at the end of a shift.

Jean shivered.

Jean: It is so cold in here too, Mair.

Mair: Yes, it is, isn't it? The heating can't cope. Someone should have warned you. We all wear several extra layers but still sit and shiver our way through each shift.

Down in front of the stage Jo had sat down and her violin was out of its case and tucked up under her chin. She was playing in this next song and was sitting to the side of the rest of the band so they could all see her. Jo nodded twice, and then on her third count she slid her bow down across the strings and all the musicians began to play.

Immediately the audience could tell that this next song was in a totally different style to the upbeat ones that had gone before and recognised the powerful and dramatic intro melody as the same tune that had ended the overture right at the beginning of the show. A version of it had also been playing when Jean first walked out onto the stage, bag in hand, at the start of the show.

Several of the workers at Bletchley had been professional musicians before the war and many were here tonight playing in the band. The beginning of the introduction to the song was truly dramatic and uplifting, but the tempo was now settling down into a haunting melody ready for Mair to begin to sing.

The atmosphere in the hall had become intense and everyone was sitting quietly and very still as Mair turned away from Jean, Joyce and Betty and began to walk toward the front of the stage.

Mair took a breath, closed her eyes, and began to sing.

Mair: *These huts are so dark*
And so little air
All those around me, astound me,
each day as they work with such care

We take it in turns
At 3 shifts a day
Midnight until 8, the one we all hate,
is coming my way

But we all love our work
Making sure it's always done right
So proud to be able to help
Be part of our country's fight
Knowing our work here is so crucial to
how this war ends

Endless Hours

Oh look around, look around, at the state of our room
Fluorescent lights cast, a haze through the gloom
A hut thick with smoke, yellow mist fills the air
It's always like night time
No sun can get in
Dimly lit, all so cheerless
It's functional but grim

Endless hours
Endless toil
Codes to break
Plans to foil
Endless hours

I won't let you down
I'm telling you now
It won't be my bit, to cause it,
to fail or error somehow

I am feeling so tired
But also so proud
Bletchley Park has my heart and I'd love
to just shout it out loud

But we all strive to win
Breaking the code our ultimate aim
Know that we'll never give in
Our tasks are so not a game
Knowing our work here is so crucial to
how this war ends

Taste that smoke, in the air, in tobacco we'll drown
Whitewashed ceilings and walls soon cast nicotine brown
Toxic fumes from the heating, that sulphurous smell
It's always like winter

Dilly's Girls

We'll shiver all shift
Extra layers give comfort
As through traffic we sift

Endless hours
Endless toil
Codes to break
Plans to foil
Endless hours

8 hours a day
6 days a week
Such concentration, but elation when
we find the answers we seek

We just do our part
Look to our own task
Such dedication, frustration not knowing
and unable to ask

But we all know the scene
Every one of us just a small cog
In the greater Bletchley machine
All part of the daily slog
Knowing our work here is so crucial to
how this war ends

Don't understand, can't understand,
what everything means
Enigma's unique, such a complex machine
Nothing's ever explained at the start of each shift
Left feeling so helpless
Inadequate too
The work is so tedious
What more can we do?

Endless Hours

Endless hours
Endless toil
Codes to break
Plans to foil
Endless hours

Our boys at the front
Our troops are the best
Any error, may mean terror, for them,
so we never can rest

I won't let them down
I'm telling you now
It won't be my bit, to cause it to
fail or error somehow

But we've all signed The Act
These secrets are so safe with me
I've sworn to not tell a soul
Ensure that my country stays free
Knowing our work here is so crucial
to how this war ends

Oh look around, look around,
and just look at the team
The girls are exhausted, conditions extreme
The Bletchley Park 'Rattle', coughs everywhere
Intense concentration
It's making us ill
Sallow skin, hacking cough
Always fighting the chill

Endless hours
Endless toil
Codes to break

Dilly's Girls

Plans to foil
Endless hours

But it's not all work
We have that one day
Once a week we can meet, come together
for theatre and play

We're blessed with this house
These beautiful grounds
Goodness sake, there's a lake, there are gardens,
come see look around

And we all love those days
Well away from the daily grind
The dancing, the singing, the plays
All help to reset the mind.
Knowing our work here is so crucial
to how this war ends

Oh look around, look around, our spirits still high
We can beat Enigma! That's our battle cry!
We'll work till we drop, but sometimes we do

We've lost some good friends here
Their sun has now set
Taken from us by sickness
It's always a threat

Endless hours
Endless toil
Codes to break
Plans to foil
Endless hours.

As Mair sang her final word on a soft and gentle note, Jo and the band suddenly swept the tempo up again as the song finished with the dramatic melody that had played out at the start, and Mair stood with her eyes closed and her hands clasped together just under her chin.

Once the music stopped everyone in the hall jumped to their feet and gave her and the band a rousing standing ovation. Mair could feel herself colouring up as she turned to head back away from the front of the stage and was suddenly aware of a figure gesturing to her frantically at the side of the stage. It was Frank.

'Bow, go on bow,' he was mouthing in an exaggerated way. 'Wonderful! Wonderful!'

Mair smiled, turned back to the audience and gave a tiny curtsy. She then walked back to the other girls who had been standing quietly as she had sung her song and who now were all excitedly smiling as they gathered around her, hugging Mair and telling her well done.

Keith suddenly stood up from the table and spoke out.

Keith: Right, ladies, it's time for your break. See you back in here in half an hour.

Mair: I am going over to the canteen. Would any of you like to come?

Betty: Oh, yes please. I am starving!

Jean: I will see you girls later. I have promised Mavis and Margaret that I will meet them down by the lake.

Joyce: Have fun, Jean.

Jean: I will!

Our Green and Pleasant Land!

DOWN WITH THE BAND Jo was still sitting with her violin and counted the others in once more to what was instantly a much more upbeat and jolly tune which straight away had some of the audience clapping along.

While the band played the introduction to the next song the lights had dimmed, and everyone quickly left the stage as stagehands ran on and began to rearrange the set. The two halves of 'Hut 6' were swung back and taken right away from the stage. The two tables were pushed back to the sides, one against the mansion office side wall and the other against the cottage side wall.

As the introduction neared its end the lights came back up and Jean skipped out onto the stage all alone, arms out and twirling around as she began to sing.

Jean: *Oh when I get some time alone,*
I always like to take
myself away from all the huts,
and head down to the lake.
Working here is such a dream,
I never doubt my luck

Our Green and Pleasant Land!

The gardens here are so serene,
straight from a story book!

Oh the ducks have come to play
The swans just glide on past
The birds are out, they sing their songs
This hour will go so fast

It's such a gorgeous sunny day
The sky's a true deep blue
The grass so soft, it's here I'll lay
To take the Bletchley view

Oh glory be! Oh what a sight!
The trees in flower, all pink and white
Ten thousand different shades of green
I'm sure the nicest sight I've ever seen!

Oh Bletchley Park, our war-time town
Don't give me cause to ever let you down.
For all of Britain, I'll pray some more
Let us prevail and win this war.

Bletchley! Oh Bletchley! You must understand
You're everything we're fighting for
Our green and pleasant land!

At this point Jean turned to look upward into an imaginary sky and continued with the next verse.

Oh there's a sound I've come to know,
an RAF air fighter
I crane my neck and look around,
and see if I can sight her.

You can't mistake that distant noise,
the Merlin engine brings
One of our handsome pilot boys,
those famous Spitfire wings!

Oh I hope he sees me wave
I'm waving sending love
I hope he hears me sing my song
Looks down from high above

I'm sure I saw him rock his wings
He's heading back our way
He must have seen me, heard me sing
He's surely made my day!

Oh glory be! Oh what a sight!
This work of art, this show of might!
He skims our lake, then pulls up sharp
Above the house, and steals my heart!

Jean waves for the Spitfire!

Our Green and Pleasant Land!

Oh RAF, our boys in blue
We owe so much, to so few.
For all of Britain, I'll pray some more
Let us prevail and win this war.

Bletchley! Oh Bletchley! You must understand
You're everything we're fighting for
Our green and pleasant land!

So let me take you on a tour,
a trip around the park.
The mansion is the centrepiece
and is the place to start
From the lake where we are now,
it peeks out through the trees
Reflected in the sliver sheen,
a sight that's sure to please!

On the left the roof is green
It's the copper tiles they say
Shaped rather like an old church bell
Unique in every way.

The house is shaped with curves and points
The chimneys stand so high
White woodwork trims and angled joints
So easy on the eye!

At this point Margaret and Mavis ran out onto the stage and joined in the singing with their friend.

ALL: *Oh Glory be! Oh what a sight!*
The window frames all painted white
The bricks in multi-shades of red
The entrance arch, the tiles of lead

But even here you see the war
Those sandbags stacked around the doors
For all of Britain, we'll pray some more
Let us prevail and win this war!

Bletchley! Oh Bletchley!
You must understand
You're everything we're fighting for
Our green and pleasant land!

Mavis: *The house is where you'll find our chief,*
Commander Denniston,
Offices through every door,
even Dilly he has one.
A kitchen and a dining room,
nothing there too strange,
But also rooms for printers and
a telephone exchange!

Margaret: *Now cover up your eyes*
Else you'll be in a fix
Upstairs is where you'll find the spies
The home of MI6.

Jean: *The house is such a special place*
New secrets by the hour
My favourite is the wireless room
That's in the water tower!

All three girls now sang together.

ALL: *Oh Glory be! Would you believe?*
Some things they do, you can't conceive
It's leading edge, they make the rules
The Government Code and Cipher School!

Our Green and Pleasant Land!

Oh Bletchley Park, our war-time town
Don't give us cause to ever let you down.
For all of Britain, we'll pray some more
Let us prevail and win this war.

Bletchley! Oh Bletchley! You must understand
You're everything we're fighting for
Our green and pleasant land!

Margaret: *Behind the house are garages,*
they smell of gasoline.
Not far from there the cottage where
there's Dilly and his team
And beyond are all the wooden huts,
and purpose-built brick blocks
All serving different functions as
they strive to tick the box!

Jean: *The huts can be so dark*
In winter they're so cold
In summer it's the opposite
Heat takes a strangle-hold.

Mavis: *I'll try to remember what*
It is each of them do
I'll do my best to list the lot
So this is just for you.

One of the members of the ensemble appeared at the side of the stage carrying a clipboard and looking very officious, and then began to call out the hut numbers one by one. Each hut number was called out in time with the girls singing the song. As the first number was called other members of the cast appeared at the back of the stage, walking across stage right to stage left, and acting out scenes from each of the hut descriptions.

Announcer: In One!
Mavis: *The first was built at Bletchley*
back in 1939
Here they plan the buses to
get the workers in on time

Announcer: In Two!
Jean: *Everybody's favourite hut,*
just come in and you will see
It's where we go to rest and chill,
and maybe have some tea

Announcer: In Three!
Margaret: *The first of all our Intel huts,*
Enigma-based of course
Translations and analysis for
the Army and Air Force

Announcer: In Four!
Jean: *In here you'll find the Navy*
team all working to translate
And analyse Enigma texts arriving
from Hut Eight

Announcer: In Five!
Mavis: *This hut is for the Military,*
Intel from Italy
From Portugal and some from Spain,
that's translation work times three!

Announcer: In Six!
Jean: *Hut Six is where they break the codes*
and send on to Hut Three
Finding how those wheels were set
all helps to solve the key!

Our Green and Pleasant Land!

Announcer: In Seven!

Margaret: *It's Intel work again in here,*
where they do what they can
To crypto-analyse the codes
they pick up from Japan

Announcer: In Eight!

Jean: *The Navy codes all Greek to some,*
like Alpha Beta Sigma
But not to Alan Turing,
and it's here he cracked Enigma!

Announcer: In Nine!

Mavis: *I-S-O-S is based in here,*
tracking all the German spies
Double agents who now work for us,
their Intel it's all lies!

Announcer: In Ten!

Jean: *In here they're all decoding*
something different altogether
As well as other bits and bobs,
they're working out the weather!

Announcer: In Eleven!

Margaret: *A hut so close to Turing's heart,*
as you will plainly see
It's where they build his Bombe machines,
that's Bombe spelt with an 'E'!

Announcer: In Twelve!

Margaret: *Let's take a break from daily work*
and if music is your thing
Hut Twelve's the one, for tunes and song,
the Bletchley choir will sing!

Announcer: In Fourteen!

Jean: *There has never been a thirteen*
as far as I remember
Go to this hut and you will find,
a communications centre.

Announcer: In Fifteen!

Mavis: *In Hut Fifteen you'll find a very*
different demographic
In here it's all about signals,
and analysis of traffic.

Announcer: In Sixteen!

Margaret: *ISK are based in here,*
that's Dilly, don't you know
When he broke Abwehr Enigma codes,
then Hut Sixteen was GO!

All girls were now standing at the front of the stage and all sang together.

ALL: *Oh Glory be! Would you believe?*
Some things they do you can't conceive
It's leading edge, they make the rules
The Government Code and Cipher School!

Oh Bletchley Park, our war-time town
Don't give us cause to ever let you down.
For all of Britain, we'll pray some more
Let us prevail and win this war.

Bletchley! Oh Bletchley! You must understand
You're everything we're fighting for
Our green and pleasant land!

Bletchley! Oh Bletchley! You must understand

Our Green and Pleasant Land!

You're everything we're fighting for
Our green and pleasant land!

Jean: *Now one more chance to close my eyes,*
and lay back in the sun.
Mavis: *Will soon be time to head back*
and another shift begun.
Margaret: *But there's one more sound I want*
to hear, before I'm on my way
Another sound that's such a part
of every Bletchley day!

At this point in the song someone backstage blew a whistle and then as the girls sang about the steam train arriving at Bletchley Station – which was in fact just a few hundred yards down the road from the Bletchley mansion – other cast members began to appear on the stage.

Some were dressed as soldiers with kit bags slung over their shoulders. There were RAF air crew and Royal Navy sailors too. Some were officers dressed in pressed uniforms and carrying briefcases. A group of Wrens were there wearing their blue double-breasted jackets, blue skirts, white shirts and ties, and of course all wearing their famous circular hats, each of which sported a small bow and a large badge. Finally, there were all the Bletchley codebreakers, which included all the rest of the girls from the cottage, along with Dilly, Keith, Alan, Gordon, Hugh and many others.

Frank was back on the stage too, still wearing his Churchill costume and still waving his huge cigar!

Jean: *Oh there's the whistle now!*
Mavis: *I felt it in the ground.*
Margaret: *You feel the tons of pressured iron*
Before you hear the sound!

Jean: *The station is just down the road*
Mavis: *The sky's now full of steam.*
Margaret: *The train is here, a brand new load*
Part of the Bletchley scene!

Jean, Mavis & Margaret:

Oh Glory be! Oh what a noise!
More troops perhaps? Our precious boys
The chugging sound, the whistle's cry
Wish we were there, to wave goodbye!

Finally, the whole cast turned to face the audience and everyone joined in with the singing to bring Act One to a rousing finale.

ALL: *Oh Bletchley Park, our war-time town*
Don't give us cause to ever let you down.
For all of Britain, we'll pray some more
Let us prevail and win this war.

Bletchley! Oh Bletchley! You must understand
You're everything we're fighting for
Our green and pleasant land!

Bletchley! Oh Bletchley! You must understand
You're everything we're fighting for
Our green and pleasant land!

You're everything we're fighting for
Our green and pleasant land!

You're everything we're fighting for
Our green
And
Pleasant
Land!

PART TWO

Dilly's Girls

ACT II

Dilly's Girls – Part II

THE INTERVAL WAS NEARLY OVER. The seven girls made their way back onto the stage behind the main curtains which were still drawn hiding the stage from the audience. A couple of the stagehands were making final checks to the set, which had been reset as the cottage stage-left and mansion office stage-right. The huge painting of the mansion still hung at the back of the stage. Frank and Bill were there too, making sure everything was set for the start of the second act.

Mavis, Margaret, Claire, Jean, Betty, Flo and Joyce were all beaming as they walked out onto the stage, all of them full of confidence after the first half of the show had gone so well. Jean in particular was on such a high and she couldn't resist yet another twirl with her arms stretched out causing the others to laugh.

'Jean's still dancing with the swans and ducks,' Flo teased.

'Oh, when I get some time alone, I always like to take,' Joyce sang softly.

'Take myself away from all the huts, and head down to the lake,' Betty continued, and they all laughed again.

Claire, Mavis and Margaret were already in position in the cottage.

'Come on, you four; let's have you over here and ready in your places!'

Frank smiled to himself. Claire was still organising the girls even here on the stage.

Bill had walked over to the girls.

'Everybody set?'

'Yes, I think so, thanks, Bill,' Margaret answered.

'I can't wait,' Jean chipped in.

'Good. I will go give Jo the signal. Good luck, ladies!' With that Bill and Frank left the stage.

'I reckon it's time we got Mavis and Keith together, don't you?' Margaret said causing the others to laugh again just as the lights in the hall dropped and a hush fell over the audience still hidden behind the curtains.

'Here we go,' whispered Claire.

The band struck up and the curtains swung back, and the stage was suddenly brightly lit once more with the main light focused on the girls in the cottage, who were now all busy working on the enemy codes.

As the introduction came to an end, Margaret drew a breath ready to sing.

Margaret: *There's been an increase in Italian signals,*
And Mavis thinks this could be really key.
So all of us are frantic at the Cottage,
We must explain this high activity.

Mavis: *It's looking like it's coming from their navy,*
They talk about the sailing of their fleet.
We've really got to get these signals sorted,
And send back all our Intel as complete.

Claire: *The Italians have upgraded their Enigma*
Dilly's sure that everything has been re-wired
All the cribs we have no longer give the answers
We must soldier on although we are so tired.

ALL: *They call us Dilly's Girls*
Or Dilly's Fillies!

Betty: *Only ladies are permitted on our crew.*
ALL: *Do we mind?*
Don't be silly!
Margaret: *Solving the Enigma's what we do!*

ALL: *We're Dilly's Girls*
Dilly's Fillies!
Joyce: *You've always got to think outside the box.*
ALL: *Clues to find*
Count on Dilly!
Flo: *So proud to be the team of Dillwyn Knox!*

Betty was standing over by the blackboard mounted on the cottage wall, which had been covered in chalk letters. But one letter was missing and as she sang Betty wrote it up on the board.

Betty: *Now Enigma has a critical design flaw*
It will never map a letter to itself
One night Mavis realised she had a dud test message
That did not have a single letter 'L'!

The stage lights then dropped so that there was now just a single spotlight on Mavis who was sitting at the table in the cottage all alone, as the other girls dropped back into the shadows. It was late at night and Mavis was pondering her discovery.

Mavis: *Our Italian friend had pressed*
the same key over
The same single key to generate his test
I'm certain this will give us all the answers
But I need help with my math to solve the rest.

As Mavis sang that last word of the verse a second light illuminated the office over on the other side of the stage, where Keith was sat working at the other desk.

Mavis jumped up from her chair and left the cottage though its side door to reappear from behind the cottage at the back of the stage. She ran over to the main house where she knew Keith was working late and persuaded him to come back with her to the cottage to help. While Mavis and Keith were acting out this scene the other girls were all back in the lights centre stage and carried on singing.

Margaret: *Mavis knew her Keith was*
over at The Mansion
Just like her he was working through the night
Claire: *And with his help and thanks*
to Dilly's rodding
We were able to decipher all by light!

As the girls all sang the next chorus, Mavis and Keith, now back in the cottage, were acting out working together on the maths needed to resolve the wiring of the rotors based on the breakthrough that Mavis had discovered. At one point Mavis deliberately knocked her pencil onto the floor by Keith. Keith looked up at his wife and saw that she was beaming back at him. He knew straight away what she was up to as she had done exactly the same thing on that fateful night. She had later told him that she had really liked him and had hoped that he would gallantly pick it up for her. But he had revealed that he had been wise to her clumsy attempt to get a reaction and had ignored it, and this time was going to be no different.

'I think you have dropped your pencil, darling,' he whispered and gave Mavis a wink.

Mavis laughed. Meanwhile the girls were all singing the song:

ALL: *They call us Dilly's Girls*
Or Dilly's Fillies!
Betty: *Only ladies are permitted on our crew.*
ALL: *Do we mind?*
Don't be silly!
Margaret: *Solving the Enigma's what we do!*

At the end of the first section of the chorus the music cut for a small piece of dialogue between the two intrepid codebreakers.

Keith: You did it, Mavis, you really did it!
Mavis: We did it, Keith.
Keith: Yes, I suppose we did.

Keith pulled Mavis toward him and gave her a massive hug, causing Mavis to act startled and Keith to mutter out an apology.

Keith: Oh! Oh my! I am so sorry, Mavis.
Mavis: Oh, for heaven's sake! What are you like? Come here.

Mavis pulled her husband toward her and gave him a massive kiss, causing a huge cheer and several loud whistles from the audience. The rest of Dilly's Girls continued to sing.

ALL: *We're Dilly's Girls*
Dilly's Fillies!
Joyce: *You've always got to think outside the box.*
ALL: *Clues to find!*
Count on Dilly!
Flo: *So proud to be the team of Dillwyn Knox!*

Margaret: *We've just heard that our*
efforts were successful,
We've really showed our Navy that we can.
This all led to our boys defeating their ships
In battle at the Cape of Matapan!

Jean: *So all thanks to that lazy signal soldier*
And to our Mavis for her working out the key
The whole Italian navy has been wiped out
No longer any threat out on the sea!

Dilly's Girls

Betty: *Dilly took our Mavis out one night to dinner*
To the Fountain Inn on Stony Stratford Road
He was keen to celebrate and say thank you
For her breakthrough in the cracking of the code!

Claire: *But when Dilly drives his treasured Baby Austin*
You really don't want to be in Dilly's way
His driving is a total highway nightmare
We so hope that Mavis makes it back OK!

Dilly's Baby Austin 7

ALL: *They call us Dilly's Girls*
Or Dilly's Fillies!
Betty: *Only ladies are permitted on our crew.*
ALL: *Do we mind?*
Don't be silly!
Margaret: *Solving the Enigma's what we do!*

Dilly's Girls – Part II

ALL: *We're Dilly's Girls*
Dilly's Fillies!
Joyce: *You've always got to think outside the box.*
ALL: *Clues to find!*
Count on Dilly!
Flo: *So proud to be the team of Dillwyn Knox!*

Joyce: *Now you won't believe what's*
just come in from London.
It's only from the Admiral of our fleet.
He's credited the victory to our work here,
And says he's on his way to meet and greet!

Keith was back sitting at the table in the cottage as his wife and the other girls continued to dance, sing and perform all around him. He knew that the girls were about to get a huge surprise, and he could not wait to see their reaction.

The battle of Matapan had been Britain's first big victory of the war and had been a huge morale boost for everyone back at home, not to mention having been so decisive as to have taken the entire Italian fleet out of the war for good. The victory was in no small part down to the Italian Enigma messages that the girls were now able to de-code in the cottage.

Dilly had fought to ensure that the Intelligence gleaned from the cottage made its way to the people who needed to see it. In this case the person that needed to see it had been Admiral Sir Andrew Cunningham who was in charge of the Mediterranean fleet. Using this crucial information made available to him, Cunningham had routed the Italian Navy and had been hailed as the 'New Nelson' by Churchill and had been reported as a British hero in the press.

But for the workers at Bletchley, and in particular the girls in the cottage, it is what happened next that had been truly remarkable. The Director of Naval Intelligence, Admiral John Henry Godfrey, had written to them to say that this victory had been completely down to them, and not only that, he and Cunningham had then gone out of their way to pay them a visit in the cottage to thank them all personally. It was most unusual, if not totally unheard of, for such high-ranking commanders to pay a tribute in this way.

This visit was now about to be played out in the show and what the girls didn't know was that Cunningham was back at Bletchley and had been in the audience that evening, and not only that, he had jumped at the chance to join in and play himself in the scene.

Nigel stepped through the cottage door.

Claire: *Here's Dilly and he's looking quite excited.*
Dilly: *Girls, there's someone here that*
you must come and see,
It's the Admiral of the British Royal Navy
And he's here to thank you for our victory!

ALL: *They call us Dilly's Girls*
Or Dilly's Fillies!
Betty: *Only ladies are permitted on our crew.*
ALL: *Do we mind?*
Don't be silly!
Margaret: *Solving the Enigma's what we do!*

ALL: *We're Dilly's Girls*
Dilly's Fillies!
Joyce: *You've always got to think outside the box.*
ALL: *Clues to find!*
Count on Dilly!
Flo: *So proud to be the team of Dillwyn Knox!*

Dilly: Ladies, may I introduce you all to Admiral Sir Andrew Cunningham, Commander in Chief of the British Mediterranean fleet.

Cunningham stepped through the door and into the cottage. Keith was watching for his wife's reaction. Mavis and the other girls did not disappoint as jaws quite literally hit the floor!

The Admiral was dressed in full uniform just as he had been when he had visited the cottage after Matapan. Although most of the audience had seen Cunningham earlier sitting down at the front with Denniston and his wife, and many had even shaken his hand before the show or during the intermission, no one expected to see him up on the stage. There was an audible gasp when he appeared, which was quickly followed by everyone getting to their feet to give Sir Andrew a standing ovation.

Frank had told Keith during the intermission that Cunningham would be coming on to the stage. It had been Denniston's suggestion since he too had been roped into a cameo appearance of himself later in this second act. According to Frank, the Admiral had not needed much persuasion and had bragged that he had been a regular star-turn in the crew revues on board his flagship HMS Warspite during the war. As the applause thundered around the hall, Sir Andrew moved straight over to Mavis to shake her hand.

'Ah, Mrs Batey, I believe congratulations on your wedding are in order,' the Admiral said, smiling. 'It's so lovely to see you again, my dear.'

'Thank you, sir.' Mavis could feel herself colouring up. 'This is an even bigger surprise than your last visit!'

By now the applause was dying down and everyone in the hall was taking their seats again and it was Claire who got things back on script once more.

```
Claire: Lovely to meet you, sir.
Margaret: Welcome to our cottage, sir.
Mavis: Thank you for coming to see us, sir.
Joyce: Some wine, sir?
```

Dilly threw Joyce a puzzled look.

```
Betty: Oh, when we heard that the Admiral was coming to
    see us, Mavis, Joyce and I rushed down to the Eight
    Bells pub at the bottom of the road and bought some
    bottles of wine!
Mavis: I hope that's alright, sir?
```

Mavis nudged the Admiral and nodded toward the sheets of paper he had been holding as he had walked onto the stage. 'It's your line now, sir,' she whispered.

Admiral: Ah, absolutely! Yes please, my dear. Now, Dilly old boy, make sure you and all your ladies have a glass to hand. I would very much like to say a few words and propose a toast.

'How was that?' the Admiral whispered back, smiling broadly, and clearly feeling very pleased with himself.

'That was just perfect, sir.' Mavis beamed back.

Jo and the band began to play a soft melody over which Sir Andrew began his piece, speaking the words at first but very soon he had settled and was right into the part, and Mavis was thrilled to see him actually beginning to sing the lines.

Admiral: *When your message first came through,*
I wasn't quite sure what to do
So much detail, all their plans
laid bare for all to see
But a friend who Dilly knew, told me
to put my trust in all of you
And what he told me of your boss
was good enough for me.

Italian intentions were astute,
to hit British convoys when en route,
from Egypt and then while sailing on to Greece
It was time to hatch a plan, and with
your Intel show we can
A plan so cunning it would class a masterpiece!

But we had to play it cool, local spies we had to fool
In Alexandria they watched my every move.

Dilly's Girls – Part II

So I had to find a way, to let us get our fleet away
In secret so surprise was ours to use.

Well golfing is my game, and I made
sure they saw my name,
as I packed my things, and booked
in at the local course
Then under cover of the night,
my men and I made flight
And our ships set sail to intercept their force.

Well the plan turned out so neat,
we destroyed their entire fleet
The Italian Navy now removed for all the war
And, ladies, this was all down to you,
oh and of course to Dilly too!
So a toast to you, your breakthroughs,
here's to many more!

ALL: *To many more! Cheers!*

Admiral: Now, ladies, what do you all get up to here at Bletchley when you are not hard at work breaking all these enemy codes?
Betty: All sorts of things, sir!
Jean: I love playing rounders.
Admiral: Rounders? Well so do I! Well, ladies, it is a lovely afternoon, so who is going to have a game with me?
ALL: Yes please, sir!

Sir Andrew laughed.

Admiral: So, you have all the equipment then?
Jean: We use part of an old broom handle for the bat,

sir. Someone drilled a hole in it and added a strap. Oh, and we have a tennis ball!

Claire: There used to be quite a lot of arguing about the rules so some of the Dons wrote them all down.

Flo: In Latin of course.

Now everyone laughed.

Betty: We use trees as our bases.

Rounders on the lawn

As Betty spoke these final words of the scene in the cottage, the band struck up the introduction to the next song and everyone in the cottage began to move out through the door.

The script had said that they should all be chatting and should appear thrilled to be going to play a game of rounders with the Admiral, but no directions were necessary as all the girls were very excited just to see the real Sir Andrew, and he was very much enjoying being the centre of their attention as they left the stage.

Keith put his arm around his wife as they followed the others through the cottage door.

'I thought old Cunningham handled that brilliantly, didn't you?'

'You knew, didn't you?' Mavis exclaimed.

Keith laughed. 'I only found out ten minutes ago, darling. Frank told me, just before I came on. I think the Admiral only agreed to do it in the interval. Apparently, it was when Denniston told him that he was appearing in the show later on that Cunningham asked if he could too. Bill wasn't so sure it was a good idea, but Frank jumped at the chance to have the Admiral involved. I knew it wouldn't faze Dilly's Girls though!'

Mavis laughed and hugged her husband. The show was going better than she had dared to dream.

The Golf, Chess and Cheese Society

GETTING BACK OUT THROUGH the cottage door was proving a slow process. Not only was everyone still fussing around the Admiral, but almost the entire cast were congregated down both stage wings excitedly preparing to get on stage for what was going to be the biggest number in terms of people on stage, apart perhaps from the two act finales.

It was to be a celebration of the social side of life at Bletchley during the war, which had certainly been very active and varied. During the first months of the war the park's population had mainly consisted of university types who were all well used to organised clubs and extracurricular activities, and so it was not too long before various organised social societies began to take shape at Bletchley. As the park expanded and its population grew, so did the range of activities available to everyone. One of the most popular of these activities had been the Scottish Dancing Club, which had been set up and run by Hugh Foss, another one of Dilly's colleagues from the early days of GC&CS.

Hugh Foss was a proud Scotsman and another larger than life and eccentric Bletchley character. It was Hugh who had readily agreed to take charge of all the choreography for this next number. Just like so many of the old-school codebreakers at Bletchley, Hugh had many eccentricities, but he was an easy going and good-humoured character and was regarded very fondly by everyone that knew or worked with him.

As Keith and Mavis struggled to make their way past the gathered cast members all eagerly waiting to go on from the cottage side of the stage, Keith glanced across the stage and smiled to himself as he caught sight of Hugh, who was waiting with the other half of the cast over in the wings stage-right.

Hugh was hard to miss. He was well over six feet tall, and his height along with a big red bushy beard made him very easy to spot under any circumstance. Hugh had persuaded his wife Alison to help with the organisation for this particular song in the show. Alison was here with Keith, Mavis and the others behind the cottage stage-left, and she was trying but struggling to get everyone lined up and ready for their big entrance.

Keith nudged his wife. 'Looks like poor Alison is in a dreadful tizz.'

'Oh, bless her,' Mavis offered, 'it's a good job she has Frank here to help her out.'

Alison Foss was the complete opposite of her husband in both appearance and outlook. She was short and dumpy while her husband was very tall and lanky, and Keith had always thought that they had made for a bit of an odd couple when he had seen them dance together at the Scottish Reels Club. She was also dreadfully disorganised, so much so that Hugh always had to leave work at four-thirty every day to head back home to their bungalow in the village of Aspley Guise, just to the east of Bletchley, to sort the daily early-evening domestic chaos, cook the tea, and then get their two young children to bed. But Hugh and Alison were such a lovely couple and everyone that knew them adored them.

Hugh Foss was a quite brilliant codebreaker and had ended the war in charge of the Japanese section in Hut 7. But away from the pressures of work Hugh loved to indulge his passion for Scottish Highland dancing. His Scottish Reels Club had proven to be one of the more popular societies at Bletchley, and Hugh quickly became known around the park as the 'King of Reels'. His dancing was as fantastically elegant as his codebreaking.

The Reels Club had begun with meetings in the mansion's ballroom, and these meetings always drew lots of interest. The gramophone would be set up in the corner and then the rumble of feet on the wooden floor could then be heard across Bletchley Park. Once the Assembly Hall had been built the club moved here, but during the summer meets would also be held outside and Scottish dancing was often seen down by the lake and even on the croquet lawn.

The Scottish dancing club became so popular that Hugh's copy of the Circassion Circle dance quite literally wore out, and a collection was quickly organised to buy him a new one. There really was no more popular club than Hugh's dancing club, and Hugh made sure that more elaborate and formal dances were held regularly throughout the war years. A full-dress dance was always held on St Andrew's Day, for example.

Tonight, Hugh and Alison were both resplendent in their full Scottish Highland dress. Hugh was wearing his black formal Prince Charlie jacket with its dazzling silver buttons over a black waistcoat, white shirt and a black bowtie. His green tartan kilt was fronted by a large furry sporran, and knee-length thick white socks were bound by black cord down to his black dancing shoes. His outfit was finished off by his matching tartan fly plaid sash which hung over his shoulder and was held in place by a large elaborate silver brooch. Alison looked just as stunning in her ankle-length tartan skirt and colour coordinated blouse. She also had a tartan sash over her shoulder with a brooch which matched her husband's, although hers was a slightly smaller version.

Although the Fosses were sporting by far the most eye-catching of all the outfits on display, there were many other elaborate offerings that were about to appear on stage. As well as all the Scottish dancers there were cast members dressed as Shakespearian actors, some were athletes and tennis players, there were bakers and cooks, some were wearing choral gowns, and many just dressed in their usual Bletchley attire.

The audience had finally settled down after the rousing response to the Admiral's unexpected appearance. The back walls of the cottage and mansion had been swung back and the stage cleared, and Jo had brought the band back to life with some wonderful violin playing as the entire waiting ensemble streamed onto the stage from both sides. Keith noted that the music definitely had a Scottish feel to it, which he thought was a lovely nod to Hugh and Alison's choreography efforts, and very quickly all the audience were clapping along.

The song was to be a celebration of all the different social activities that had been embraced by the Bletchley Park workers during the war years.

As the Bletchley social calendar had become ever more expansive, a board on a wall in the canteen had been given over to club announcements and notices. It had not taken long before some unknown Bletchley worker had coined a generic name for this alternate GC&CS world and had stuck a large wooden sign above the notice board which simply read: 'The Golf, Chess & Cheese Society'.

As the introduction to the song played, the cast all danced onto the stage. The Scottish dancers formed a circle in the middle and began to skip and twirl to the music, and Keith smiled from the wings as he noticed that Hugh's old gramophone had even made an appearance, having been placed on a table at the back of the stage.

Over on the side two Bletchley workers sat at a table deep in concentration as they played a game of chess, moving the pieces about the board in an exaggerated way in time to the music. A group of actors recreated a scene from a Shakespeare play, the men in tights, codpieces and ruffs, and the ladies dazzled in their recreations of Elizabethan dresses. Two more of the cast were acting out a game of tennis and there were several in their sports kit exercising and stretching ready for their daily run. Another table had been placed on the other side of the stage and had been covered in tins and bowls. Three members of the cast were sporting aprons with one wearing a giant chef's hat, and they were busying themselves baking; tossing tins to one another and waving large wooden spoons in the air. Finally, there were several of the cast dressed in winter clothes with thick woolly hats and scarves pretending to skate around the circle of Scottish dancers.

The Assembly Hall stage really was a colourful and magical sight, with everyone skipping, dancing or simply performing in time to Joanna's upbeat Bletchley jig. As the opening melody came to an end the Scottish circle split apart, and Hugh and Alison danced their way to the front of the stage and began to sing.

Hugh & Alison: *Oh Bletchley's not all work,*
you know, sometimes we do have fun.
Just get yourself along one night and
we'll show you how it's done.

Fancy being in a play?
Or baking cakes for tea?
Then the only place for you is the Golf,
Chess and Cheese... Society!

One of the other Scottish dancers took over the singing as Hugh and Alison performed some especially intricate Highland Reel manoeuvres.

Scottish Dancer: *If Scottish dancing is your*
thing then Hugh Foss is your man.
Those Highland Reels hold such appeal
so come and join his clan.
His gramophone will grab you,
The music sets you free!
Then the only place for you is the Golf,
Chess and Cheese... Society!

Down with the band Jo now led the musicians through a break to a piece of typical Highland music as Hugh and his wife completed their routine before seamlessly switching back to the main melody as the whole ensemble turned to the front and sang the first chorus together.

ALL: *Oh it's the Golf!*
And the Chess!
It's the Cheese!
Society

Oh it's the Golf!
And the Chess!
It's the Cheese!
Society

The Scottish dancers all returned to their circle toward the back of the stage as the Shakespearian actors moved front-centre and continued the singing, with one holding up Yorick's skull as he sang the famous words.

The Golf, Chess and Cheese Society

Actor: *The drama scene at Bletchley runs*
productions by the score.
Our actors strut their stuff and always
leave them wanting more.
Tonight they're doing Shakespeare,
To be or not to be
Then the only place for you is the Golf,
Chess and Cheese... Society!

Now it was the turn of the two chess players to take over the singing at the front of the stage.

Chess Players: *If you're into quizzes then*
we'll see you down the pub.
Test your brain against the best,
and then relax with beer and grub.
Do you know the answers?
Well come along and see,
Then the only place for you is the Golf,
Chess and Cheese... Society!

ALL: *Oh it's the Golf!*
And the Chess!
It's the Cheese!
Society

Oh it's the Golf!
And the Chess!
It's the Cheese!
Society

Next the sportsmen and women took up the prime position centre-front and took over the singing.

Athletes: *There is athletics in the summer;*
Turing is the man to beat.
Dig out your spikes; get on your marks,
if you can stand the heat.
Fancy running, or some jumping?
All there for you for free.
Then the only place for you is the Golf,
Chess and Cheese... Society!

Anyone for tennis? We have courts here in the Park.
Some of us are so keen we even knock-up after dark.
You're looking for the balls?
Oh Dilly's hit them in the tree!
Then the only place for you is the Golf,
Chess and Cheese... Society!

ALL: *Oh it's the Golf!*
And the Chess!
It's the Cheese!
Society

Oh it's the Golf!
And the Chess!
It's the Cheese!
Society

Just before her call up to Bletchley Joanna had been studying classical and choral music at university, and for this point in the song she had used all her skills to turn this mid-section into a piece which would not have sounded out of place in a church or cathedral. She led the musicians as the band elegantly switched to a more classical and softer take on the song's core melody.

At the same time the entire ensemble lined up toward the front of the stage in a gentle curve around the four cast members who were wearing the choral gowns, and who were now stood front-centre on the stage.

Jo had put down her violin and had moved to stand in front of her choir below the stage, and with her arms stretched out began to carefully orchestrate the four-part harmonies she had written and which the group had painstakingly rehearsed for the next segment of the song.

Choir: *The Bletchley choirs are to behold,*
you need to hear them sing.
They'll have a go at anything from
carols through to swing.
Keep your eye on the conductor,
She will count you one two three
Then the only place for you is the Golf,
Chess and Cheese... Society!

The improvised choir were not finished yet and the harmonies continued as the singers played with the words from the song's title.

Society, society,
Golf and chess
Chess and cheese
Cheese and golf
Society
Chess and golf
Cheese and chess
Golf and cheese
Society
Golf, chess, cheese, chess, chess, golf, cheese, chess!
Society, society, society, society
Then the only place, the only place, the only place,
for you, for you to be!
Then the only place for you is the Golf,
Chess and Cheese... Society!

As the choristers held that last note Jo swung back to face her musicians, and with a crisp hand signal brought the band back in with the original up-beat Bletchley jig. Most of the cast on stage then skipped back to their original positions, just leaving the ones dressed as bakers down at the front.

The chief chef – who had been holding his hat during the choral piece – now popped his toque blanche back on his head and as their table was pushed into the centre of the stage the three cooks continued the singing.

Cooks: *The cooking classes are the best;*
there are always lots to eat.
To have these cakes, the buns and tarts,
is always such a treat!
Coming back for seconds?
Some more I hear you plea
Then the only place for you is the Golf,
Chess and Cheese... Society!

As the whole cast sang the next chorus they danced around the chefs, pretending to take and taste the various cakes, buns and tarts that they had been singing about.

ALL: *Oh it's the Golf!*
And the Chess!
It's the Cheese!
Society

Oh it's the Golf!
And the Chess!
It's the Cheese!
Society

Finally, it was the turn of the cast who were all decked out in their winter clothes to lead the singing through the final two verses of the song.

Skaters: *In the winter we have fun and games*
just messing in the snow.

The Golf, Chess and Cheese Society

I know it's cold but always fun,
so come and have a go.
The only thing we might not do
Is if you want to ski
Then the only place for you is the Golf,
Chess and Cheese... Society!

If the winter's really cold there is
something sure to please.
As all the water turns to ice the
Bletchley Lake will freeze.
So it's time to get your skates on,
Now balance is the key
Then the only place for you is the Golf,
Chess and Cheese... Society!

For the final chorus all the cast were on their feet singing and dancing together. Chess players linked arms with Scottish dancers. Tennis players and athletes danced with chefs. Shakespearian actors skipped around with ice skaters. The stage just became one huge joyful collection of Bletchley workers having the time of their lives.

ALL: *Oh it's the Golf!*
And the Chess!
It's the Cheese!
Society

Oh it's the Golf!
And the Chess!
It's the Cheese!
Society

It's the Golf, Chess and Cheese... Society!

Society!

The audience had not known quite where to look and who to follow as the cast had danced and sung their way through the last part of the song. But what appeared to be a random Bletchley celebration up on the stage had in fact been very carefully choreographed by Hugh and Alison. Hours of practice had ensured that everyone up on the stage knew exactly where they were meant to be. As the dancers weaved in and out of the various circles and lines, when the song finally hit its rousing conclusion, they had formed two rows across the front of the stage, and on the final note the front row dropped down to its knees as everyone threw their hands into the air.

The Assembly Hall erupted once more with clapping, cheers, whistles and calls for more.

Frank, Mavis, Keith and the girls were all cheering too from the wings.

'Oh Frank, that was amazing,' Mavis shouted over the thunderous noise in the hall.

'Jo and Hugh did a pretty spectacular job, didn't they?' Frank beamed back.

Out on stage everyone was taking their well-deserved bows, probably for the seventh or eighth time at least.

'Right.' Frank looked toward Mavis and the others. 'You are back on, ladies!'

Lobsters & Crabs

THE LIGHTS CUT sending the stage back into darkness. As Hugh, Alison, their dancers, and the rest of the ensemble headed back off into the wings, stagehands were already busy adjusting the set ready for the next song.

Once the audience had settled down, Jo started up the next number which opened with a sinister sounding melody played on just the piano.

It was even darker now in the wings where Mavis was waiting with the other girls ready for the next song. Mavis jumped as a man dressed in a dark suit and wearing a hat tipped forward over his eyes brushed past her.

'Oh, Peter, I didn't see you coming there!'

'Sorry, my dear,' he whispered back, 'I can barely see where I'm going in this light.'

It was her boss and Keith's best man, Peter Twinn, who had taken over their section when Dilly had left Bletchley.

'Good luck,' Mavis whispered back as Peter was followed onto the stage by three other members of Dilly's ISK Team, who were all dressed in a similarly shifty way. All were playing the part of a Nazi spy and each took up position in a corner of the stage.

'Come along, Margaret, we need to be over the other side.' It was Nigel, and here in the darkened wings Mavis could not help but think of how much he looked like Dilly. This next song was so important to her and she had spent a long time working with Jo and Frank on the tune and the words.

Dilly had loved Lewis Carroll's stories since childhood, and he had brought the magic of Alice and all the other characters into the daily routine in the cottage, which had made the challenge of code breaking so much more inspiring. The skit he wrote with Frank at the end of the first war had been based on Alice's adventures, and Mavis had wanted some of that Carrollian magic to feature in their tribute to Dilly here tonight.

'I'll see you others on stage shortly,' Margaret said to the other girls as she and Nigel disappeared off back down the stairs to cut across through the kitchen area behind the stage to get to the other side.

The lights were still down and the audience was now hushed as the music continued its gentle but sinister melody.

Suddenly a light came on focused on the first spy. His trilby was pulled down over his eyes and he had a newspaper tucked up under his arm as he cupped his hands around his mouth, lighting a cigarette. Once lit, he took a drag, puffed out the smoke, and then began to speak.

Nazi Spy 1: I spy, with my little eye, an Enigma beginning with 'A'.

The rest of the band suddenly struck a loud note causing several people in the audience to jump, and then it was back to just the piano. The first light went out and a second now came on, this time lighting up German spy number two.

Nazi Spy 2: A more complex machine has never been seen, totally unbreakable some may say.

Another loud couple of notes from the other musicians caused many of the same people to jump for a second time, and then just as before, the light went out and it was back to just the piano. Now the third spy was lit, and this time it was a lady's voice that spoke out from under another large trilby.

Nazi Spy 3: Up the quota, an extra rotor, that's four now to scramble the text.

The same sudden notes sounded from the band, followed by the same switching of the spotlight, and now it was the turn of spy number four.

Nazi Spy 4: As it happens, there's no pattern, to predict which rotor turns next.

The cycle of lights and spies repeated one more time.

Nazi Spy 1: Hut 6 is in a fix, they can't crack it so what should they do?

Nazi Spy 2: You need unorthodox, so give it to Knox, his ladies will find the clue.

Nazi Spy 3: I spy, with my little eye, an Enigma beginning with 'A'.

Nazi Spy 4: Abwher Enigma.

The stage lights dropped once more. The four Nazi spies slinked away into the darkness and the sinister piano refrain abruptly stopped.

There were a few seconds of dark silence and then suddenly the stage lit up and Jo brought the band in with the introduction to the next song, which was bright and upbeat and an immediate contrast to the previous section with the German spies.

Mavis and the girls burst through the cottage door and began to go about their work in the cottage.

Margaret and Dilly then appeared from behind the mansion office and walked toward the front of the stage.

Margaret began to sing.

Margaret: *'Spy Enigma', is what Dilly calls it,*
used by Intelligence.
'Abwehr Enigma', is its real name,
that's German for Defence!

An answer Hut 6 could not find
So let's see if we can

With Dilly's ever inventive mind
I'm sure he'll hatch a plan!

Jo softened the music for the next lines of dialogue before Margaret started to sing once again. The girls in the cottage had now gathered around Margaret and Dilly in the middle of the stage.

Dilly: Ladies, I am going to call this 'Operation Double Cross!', and I think our team needs a special name too.

Mavis: How about 'Illicit Signals Knox'?! Or even better 'Intelligence Service Knox'!

Dilly: Yes, yes, yes! ISK, I love it! That is it!

Margaret: *Dilly's buzzing, he's so excited,*
great to see him back on form.
Hear him humming, we're so delighted,
it's all one great brainstorm.

It's used by German High Command
It's not been seen before
Enigma yes, but different brand
We'll give this thing what for!

Dilly: *All that Abwher traffic that we get to see,*
Shows this new machine has changed the way
that messages are marked
Letters listed in two blocks of four
Is not their method anymore,
It's now a single string of eight that sets the key!

This leads me to deduce a crucial fact,
That four rotors not the normal three are
used to mix the text
Not only this, but you will find

Lobsters & Crabs

These four can turn at any time
But it's when all four turn together
we must act!

To solve this there's a plan I have evolved
Take each message key, and break it down,
and link the letters thus
One-five two-six, three-seven four-eight
Extend the chain to illustrate
A repeated sequence means all four revolved!

ALL: *Wonderland! Wonderland!*
Wonderland! Wonderland!
The Cottage has become our Wonderland!
It seems so easy to our Dilly
Just look again and you will see
His inventive mind gives us the upper hand!
In our Wonderland.

Dilly: *When all four rotors, turn together,*
that's when we'll find our proof.
But there's more, question whether,
it's an isolated move.

These chains of letters move sideways
When checking keeping tab
As all four wheels turn that's the phase
That we'll now call a crab!

These crabs are fairly common, look and see
They almost always come in groups which
makes deciphering so hard
So we need to find a lonely crab
All by itself, that would be fab
A lonely crab's our lobster and the key!

Dilly: Ladies, you are now on a lobster hunt.
Find me a lobster!

ALL: *Wonderland! Wonderland!*
Wonderland! Wonderland!
The Cottage has become our Wonderland!
It seems so easy to our Dilly
Just look again and you will see
His inventive mind gives us the upper hand!
In our Wonderland.

The group of intrepid codebreakers now began to act out a scene that represented day after day of hard work in the Cottage working at breaking this new German Enigma. Dilly in particular was looking really exhausted and was struggling to move around, stumbling against the table. Then Mavis started up the singing again.

Mavis: *Night after night, Dilly's working,*
surviving just on tea.
It isn't right, Dilly's hurting,
he needs to let it be!

Claire: *He needs to head back to Courns Wood*
He needs to take it slow.
Now Olive's told him that he should
His illness won't let go.

The audience watched as the girls waved Dilly off as he headed back home, leaving them to work on the code breaking alone.

Mavis: *Dilly's home now, and we're so busy,*
on his lobster trail.
We'll do this somehow, we know it's tricky,
but we're sure we will prevail!

Lobsters & Crabs

Who was it said cryptology couldn't be fun?
Thanks to Dilly the most boring of our tasks are brought to life
Using poetry and crazy names
No decoding job becomes the same
His wacky word games help so much to get it done

Lewis Carroll is the writer he loves best
A question Dilly loves to ask is which way a clock hands turn?
Oh clockwise is what you all will say
But if you're the clock it's not that way!
Think inside Enigma and you will pass the test.

The Cottage has become our Wonderland
Just like Alice he has taught us always look behind the glass
Starfish, beetles, slugs and even snakes!
Crabs and lobsters are now what it takes
Look out beyond the box and you will understand!

ALL: *Wonderland! Wonderland!*
Wonderland! Wonderland!
The Cottage has become our Wonderland!
It seems so easy to our Dilly
Just look again and you will see
His inventive mind gives us the upper hand!
In our Wonderland.

Margaret: Then on the 8th December 1941 it happened!

Margaret: *Mavis has cracked it, she broke a message, and from then on we were in.*
We attacked it, read every message, transmitted to Berlin.

Dilly's Girls

Claire: *The cottage needed to expand*
So Dilly gained a hut.
I.S.K. was now the brand
Not even Denniston could shut!

Mavis: *It's never ending, so much traffic,*
their entire network laid bare!
Always sending, typographic,
so much data to compare!

Those Abwher keys gave Bletchley such a say
This was the crowning moment of our
Dilly's brilliant career
Knowing how this new Enigma mapped
All Nazi spy talk could now be tracked
From Pearl Harbor through to Europe's victory day!

Decoding all their signals with such speed
Confirmation from Berlin that all our agents
are believed
And tracking all those Nazi mobsters
All thanks to Dilly's search for lobsters
Gestapo plans laid bare for
Bletchley Park to read!

ALL: *Wonderland! Wonderland!*
Wonderland! Wonderland!
The Cottage has become our Wonderland!
It seems so easy to our Dilly
Just look again and then you will see
His inventive mind gives us the upper hand!
In our Wonderland.

Margaret: *All down to Dilly's rotor hunch*
And Mavis keeping tabs

Now all we want to eat for lunch
Are lobsters please, no crabs!

ALL: *All down to Dilly's rotor hunch*
And Mavis keeping tabs
Now all we want to eat for lunch
Are lobsters please, no crabs!

Are lobsters please, no crabs!

The audience responded to the end of the song with their usual enthusiastic applause and cheering. Just as things begin to settle down once again the main stage light swung over to the mansion office. The office door opened, and Commander Denniston stepped out onto the stage and sat down at the desk. The Assembly Hall erupted with cheering and more applause and everyone in the hall immediately got to their feet. Mavis was watching Dilly's old friend and boss closely, and could see that he appeared genuinely taken aback by everyone's reaction to his appearance on stage.

Denniston had been ousted as the commander of Bletchley not long after Dilly had had to leave Bletchley to work from home due to his illness and Mavis knew just how upset Dilly had been when he had heard that Denniston had been moved on.

Instinctively Mavis went over to her old Commander and took his hand, urging him back onto his feet. She turned him toward the audience and then stood back to clap along with everyone else in the hall.

Alistair Denniston acknowledged the applause with a smile, a small wave, and by mouthing a very clear 'Thank you'. He then turned back to Mavis with a look that said, 'what on earth do I do now?'.

Mavis gave Denniston a hug and led him back to the table in the mansion office.

Dilly and Denniston had often disagreed about code breaking matters and this had often resulted in Dilly writing a long letter to his old friend, which more often than not included a threat to resign. But Denniston knew Dilly too well to be worried about such letters, and always knew exactly how to calm and smooth things over with his Chief Cryptographer.

The girls moved back over to the cottage and Denniston sat back down at his desk. Eventually the applause died down and everyone in the hall took their seats again.

There was a loud knock at the office door. It was Denniston's old secretary Barbara Abernethy; the lady who had opened the show with her old camera.

Denniston: Yes?

Barbara: You called, sir?

Denniston: Ah. Yes, please come in and sit down, Barbara. Please can you get the following message to Stewart Menzies at MI6 for me?

Barbara: Of course, sir.

Denniston: For Menzies' eyes only and to be delivered by courier.

Barbara: Yes, of course, sir.

Denniston: Regarding Abwher. Knox has again justified his reputation as our most original investigator of Enigma problems. First message read in full on December 8th. He attributes this success to two young girl members of his staff, Miss Rock and Miss Lever, and he gives them all the credit. He is of course the leader, but no doubt has selected and trained his staff to assist him in his somewhat unusual methods.

Alistair Denniston smiled to himself. He had hardly needed a script as these were the exact words he had messaged Menzies following the cottage's break of Abwher.

As soon as Denniston had finished speaking, the band burst back into action and Dilly's girls ran out from the cottage into the centre of the stage once more, singing as they went. Mavis and Claire went over to the mansion office and took Alistair and Barbara by the hand, leading them back out into the centre of the stage as the song came to its finale, so that they were all there centre stage to take another bow.

ALL: *Who was it said cryptology couldn't be fun?*
Thanks to Dilly the most boring of our
tasks are brought to life
Using poetry and crazy names
No code breaking job becomes the same
His wacky word games help so much to get it done

Wonderland! Wonderland!
Wonderland! Wonderland!
The Cottage has become our Wonderland!
It seems so easy to our Dilly
Just look again and then you will see
His inventive mind gives us the upper hand!
In our Wonderland!

As the stage lights dimmed after another rousing reaction from the audience, Claire led Denniston and Barbara to the back of the stage and then off into the wings while the other girls all headed back to the cottage.

Dilly's Girls – Part III

WHEN THE LIGHTS RELIT THE STAGE, Margaret, Mavis, Joyce, Betty, Flo and Jean were all busy at their work in the cottage checking messages and working with their rods on the day's Enigma traffic.

Down below the stage at the front, Jo started up the next song. The melody was instantly recognisable as the one that had appeared twice before in the show, but this time it was a softer, gentler interpretation, and Jo led the way on her violin.

Claire Harding appeared again from behind the office wall at the back of the stage and slowly walked forward toward the audience. She was reading a piece of paper and looked visibly upset by something.

As Claire began to sing, the other girls looked up from their tasks and moved out onto the stage and gathered round their friend and manager.

Claire: *A note has just come in from the Commander,*
It says here that our Dilly's taken ill.
Oh what are we to do without our leader?
Dilly says we must all show a strength of will

The letter says he can no longer travel.
But that he'll continue working from his home.

Dilly's Girls – Part III

We must keep things progressing at the cottage,
While our Dilly does his best out on his own.

The girls all sang the chorus together. But the song was not the upbeat joyful one that it had been before. This time it was being sung with sadness and heavy hearts.

ALL: *They call us Dilly's Girls*
Or Dilly's Fillies
Betty: *Only ladies are permitted on our crew*
ALL: *Do we mind?*
Don't be silly
Margaret: *Solving the Enigma's what we do*

ALL: *We're Dilly's Girls*
Dilly's Fillies
Joyce: *You've always got to think outside the box.*
ALL: *Clues to find*
Count on Dilly
Flo: *So proud to be the team of Dillwyn Knox*

Claire: *He will always be a key man*
here at Bletchley,
So dear to us and we all love him so.
He built his team of girls and we adore him,
Dilly, bless you, we will never let you go.

As Claire sang, Margaret was saying her farewells to the other girls and then left the stage through the cottage door.

Claire: *Margaret's gone to work with him*
at Courns Wood,
The two of them get back here when they can.
Mavis is now in charge here at the Cottage,
While Dilly carries on as our main man!

ALL: *They call us Dilly's Girls*
Or Dilly's Fillies
Betty: *Only ladies are permitted on our crew*
ALL: *Do we mind?*
Don't be silly
Margaret: *Solving the Enigma's what we do*

ALL: *We're Dilly's Girls*
Dilly's Fillies
Joyce: *You've always got to think*
outside the box.
ALL: *Clues to find*
Count on Dilly
Flo: *So proud to be the team of Dillwyn Knox!*

There was just a spattering of clapping as this short rendition of the song ended. The people watching were clearly not sure whether or not to clap following such a sad message. The lights dimmed and then came back up very quickly. The girls were still busy in the cottage working on Enigma. Just out of sight behind the mansion office wall Margaret stood with Nigel de Grey waiting to walk out onto the stage.

'All set, sir?' she whispered.

'Ah, Nigel will be fine,' answered Frank Birch who had just appeared and had spoken before de Grey had the chance to respond. 'You almost forgot these, old boy!'

Frank handed Nigel three exercise books which had been decorated to look like German code books.

'Goodness me, thank you, Frank.' De Grey had been so focused on the song he was about to sing that he had totally forgotten to pick up these key props. 'All set now, my dear,' Nigel answered Margaret. He leant to one side, putting his weight onto Dilly's old walking stick and smiled as he offered his other arm to Margaret.

Together Margaret and Nigel walked forward and out onto the stage; de Grey hunched over his stick and Margaret helping him along.

Jean: It's Margaret and Dilly!

Claire: Oh, welcome back, sir! It is so lovely to see you both.

Mavis: Oh, sir you must take care. Why have you come all this way?

Dilly: Good morning, ladies.

Girls: Morning, sir!

Dilly: How is it going today?

Mavis: Very slowly, sir, and very frustrating. After our breakthrough the other month we seem to be on a run of bad luck.

Dilly: Well, we hope that Alan Turing and his team are about to make a breakthrough on solving the latest 'Shark' German Naval Enigma codes. As you know the situation in the Atlantic has been desperate for months now.

Dilly turned toward the audience ready to begin signing the next song, which initially would not be much more than spoken word over a soft melody.

Atlantic Convoy

AS DE GREY STOOD at the front of the stage acting out the role of his old friend Dilly, he could just about see the front few rows of the audience and he caught sight of Olive Knox, Dilly's wife. Nigel had worked with Dilly and Olive in those very early days of Naval Intelligence in Room-40 during the first war and it suddenly struck him that he desperately hoped that he was not causing his old friend's wife any offence or upset by his portrayal of her husband. Whether Olive had noticed a look on his face, or whether purely by chance, she chose that precise moment to smile and blow him a small kiss. Nigel smiled and nodded back. Now seemingly having Olive's approval, it was time to really do her and Dilly proud.

Unlike Dilly, who had stayed on at Room-40 and had been a key player in the formation of GC&CS between the wars, de Grey had left when the Great War ended in 1918. He had been recalled at the outbreak of the Second World War and had arrived at Bletchley Park in 1939. By the end of World War Two he had risen to the position of Deputy Director of the Park under Commander Edward 'Jumbo' Travis.

As Jo and the band began the gentle and somewhat haunting introduction to the next song, he was suddenly stuck by the poignancy of the words he was about to sing. Since the war ended everyone had been in what seemed to be an endless but understandable state of celebration. Even the rehearsals for this evening's show had been held in an excited and happy atmosphere throughout.

The war had been won by a combination of many things. There had been the almost incomprehensible sacrifice by so many. The bravery, the determination, resourcefulness, invention, and imagination of the Allied forces and of the British people would surely be forever etched into the memorial of history. Then of course there was also the genius and dedication of all the people sat out in front of him here tonight in the Bletchley Assembly Hall; all his friends and colleagues.

But luck too had played its part. My goodness it had been such a close thing in the early days. De Grey remembered how the threat of imminent invasion had hung over the whole country during the summer of 1940. This threat had been especially felt at Bletchley as they began to regularly see references to an operation named 'Sea Lion' in intercepted Luftwaffe Enigma traffic. Everyone knew what this must refer to and what the Germans were planning; the Nazi invasion of Britain. But two unbelievable pieces of luck had presented themselves in the shape of two inexplicable German High Command decisions.

First, Adolf Hitler had told his Panzer tank divisions to halt their advance for two days just a few miles from Dunkirk when the German Army had the British Expeditionary Force at its mercy. This lucky break along with determined defensive fighting against all odds by many in the BEF allowed the miracle of the evacuation of over three hundred thousand troops – which included over one hundred and twenty thousand French troops – back home to British soil. Not only that, but the normally rough English Channel had been a millpond for the nine days of the evacuation. Only on one morning did an onshore breeze cause any sort of serious trouble. In the skies overhead, clouds, mist, and rain always seemed to appear at just the right times to limit the damage being caused by the terrifying Stuka dive-bombers and other Luftwaffe fighters and bombers. Quite literally on the day after the evacuation was over, the wind switched to the north and the beaches were once again being hammered by huge breaking waves. It really did seem that some higher divine influence might be at work.

Then at the height of the Battle of Britain the Luftwaffe suddenly turned their bombing away from the Royal Air Force Fighter Command airfields to London, just at the point when our pilots would soon have nowhere left to land their Spitfires and Hurricanes.

Would future generations ever be capable of understanding how close it all had been? How could they ever possibly fully understand just what this generation had gone through?

There was the bravery and sacrifice of so many, some whose actions and sacrifice would perhaps never be fully recognised or understood. He thought of the tens of thousands of British soldiers that had not made it home from the Dunkirk beaches, and who had fought a desperate rear-guard action to allow their comrades the chance of escape. Enigma had revealed that, of those not killed while trying to hold back the German advance, many had been immediately executed while the others had been taken as prisoners of war and made to march hundreds of miles east to be incarcerated under desperate conditions.

And there were the men and women who had given their lives on the chance of recovering some vital piece of intelligence that might just find its way to Bletchley so that the people here in the hall tonight could use it to potentially save thousands of other lives. The chances are that nobody would ever get to hear their stories.

De Grey looked down at the three code books he was gripping in his hands, thought of his old friend, and now, continuing his portrayal of Dilly, Nigel began to sing.

Dilly: *I'd like to make a bet tonight,*
That as years go by you will all lose sight,
Of the fear we faced and the sacrifices made.

Imagine waking every day,
And know that just some miles away,
The German Army is waiting ready to invade.

In 1940 we were it.
No U.S. yet, just British grit.
We faced the Nazi tyranny alone.

If Britain's Battle had been lost
Can you begin to count the cost?

To lose your way of life, your country,
lose your home?

At this point Jo and the band picked up the tempo of the song, changing the timing of the melody.

But while so many of you know,
of that battle in the sky,
Another's being fought that's just as key.
As important to our future, I'm telling you no lie,
Not planes, but ships, this one was fought at sea.

As the girls watched on from the cottage several other members of the cast had come on to the back of the stage all dressed as men and women of the Royal Navy and of the Merchant Navy. These sailors now joined with Dilly in the singing of the chorus. They stood across the stage between the back walls of the office and the cottage, and once they were in position a new back drop was lowered into place depicting a scene of some ships at sea.

ALL: *Oh, oh, oh, Atlantic convoys.*
Our lifeline in this time of misery.
Oh, oh, oh, a frantic deploy,
Of fuel and food supplies across the sea.

Oh, oh, oh, Atlantic convoys.
Hunted down by packs of U-Boats on the way,
Oh, oh, oh, Germanic war ploy,
To sink our ships and block our passageway.

As the congregated ensemble sang the rousing chorus, Margaret and Mavis moved over to stand by Dilly at the front of the stage and the three of them continued the story in song.

Margaret: *The German Navy Enigma was more*
complex than the rest,

Dilly's Girls

Code-named Dolphin it was proving hard to break.
Even Turing, and his team, working at their best
Couldn't solve the rotors now that they
were three from eight.

Mavis: *German U-Boats all lined up,*
right along those shipping lines.
Like hungry wolves they'd always operate in packs.
They had broken all our codes,
so it didn't take much time,
Before those U-Boats were set ready to attack!

Dilly: *1940 in just three months,*
several hundred ships were struck,
Countless perished every one of them a hero.
With Dolphin still unbroken,
we prayed to get some luck,
And then at last it came with
U-Boat U – 1 – 1 – Zero!

ALL: *Oh, oh, oh, Atlantic convoys.*
Our lifeline in this time of misery.
Oh, oh, oh, a frantic deploy,
Of fuel and food supplies across the sea!

Oh, oh, oh, Atlantic convoys.
Hunted down by packs of U-Boats on the way,
Oh, oh, oh, Germanic war ploy,
To sink our ships and block our passageway.

Margaret: *Forced to the surface it gave up,*
a complete Enigma kit.
In our battle to solve Dolphin such a clue.
Turing broke the code, and quickly from,
one hundred being hit...

... a month, this number very soon
had dropped to two!

Mavis: *But early on in '42, this all came to an end.*
Shark replaced Dolphin, three rotors became four.
U-Boats quickly massed again, no way we could defend...
.... Convoys at the mercy of those
submarines once more!
Dilly: *This carnage lasted for eight months,*
though Bletchley tried so hard.
There seemed no way to stop this Shark advance.
But when a sub was forced to scuttle,
by our H.M.S. Petard,
Three hero sailors knew that
this could be our chance!

HMS Petard

ALL: *Oh, oh, oh, Atlantic convoys.*
Our lifeline in this time of misery.
Oh, oh, oh, a frantic deploy,
Of fuel and food supplies across the sea!

Oh, oh, oh Atlantic convoys.
Hunted down by packs of U-Boats on the way,
Oh, oh, oh, Germanic war ploy,
To sink our ships and block our passageway!

Margaret: *That night three men dived in the sea,*
And swam toward the enemy...
... U-Boat as it floundered in the waves.

Mavis: *This sub was sinking, no mistake.*
This was a chance they had to take.
These three young men, the bravest
of the brave!

Dilly: *One was just a NAAFI lad,*
To go to sea he'd been so glad.
Young Tommy Brown, was just sixteen years old.

Margaret: *The Lieutenant told Tommy what to do,*
"The codes we find we'll pass to you."
"Just hold on and try to brave this
wet and cold!"

Mavis: *The three climbed in and went below.*
Dived down, so dark, against the flow...
... of sea water as it filled the sinking ship.

Dilly: *Tommy took the books his crewmates found,*
Climbed the tower, then went back down,
Three times in all young Tommy made this trip.

Margaret: *Then Tommy called down to his friends,*
could see the sub was near its end,
"Please, get out now, before it is too late!"

Mavis: *The sea rushed past him down the tower*
He knew this was his darkest hour
No choice but leave his crewmates to their fate.

Dilly: *Tommy let go as the sub went under,*
No way to hold on any longer,
He tried to swim, those priceless codebooks
in his grip.

But as it sank it dragged him down
Just like his friends he almost drowned
But Tommy fought like mad and made it to his ship!

Sea water rushed past Tommy down the conning tower.

ALL: *Oh, oh, oh, Atlantic convoys.*
Our lifeline in this time of misery.
Oh, oh, oh, a frantic deploy,
Of fuel and food supplies across the sea.

Oh, oh, oh, Atlantic convoys.
Hunted down by packs of U-Boats on the way,
Oh, oh, oh, Germanic war ploy,
To sink our ships and block our passageway.

Jo then cut the music back to the quieter haunting melody that had started the song and Dilly continued.

Dilly: *I am certain as they made those dives,*
They knew they had forfeit' their lives,
I know it's hard as years roll on,
and memories get hazier.

But as my story ends, please no applause.
I ask you, take some time and pause,
remember Lieutenant Fasson and
Able Seaman Grazier.

The music stopped and Dilly, Margaret and Mavis moved over to the cottage where Dilly placed the three code books on the table. The three then moved back to stand with the other girls. The lights on the stage went down apart from a single spotlight focused on those German code books on the table.

After several seconds of silence, a second spotlight then illuminated three sailors who had moved forward from the rest of the cast. These men were now standing at the front of the stage over on the other side by the office. One was dressed as an officer, one as an able seaman and one was a young boy in basic NAAFI attire. Fasson and Grazier tousled Tommy's hair and then hugged him before he walked away into the dark leaving just the two mean who had died.

The melody of the last part of 'Our Green and Pleasant Land' began to play quietly, and then the two sailors, Dilly and the Girls, and all the cast gathered at the back of the stage began to sing quietly at first, but then building up to a big crescendo.

ALL: *Bletchley! Oh Bletchley! You must understand*
You're everything we're fighting for
Our green and pleasant land!

Bletchley! Oh Bletchley! You must understand
You're everything we're fighting for
Our green and pleasant land!

You're everything we're fighting for
Our green and pleasant land!

As the final notes of the song rang out around the hall the two sailors turned to face the audience. They smartly stood to attention and saluted. The spotlight on the two men then cut and the stage fell into darkness, apart from that single light trained on the codebooks on the table once more.

The hall was silent, with people not knowing quite whether they should applaud or not. But someone somewhere began to clap, and the hall quickly erupted in a thunderous round of respectful applause.

There was no time here for anyone to pause on the stage. All the naval cast members began to leave the stage through the mansion office door and over on the other side of the stage the lights came up on the cottage where the girls were gathered around the table excited to see the code books.

Dilly: These are the actual code books that were captured by our Navy and might give us the breakthrough we need to crack Shark Enigma. Turing thought you might like to see them. Ladies, Alan has asked for your help over in Hut 11 tomorrow. They are almost ready to run the first Shark Enigma cribs through the Bombe.

The Bombe Song

ALL THROUGH THE SINGING of the previous song there had been quite a commotion backstage as preparations were being made for the revealing of the night's biggest prop.

Keith was there to help out and couldn't help but smile as all work had to stop between each of the choruses so that no noise would be made during the solemn story being told by Nigel and the girls on stage; only to quickly start up again as soon as the next chorus kicked in.

This organised chaos was being managed by Alan Turing who had been tasked by Frank some weeks ago to create a version of his Bombe machine that could be used on stage as part of the show. Frank was there too, giving directions, still dressed as Churchill and still barking instructions as if he were the Prime Minister.

The Bombe was an electromechanical machine that had been designed by Turing at the start of the war and then had been used throughout the war to help break the Enigma messages. It had been crucial to Bletchley's Enigma success and Frank had been determined that it should feature in this production somehow.

But each Bombe had been built within a bronze-coloured metal case which was about seven feet wide, over six feet high, and two feet in depth. On its front it could be loaded with over one hundred coloured drums that would click around simulating the rotors of an Enigma machine. The drums were lined up in nine rows across the front of the machine. There were three rows of 12 drums in the top section of a Bombe, three rows of 13 in the middle section, and three rows of 12 drums in the bottom section. Inside a Bombe it was rammed full of metal levers, cogs, connectors, gears, rotors, hinges, patch-panels, switches, and miles of electrical cable. In total each machine weighed over a ton and so clearly an actual machine could never be used in the show.

Turing loved being presented with a problem that needed to be solved and he had happily set to work on this new challenge as musical theatre prop builder. Once more he hunkered down in the old plum shed that Dilly had arranged for him to use as a workshop when he had first begun work on his designs for the actual Bombe machines at the beginning of the war. To be honest, he had been happy to hide away from all the end of war celebrations and was never happier than when working by himself.

Since the order had already come in from Whitehall that all Bombes and other code breaking devices were to be destroyed so that the Bletchley story would forever remain a secret, there was no shortage of parts available, and Alan and Frank had been very quick to squirrel away pieces of machine that they thought they might be able to use. In particular, a set of the multi-coloured drums were procured since these were the iconic feature of a Bombe machine.

Alan knew that any successful theatre prop had to look real. But the key factor in this case would be all about the weight and of keeping it down. The innards of all the drums were removed and the bronze metal casing had been replicated via four wooden frames that could be lined up next to each other on the stage and then clipped together. He had then used cloth under tension on each frame to simulate the front panels of the machine. The cloth was tacked to a light wooden trellis frame and it was through this frame that each of the drums was connected.

The Bombe drums replicated the Enigma rotors. Each day an Enigma machine would be loaded with three rotors from a selection of five by its operator. Each one of the five available rotors had a different internal wiring fingerprint. The Bombe drums were colour coded to represent each of the different Enigma rotors; the wiring of rotor one was replicated by a red drum, rotor two was a maroon drum, number three was green, four was yellow, and rotor five a brown drum. The three drums required would be selected and loaded onto the front panel of the Bombe, one above the other.

When fully loaded, the drums along the top row in each section – thus from the top of the Bombe down: rows one, four, and seven – represented the primary rotors, and when the Bombe was running these would fully revolve about once every second. The drums loaded on the middle row in each section would click on one letter each time the primary drums completed a full revolution. Finally, the drums on the third row in each section would click on one letter for each completed revolution of the middle drums.

Each of the four trellis frames was divided into three horizontal panels, where each of these panels could be loaded with three sets of three drums. The drums in each set were fitted one above the other. Three of the four frames were fitted with 27 drums which represented nine sets of three Enigma rotors. The fourth wooden frame was a little wider than the others, and carried an extra drum set on the middle panel, just as per a real Bombe machine. This extra set of drums would be the one that gave the reading when the Bombe 'stopped'. All these drums were held in place on Alan's prop via rods through the wooden trellis which allowed the drums to rotate.

But it was round the back of each of the four frames where Turing had worked his magic, and where it appeared to Keith that someone must have found Alan several sets of Meccano. All the drums were linked via belts around metal wheels of various sizes, and when the four frames were all clipped together everything connected to a single handle in the centre. Turning the handle caused the top row of drums on each horizontal panel to rotate, and then the centre rows to click on one position for every full turn on those first drums, and then the bottom row of drums to move on one position for every full turn of the centre drums: just like a real Bombe.

These four prop sections were still quite heavy, and it was taking a good deal of effort to get them up and out onto the stage. The new backdrop that had appeared just behind the ensemble during the song Atlantic Convoy crucially left space for the imitation Bombe sections to be moved into place and to then be clipped together out of sight of the audience while the cast were singing.

The Bombe Song

Not only were there several stagehands and cast members busy manoeuvring Turing's Bombe machine sections up onto the stage and into place, but there was also a dozen or so very excited Wrens gathering in the wings waiting for their big moment in the production, and all of this while the stage was packed with the cast all singing the song Atlantic Convoy.

Finally, the applause for the end of the song died down and the cottage lit up. Keith could hear Nigel as Dilly inviting the girls to visit Hut 11 the next day. This was the signal for Jo to fire up the band for the start of the next song; the 'Bombe Song'.

The Atlantic Convoy backdrop lifted to reveal the Bombe machine at the back of the stage stood just in front of the original painting of the Bletchley Mansion.

Turing's machines were called Bombes following on from the Polish versions which were known as *Bomba*. One theory to the origin of the name was that they were named such because they made a clicking noise like a time-bomb as they ran. With this in mind, Jo had written the start

A Wren loads a Bombe

of this next song based on the very rhythmic click, click, click, click, of a Bombe machine drums continually turning.

As the stage was lit up the Wrens walked out onto the stage all looking very smart in their uniforms. Each was wearing a dark blue tailored skirt to just below the knee, a white shirt – with sleeves rolled up ready for their shift operating the Bombes – and a blue tie and black shoes. The Wrens began to act out the tasks needed to operate the Bombe machines. All of them were moving in a very mechanical, almost robotical way in time with the opening bars of the music.

Mavis and Margaret were there too, trying not to get in the way but looking very interested in proceedings.

Then the Wrens began to sing with the lyrics and their movements around the stage matching the endless click-click-click of the Bombe drums and the rhythm of the music.

Wrens:

Here's our hut, the doors locked shut.
We have to find the answers and there's no short cut.
A day of toil. The smell of oil.
Suffering with the heat from the electric coils.
Drums to lift. Codes to sift.
It's another day of pressure on a 12-hour shift.
Panels patched. Doors all latched.
Time to tackle all the codes the Nazis hatched.
If we're late, then it's not great.
We'll have to start all over with a brand-new slate.
Let's turn it on. Start the fun.

At this point the music and the rotating drums on the Bombe suddenly stopped. The supervising Wren – who was looking very officious with a large clipboard in her hand – turned to the audience and announced that.

Supervisor: The process to identify potential initial positions for the rotor cores has begun.

The Bombe Song

Alan's model of the Bombe machine had also been fitted with five large over-sized black bakelite chicken-head switches on one side and the operators took turns to twist these one at a time.

These switches served no function other than to give the impression that the Wrens were switching on the machine. On each turn of a switch Jo flicked her arm and the band played a loud note as the Wrens sang out the following letters in turn.

Wrens: 'B'
'O'
'M'
'B'
'E'

On turning the final switch the band struck up with a really upbeat melody. The Wren supervisor turned toward the audience and burst into song, encouraging all the Bletchley workers watching to clap along.

Supervisor: *Alan's genius has given us the key*
To see our convoys safe across the sea
Rotors, levers, gears and cables
All connect so we are able
To break the codes and set our country free
All down to Turing's Bombe ...
... that's bombe spelt with an 'E'!

Wrens: *Oh it's our Bombe with an 'E',*
Alan Turing's legacy.
Beat the stigma of Enigma
Bletchley Park cryptology!

Oh it's our Bombe with an 'E',
drums are turning franticly,
We were heading for disaster but
Gordon Welchman made it faster

Oh it's our Bombe with an 'E',
all now linked diagon-ly
Gordon's board has made it slicker
So the answers come much quicker

Rotors, levers, gears and cables
All connect so we are able
To break the codes and set our country free
All down to Turing's Bombe ...
... that's bombe spelt with an 'E'!

Margaret moved round to the front of the stage as the melody of the song changed once more and took over the singing. She and Mavis were now to sing a series of verses that explained the mechanics of these amazing machines and the process of breaking the code.

Margaret:*Each Bombe is set with coloured drums,*
Each drum maps to a rotor.
Over 30 tests done in one go,
We're sure to meet our quota.

Mavis: *Codebreakers try to find a crib,*
That's text hidden in the message.
Then write a program for the Bombe,
A menu to what success is!

Once more the Wrens took over singing duties as they and Dilly's Girls switched between chorus and verses.

Wrens: *Oh it's our Bombe with an 'E',*
Alan Turing's legacy.
Beat the stigma of Enigma
Bletchley Park cryptology!

Oh it's our Bombe with an 'E,
Alan Turing's legacy,

The Bombe Song

It's got to get this job right,
As we've only got 'till Midnight

Margaret: *The operators load the drums,*
And wire-up per the menu.
Sometimes they have to clean the wires,
Watch closely what the Wrens do.

Mavis: *We're waiting for the Bombe to stop,*
Potential rotor setting.
Readings are taken from the Bombe,
And then passed on for checking.

Wrens: *Oh it's our Bombe with an 'E',*
Alan Turing's legacy.
Beat the stigma of Enigma
Bletchley Park cryptology!

Oh it's our Bombe with an 'E,
Alan Turing's legacy,
It's got to get this job right,
As we've only got 'till Midnight

A sudden change in tempo returned the Wrens to their mechanical movements and singing.

Wrens: *Until Midnight*
To get it right
Watching the clock,
When will it stop?
Oh will it stop
Please let it stop,

Until Midnight
To get it right

Watching the clock,
When will it stop?
Oh will it stop?
Please let it stop,
CLICK!
It's stopped!!

Wrens: *So, how's our stop? Is it great?*
Or is it nothing more than just a candidate?
The Typex test, will let us know, if what
we have decrypted is now good to go.
The result looks bad, but don't be sad. Just plan
another sequence on the old note pad.
Instructions come, reset the drums.
Everything relies on Alan Turing's sums.
If we're late, then it's not great. We'll have
to start all over with a brand new slate.
Let's turn it on, start the fun,

Supervisor: The process to identify potential initial positions for the rotor cores has begun

Once more the Wrens turned each of the large black switches on the side of the replica Bombe and as each switch clicked over the operators sang out the letters.

Wrens: *'B'*
'O'
'M'
'B'
'E'

Supervisor:*At Bletchley Alan's quite the V.I.P.*
Known as 'The Prof' no one would disagree
That his work here is so vital

The Bombe Song

He's so worthy of that title
Broken Naval codes are now reality
All down to Turing's Bombe ...
... that's bombe spelt with an 'E'!

Wrens: *Oh it's our Bombe with an 'E',*
Alan Turing's legacy.
Beat the stigma of Enigma
Bletchley Park cryptology!

Oh it's our Bombe with an 'E',
it's no longer fantasy,
We're going to make our quota,
As it simulates the rotors!

Oh it's our Bombe with an 'E',
though there is no guarantee
Each drum turn means we're getting
Close to knowing all their settings

Rotors, levers, gears and cables
All connect so we are able
To break the codes and set our country free
All down to Turing's Bombe ...
... that's bombe spelt with an 'E'!

Margaret: *Now hoping for a "Job Up!" shout,*
We need some good news soon.
That's it! So on to Hut 6 now,
And to the Typex room!

Mavis: *Our Typex beats Enigma's style,*
Of that there is no doubt.
Why bother with just lighting bulbs,
When we can print it out!

Wrens: *Oh it's our Bombe with an 'E',*
Alan Turing's legacy.
Beat the stigma of Enigma
Bletchley Park cryptology!

Oh it's our Bombe with an 'E,
Alan Turing's legacy,
It's got to get this job right,
As we've only got 'till Midnight

'til Midnight
To get it right
Watching the clock,
When will it stop
Oh will it stop
Please let it stop,
CLICK!
It's stopped!!

As the machine and the music came to an abrupt stop the Wren Bombe operators acted out the stages that Mavis and Margaret had just been singing about. They carefully read the 'stop' position off the Bombe and passed the results on to a Typex operator. The whole process ended up with a loud shout of "Job Up!"

ALL: *We've done it! We've beaten Shark!*

Everyone in the hall that night knew of Alan Turing or 'The Prof' as he was fondly referred to by all at Bletchley. Everyone also knew just how important his Bombe machine had been in the battle against Enigma. Everyone well remembered just how alone Britain had been in that first year of the war and how dependent we had been on those priceless Atlantic convoys.

While the previous song had been a sobering reflection on the sacrifice and bravery of sailors like Fasson, Grazier and young Tommy Brown, this last song had been a real celebration. The audience had clapped along with the Wrens during each joyful chorus and had been whistling and cheering too as Margaret and Mavis sang them through the whole Bombe process. So, when those last words were sung out loud, the whole place erupted in loud cheers and frantic clapping with everyone up on their feet once more.

Mavis and Margaret encouraged all the Wrens to line up at the front of the stage and to take an extended bow. A pocket of Wrens in full uniform over on one side of the hall were whistling and cheering loudly for their friends and colleagues up on the stage, and all the ladies on stage beamed and waved back with joy.

The band struck up with a short burst of the Bombe song chorus as the Wrens waved and the audience clapped in time for a final time, and then all the girls turned to leave the stage as the lights on the stage went down.

Missing Dilly

WHEN THE STAGE LIGHTS finally came back up after Alan's Bombe prop had been cleared from the stage the cottage was once again the focus of everyone's attention. Several of the girls were excitedly gathered around Mavis. The cottage door suddenly opened, and Jean rushed in looking a bit flustered and all out of breath. She quickly noticed that something unusual was going on.

Joyce: Morning, Jean!

Claire: Hello, Jean.

Joyce: What time do you call this, Jean?

Jean: Oh, I am so sorry I'm a bit late but the queue for the bath just wasn't moving this morning and I got up extra early especially. I desperately needed a proper wash as I missed my slot last week.

Mavis: Have you warmed up yet then, Jean?

Jean: Not really. It was even colder than usual today. What has happened here then?

Joyce: Oh, Jean, it is Mavis, she's got some news.

Jean: Oh, Mavis, he hasn't, has he?

Mavis: Yes, Keith proposed to me last night and I said yes!

Mavis held out her hand to show Jean her ring and then the two girls hugged.

Jean: Oh, Mavis, it is beautiful!

Mavis: Keith told me that it belonged to his Grandmother. I am so happy, Jean.

Joyce: Good old Keith, I never knew he had it in him!

All the girls were laughing apart from Flo, who was sat quietly at the table aimlessly shuffling some of Dilly's famous rods around. Jean had spotted her.

Jean: Morning, Flo.

Flo: Hello, Jean.

Jean: Oh, Flo, what is wrong? You look so sad.

Flo: Oh, I'm sorry, Jean. I don't mean to be down especially with Mavis's big news, but I'm on a run of bad luck with my work, Jean, and I'm missing Dilly so much. I know he phones most days, but it's just not the same now that Dilly's gone.

With that Jo brought in the band for the show's next song and Flo stood and began to sing:

Flo: *Oh it's just not the same, now that Dilly's gone*
I so miss his support, infectious drive.
We're all feeling so flat, as we sing our songs,
We must keep his spirit here alive.

Mavis moved over to Flo, put her arm around her friend, and joined in the singing.

Mavis & Flo: *Oh it's just not the same,*
now that Dilly's gone
All our work here, it's all down to him.
We're all hoping so much that it won't
be very long,
Before he's back here to listen to us sing.

Joyce and Jean now took charge of the next part of the song as the rest of the girls all gathered round.

Joyce & Jean: *He phones most every day,*
Keeping us on track.
If he could have his way,
We know that he'd be back.
Enigma's still the same,
We're focused on our task.
It's never quite the pain though
When Dilly's here to ask.

All the girls in the cottage now joined in.

ALL: *Oh it's just not the same now that Dilly's gone*
The cottage lacks its guiding light.
But we're still full of hope and our
spirit's always strong
Thanks to Dilly we'll win the coding fight!

The cottage door opened once more and Claire stepped through and onto the stage. She was waving some sort of official looking letter and immediately picked up the singing of the next verses.

Claire: *Exciting news just in!*
Quick, girls, come and see.
He's been honoured by the King,
Awarded CMG!
St Michael and St George,
All for chivalry.
For us there is no better cause,
Than our wonderful Dilly!

What with the news of Mavis and Keith's engagement and now this news about Dilly's royal recognition, even Flo's spirits are lifted and all the girls joined together to joyfully sing on.

ALL: *Oh it's just not the same, now that Dilly's gone,*
We bet that medal's done the trick.
There's nothing like the King, giving you a gong,
To make you want to smile when you are sick.

Oh it's just not the same, now that Dilly's gone
All our work here, it's all down to him.
We're all hoping so much that it won't be very long,
Before he's back here to listen to us sing.

Down with the band Jo kept the song's melody bouncing along as the girls continued to excitedly gather around Claire, all taking turns to look at the letter. Mavis showed Claire her ring and the two good friends hugged and laughed.

But throughout the scene there had been one of the girls missing. Betty had been stood in the wing across the stage with Frank and Keith watching from behind the office wall. She too was holding an official looking letter and as Frank just happened to glance down he noticed that her hands were shaking. He put his hand on hers and squeezed them gently. Betty looked up and smiled back.

'Good luck,' he whispered, 'off you go.'

So, with Frank's encouragement Betty walked out onto the back of the stage and began to make her way forward and over to the others in the cottage.

It was Jean that spotted her, and at that moment the mood of the song shifted to a slower and more sombre outlook. Down with the band Jo was leading the others on her violin.

Jean: *Here comes Betty now,*
Oh, she's looking pretty sad.
Pale face and furrowed brow,
Something's looking bad

Betty: *Hey girls can you stop?*
I must halt you in your tracks.

I've just received word from the top,
Dilly's never coming back

Oh it's just not the same now that Dilly's gone,
The news is bad, I will not lie.
It's cancer, it's spread, and poor Dilly hasn't long
Before they say he's going to die.

All of Dilly's Girls sang the last line of the song together.

ALL: *Oh it's just not the same now that Dilly's gone.*

The band continued to play, building the melody back up and bringing the song to an emotional climax as the girls sadly returned to work in the cottage. As the final note faded the stage lights suddenly dropped and the song was over.

The Visit

MRS BALANCE HAD BEEN the cottage tea lady all throughout the war years. It had been Dilly's idea to bring someone in to look after all the girls with regular cups of tea and coffee while they concentrated on their codebreaking work. One of the girls suggested her mother for the job. Mrs Balance was duly called in to meet everyone and was made to sign the Official Secrets Act just like everyone else at Bletchley. It was not very long before she became a much-loved mother figure to everyone in the cottage.

It had been Keith's idea to cast Mrs Balance as Dilly's wife Olive in Frank's show and as soon as he had suggested it Mavis thought that their 'Cottage Mum' was the perfect choice for the part.

Mrs Balance, however, had not been as sure and she had taken quite a bit of persuading to take part in tonight's production. But once at rehearsals she had been a complete natural on the stage and soon became a very popular and much-loved member of the cast. As well as being a very able and fully cooperative cast member, the cups of tea had also regularly flowed during all the rehearsals.

Mavis remembered how Dilly had always made Mrs Balance feel like she was one of the team and that her role in the cottage was just as important as any of the others. As far as Mavis was concerned this was just yet another example of one of Dilly's many wonderful character traits; of how he truly valued everyone's contribution to life in the Bletchley cottage.

As Mavis stood at the side of the stage watching Mrs Balance take up her place for the next scene, she thought about Matapan, which had been one of the cottage's biggest breakthroughs during the war. She smiled as she recalled the poem that Dilly had written after they had broken the Italian Enigma and cracked the messages that had led directly to the destruction of Mussolini's fleet. Dilly was always writing verse and poems, and this one he had named 'Swollen Heads', which even now made Mavis chuckle to herself when she thought about it. It had been Dilly's tribute to his team.

Each one of Dilly's Girls had their own verse in the poem and right there in the middle was a verse for Mrs Balance too, which had included a line that said the cottage team was 'a team of all the talents'. Mavis remembered also how Mrs Balance's verse had not just been tagged onto the end, but that it had been mixed in with all the other codebreakers just to reinforce that message that as far as Dilly was concerned everyone's contribution had been equally important.

All the girls in the cottage had very quickly become labelled by everyone at Bletchley as 'Dilly's Girls', or even as 'Dilly's Fillies', and Mavis was certain that some people thought that this was a tag that might annoy her and the other girls. But Mavis had loved working with her old boss, and she knew that all the other girls had too. Every single one of them was proud to have been one of Dilly's Girls and none more so than Mrs Balance the tea lady and Cottage Mum.

The lights finally came back up on the stage which was now displaying several new props. There was a metal framed bed in the middle, another table had appeared on the stage, some chairs, and various props such as a lamp stand and a small chest of drawers. All of these had transformed the set into a representation of Courns Wood, Dilly and Olive's house. The office had also been adapted to look as though it was now part of their home. Over on the other side of the stage the cottage remained, but it was only dimly lit and barely noticeable.

Mrs Balance was there as Olive, and Nigel was in the bed as Dilly. Olive was tending to her sick husband when there was a knock at the door.

Jean: Hello, Mrs Knox, my name is Jean and I work with your husband at Bletchley.

Olive: Ah yes, Jean, I was told you were coming today and have been expecting you. You have just missed Margaret, I am afraid; she's just popped down to the village. It is so nice of you to come down to see us. How was your journey? Please do come in.

Jean: Oh, it was fine, thank you. How is Mr Knox?

Olive: He is not good, I'm afraid, Jean. The doctor is here daily now. Dillwyn has gone downhill very quickly just these last two weeks. I am not sure if he will be up to speaking to you today, to be honest. I am so sorry after the trouble of your journey. Please, this way, he is just through here. Go sit with him a while. I will make some tea.

Jean: Thank you, ma'am.

While Olive busied herself in the converted office – now the kitchen at Courns Wood – Jean walked across the stage and over to the bed where Dilly was lying seemingly asleep. The bed had clearly been set up especially in the front room for him. Jean sat down on a chair that had been placed by the bed.

Jean: Hello, sir, it's Jean. We thought it was about time one of us came to see you. Denniston wasn't keen when we first asked but you know us, nobody messes with Dilly's Girls. We all wanted to come, sir, but they would only allow one of us a pass, so we drew lots in the end. I am so glad it was me. We miss you, sir. The cottage just is not the same without you. But we are winning, sir. Results have been particularly good over the last few weeks. Oh, and the biggest result of all is that Mavis has got engaged to Keith!

Oh, sir, you are smiling, I will tell Mavis. Sorry, sir? What did you say?

Jean leant forward and in toward her beloved boss trying her best to hear what he was saying. Everything in the hall was very still. No one was moving, speaking, or even whispering. Everyone was intently focused on the scene unfolding before them up on the stage.

Down with the musicians Jo picked up her violin once more and began to play the Endless Hours melody. She was playing alone. The notes from her instrument gently rang around the hall, hanging almost hauntingly in the air. Her playing was simply beautiful, and standing in the wings Mavis felt herself shiver as the music and the scene playing out on the stage before her caused her to fill with an emotion that she had not experienced during any of the rehearsals. Somehow having the hall full of people all sat respectfully silent and intently concentrating on this moving scene had generated an intense atmosphere that Mavis was certain everyone was feeling.

Standing next to her husband, Mavis squeezed Keith's hand and felt him respond in kind.

Mavis looked at her friend sitting next to the bed and felt relief that it was not her that had to now find her voice and sing for everyone.

Out on the stage Jean began to sing.

Jean: *There's his last breath.*
Our Dilly has gone.
I can't find the right words, to say
how I feel now, to put in this song.

He looks so at peace.
Oh what can I do?
I once told him in fun that I loved him,
it was probably true.

We all love our work.
Because of this man.
He showed us the way.
He proved that we can.

Endless hours
Endless toil

Codes to break
Plans to foil
Endless hours

It's back to the Park.
I must tell the Girls.
I know they will all feel it's over, the end;
it's the end of our world.

We must carry on.
Finish his quest.
Everyone knows that the team he built,
we were taught by the best.

We all love our work.
It's because of this man.
He showed us the way.
He proved that we can!

Endless hours
Endless toil
Codes to break
Plans to foil
Endless hours

As Jean sang, the stage lights slowly closed in to focus just on her and Dilly, until by the time she sang her final note there was just a single spotlight on her and her old boss and the rest of the stage was in darkness.

Then as the band started to play the coda the spotlight itself gently faded until on the very last note the stage fell into complete darkness.

The audience responded with a respectful applause. Many were not sure whether they should be clapping or not at the end of such a sad scene.

Over in the wings Mavis peered out into the darkness trying to spot Olive whom she knew had been sat with Denniston on the front row, but she was unable to catch sight of her through the gloom.

'I hope Olive is alright,' Mavis whispered to her husband. 'I hope this hasn't all been too much for her.'

Keith put his arm around his pretty young wife, pulled her close, and gave her a gentle kiss on her head.

'I'm sure Olive is fine, darling.'

'Hey there, you two love birds!'

It was Margaret and the other girls who were now heading around the back area toward the stage ready for the next scene in the cottage. Margaret stopped for a moment when she caught sight of her friend's face and just how sad and upset she was looking.

'Oh, Mavis, are you alright?' she asked as she gave her friend a hug.

'Yes, I'm fine thanks. I just came over a bit emotional, that is all. You sang that so beautifully, Jean.'

Jean had joined the others heading for the cottage.

'Thank you, Mavis, that means a lot. But goodness me, you have an even bigger song now. Will you be alright?'

'Ladies, ladies, come along now, we need you in the cottage.'

Frank had appeared and was now busily hurrying everyone along to their next positions.

'I'll see you in a moment.' Mavis smiled. 'Don't you all worry about me, I'll be fine.'

Mavis could always rely on Frank to lift the mood and to put a smile on her face.

The lights were now coming back up on the stage and were focused once more on the cottage.

'Good luck, darling,' Keith said, giving his wife another gentle kiss on the top of her head. 'I will be right here watching you.'

Mavis gave her husband a hug and then moved down the wing to stand behind the cottage door.

'Right–' it was Frank– 'off you go, my dear.'

Naphill Wood

OUT ON THE STAGE in the cottage the girls were all quietly going about their daily codebreaking business. Everything was very subdued following the sad news about Dilly's passing.

The cottage door opened and Mavis walked in. Jean was the first one of the girls to look up.

Jean: Hello, Mavis.

Mavis: Hello, Jean. Hey everyone, this has just arrived from Courns Wood, it is from Olive. It is a letter that Dilly wrote for us before he died and look at this: he has sent us his medal.

All the girls all gathered around Mavis.

Claire: What does it say, Mavis?

Mavis quickly scanned the letter and began to fill up with emotion.

Mavis: Oh, girls. He says that the medal belongs to us. That it was our work that made it all possible. He also says that the 'Cottage Tradition' was the fulfilment of his career. Here, Claire, you read it to the others.

Mavis handed the letter to Claire and Claire began to read it out loud for the girls. As Claire read the letter, Mavis walked over to the cottage wall and hung-up Dilly's CMG medal.

Claire: 'Very many thanks for your, and the whole section's, very kind messages of congratulations. It is, of course, a fact that the congratulations are due the other way and that awards of this sort depend entirely on the support from colleagues and associates to the Head of the Section. May I therefore refer them back. In bidding farewell and in closing down the continuity but not, I hope, the traditions of the Cottage, I thank once more the section for their unswerving loyalty. Theirs I remain. Affectionately, A. D. Knox.'

Once Claire had finished reading Dilly's letter, Jo and the band struck up with the introduction to the next song. Mavis turned back toward the audience and began to sing.

Mavis:

It's time to move on
His story's been told
His life is now gone, it's over, he's left us
He's not growing old.
But because of the man that he was
And the values that he held so dear
His spirit will never be lost
His soul will always be near
Safe in our hearts
Our memories too
Locked in our thoughts
In all that we do.

We all should have a special place,
a place to get away

Naphill Wood

A place to find our inner self,
to maybe meditate, or pray
To feel the pulse of nature
Be immersed in all things good
And yours was here among the trees
The trees of Naphill Wood.

The lights on the cottage dimmed and a spotlight followed Mavis as she sang and walked out into the middle of the stage. As she went she gestured around as stagehands wheeled on props cut to look like trees. These new props were magically transforming the Assembly Hall stage into Dilly's treasured woodland.

Naphill Wood
Naphill Wood
I can see
You understood
That your legacy for ever more
Is here among your trees
Your spirit will forever soar
Carried on the breeze!
In Naphill Wood.

I remember last spring.
You asked me come stay
With you and your wife, your boys, at Courns Wood
I treasure those days.

And I remember the view from my room
That small window but Oh what a sight
Cherry blossoms out in full bloom
Shades of pink reflecting the light.

Picture the scene.
The wonder of spring.

Dilly's Girls

God's beauty behold.
Such a wonderful thing.

The Chiltern Woodlands were your special place,
the place you had to seek
You loved to plant, split wood and saw,
but last spring you were so weak
So we settled for some seeding
And took walks when you could
We'd walk and talk among your trees
The trees of Naphill Wood!

Naphill Wood
Naphill Wood
I can see
You understood
That your legacy for ever more
Is here among your trees
Your spirit will forever soar
Carried on the breeze!
In Naphill Wood.

Understand when I say
I will never forget.
You were my teacher, my mentor, my friend
I owe such a debt.

But because of the man that you were
And the values you held so dear
Your spirit will never be lost
Your soul will always be near
Safe in our hearts
Our memories too
Locked in our thoughts
In all that we do.

Up until this point the rest of the girls had been quietly watching Mavis sing her tribute from the darkened cottage. Now they also moved out onto the stage to stand with Mavis by Dilly's grave. His grave was represented here by a block of wood painted to look like stone, which had been placed at the foot of one of the trees.

All gathered at your special place,
the place you loved to stay
So rest in peace, our dearest friend,
for ever here you'll lay
To feel the pulse of nature
Be immersed in all things good
Rest here in peace among the trees
The trees of Naphill Wood.

Naphill Wood
Naphill Wood
I can see
You understood
That your legacy for ever more
Is here among your trees
Your spirit will forever soar
Carried on the breeze!
In Naphill Wood.

In a similar way to the end of the previous song, the stage lights slowly faded on the girls by the grave until the stage fell into darkness as Jo and the band raised the volume to repeat the main melody in a wonderfully tender end to a very emotional song and scene.

As the final note ended the audience once again responded with a slightly subdued round of applause. Once again no one was sure whether they should actually be clapping or not.

Church Service

AS THE GIRLS LEFT the stage there was no time to pause and reflect on the last scene in Naphill Wood as they found themselves having to dodge dozens of members of the cast who were making their way in the opposite direction as well as stagehands who were now wheeling off the trees and bringing on the pieces of set ready for the next part of the show.

When the lights came back up there were already a number of the cast at the back of the stage standing behind a make-shift church pew. The ensemble began to sing a section of the hymn Jerusalem.

Congregation: *Bring me my bow of burning gold!*
Bring me my arrows of desire!
Bring me my spear! O clouds, unfold!
Bring me my chariot of fire!
I will not cease from mental fight,
Nor shall my sword sleep in my hand,
Till we have built Jerusalem
In England's green and pleasant land.

As the cast members on stage sang, a church quickly began to take shape all around them as props and chairs were brought out onto the stage and more and more of the cast took up their places. The last person to appear was someone dressed as a vicar in full-service robes, and as the singing came to an end he turned to address his congregation.

Church Service

Vicar: Please be seated.

As everyone up on the stage sat down, Commander Denniston appeared from the back and walked forward to stand behind a rather impressive mock-up of a church lectern. The hall fell very quiet and very still and Denniston began to speak.

Denniston: I once wrote the following to Dilly on receiving a letter of resignation from him. He felt that I was not allowing him to follow up on his breakthroughs, and that I was passing his work onto the new much younger code breaking generation who were now running the other departments. Here is what I wrote:

> 'My dear, Dilly. I know we disagree fundamentally as to how this show should be run but I remain convinced that my way is the better way and likely to have wider and more effective results. If you design a Rolls-Royce, then that is no reason why you should be the one to drive it up to the house. Do you want to be the inventor and the car driver?'
>
> 'You are Knox, a scholar with a European reputation, who knows more about the inside of a certain cipher machine than anybody else. The exigencies of war need that latter gift of yours, though few people are aware of it. The exploitation of your results can be left to others so long as there are new fields for you to explore and explore them you must.'

Denniston stepped aside and Mavis stood up and walked over to the lectern. At the same time the cottage door quietly opened, and Dilly stepped through onto the stage, unnoticed by many in the hall. He closed the door gently behind himself and leant on his walking stick, intently watching his beloved Mavis speak.

Mavis: I was 19 when I arrived at Bletchley and was taken to Dilly's section in the cottage. It was very much a research unit. Hut 6 was up and running, but Dilly had been one of the great pioneers of it all. He was working on things that had not been broken. It was a strange little outfit in the cottage because, well, organisation is not a word you would associate with Dilly. When I arrived he said, 'Oh, hello, we're breaking machines. Have you got a pencil?' He then handed me some sheets of a coded message which just looked like gobbledegook to me. It was all covered in inky scrawls which didn't help. 'Have a go,' he said. Well, I just looked at it and in despair told him that it just looked all Greek to me. Dilly roared with laughter and told me that he wished it were. Of course, I didn't realise then that he was a distinguished Greek scholar. But that was it. I was never really told what to do. He taught me to think that you could do things for yourself without always having to look what the 'book' said. That was the way the cottage worked. He could be so woolly minded, yet he was brilliant, absolutely brilliant. It just seemed to come so naturally to him.

Dilly's Message

THE LIGHTS FADED a little on the church service and a spotlight suddenly lit up Dilly, causing a few gasps from those members of the audience who had not noticed his arrival. Dilly turned to address the audience as the cast in the church quietly continued as if the service was still happening in the dimmed background.

Dilly: Ah, Mavis and Margaret, my Lever and my Rock.

Jo and the band started to play the next song, which at first was following the Endless Hours melody familiar now to everyone in the hall. Dilly moved out toward the centre of the stage and began to sing.

Dilly:

Oh this scene is so fine
These great friends of mine
I am so moved I don't really know
what words I can say

All I know is for sure
That life's just a door
And that I'll be back with them all
codebreaking again some day

People say I'm reserved
But I so don't deserve

The accolades being given my way at
this service today

Can't help sometimes but laugh
After all, 'twas just logic and maths
I just had some ideas and helped show my
colleagues the way

My girls were the ones
They got the job done.
They deserve recognition, all the thanks,
the credit, the medals, and the praise.

As he sang that last line Dilly swung his stick round to point at all his friends toward the back of the stage, and the church scene once again lit up but now it had switched from being a service of remembrance to that of a wedding. Mavis was wearing her wedding suit and was standing with Keith, who was resplendent in his Fleet Air Arm uniform, in front of the vicar. Margaret was her maid of honour and was standing just behind Mavis holding a small posy of flowers, while Peter Twinn, Keith's best man, was standing just back from Keith. All the other cottage girls were gathered round, and as they threw confetti over the happy couple the hall erupted in cheers and whistles.

Dilly: *Oh, and it all went to plan*
Mavis married her man
So happy in love, forever together right
through till the end of their days

Dilly turned back to face the audience as the melody of the song changed.

But I don't want to talk about me
That's not why I'm here now you see
I've a message I want you to hear
Some facts I need to make clear
About life here at Bletchley.

Dilly's Message

The song's melody changed again, now much quicker and more up-beat.

When we started work at Bletchley
we all signed up to the Act
Official Secrets meant that we had
agreed to take the pact
Thirty years of silence we just
couldn't tell a soul
That person sitting next to you
could be a German mole.

So no one here could say a thing
of life here at the Park.
Family, friends, even my wife,
were all kept in the dark.
But hopefully I've made it clear
and now you all can see
That a gathering of friends like this,
well it really couldn't be.

There's something else I want to say,
a fact I must make clear.
A fact that's not well known but
one you have to hear.
That ladies made up three quarters
of the workers at our base
Eight thousand women helping fight
the so called 'Master Race'!

So these code breaking ladies are
just a fraction of the crew
So many other women contribute to everything we do.
The codebreakers in the cottage are really just the tip
Of the Bletchley female workforce that made
us such a hit!

Then there was yet another tempo change as Dilly reeled through a list of all the jobs done by the thousands of women that had worked at Bletchley Park during World War Two.

Dispatch riders, couriers
They say 'nothing worries us'
They really like their motorbikes
No need to hurry us!

As well as all the Cyphers
We have our lady drivers
They get us there with time to spare
Our A to B providers!

Not only do they drive
But they keep their cars alive
With bolts and spanners, oil and hammers
Fine tuning nine to five!

The typists and the clerks
Hold a big place in our hearts
We so need their typing speed
Their memos and their charts!

To work some girls are keen
Crypto-logical machines
They stack the slate, then operate
To make a winning team!

Once we've cracked the text
Translating it comes next
Italian? I know they can!
These ladies are the best!

Another tempo change followed to a bridge section in the song.

So you can see, it's meant to be
That these ladies are
Right from the start, the very heart
Of life here at Bletchley!

The very heart, the very soul
These eight thousand are our Bletchley gold!
That these ladies are the very heart
Of life here at Bletchley!

Several of the cast now moved forward to stand with Dilly toward the front of the stage. All were ladies. Some were dressed as motorcycle despatch riders. Some were wearing overalls with tool belts. Others carried clipboards and files. These ladies now took over the singing.

Bletchley Ladies: *Dispatch riders,*
Staff car drivers
All weather road survivors!

Electricians
Wire technicians
We ladies are magicians!

Pioneering
Engineering
Construction with such feeling!

Administrators
Operators
De-coded text translators!

Linguistic
Annalistic
You could say Crypto-listic!

Dilly's Girls

So you can see, it's meant to be
That we ladies are
Right from the start, the very heart
Of life here at Bletchley!

The very heart, the very soul
We eight thousand are the Bletchley gold!
That we ladies are the very heart
Of life here at Bletchley!

So very smart, the very heart
Of life here at Bletchley!

Right from the start, the very heart
Of life here at Bletchley!

Right from the start, the very heart
Of life here at Bletchley!
Of life here at Bletchley!

As the song came to a rousing end the music continued straight into the next one, which was to be the grand finale to the night's production. All the cast now moved forward to surround Dilly at the front of the stage, and Dilly began to sing.

Two Years

Dilly: *Bletchley did not win the war alone*
No single allied force can make that claim
But history has judged us, with the highest accolades
All ten thousand of our staff should share the fame.

ALL: *At least two years*
That's what historians will say
At least two years
Of death and pain were taken from the war
At least two years
Were saved for your and my today
At least two years
Some studies say it could be even more

Saving countless lives on both sides
We look back now with such pride
At those endless hours of working on the codes
Using our imagination
Our insight, dedication
Maths and logic led the trek down
Bletchley's road.

At least two years,
Two years, two years, at least two years
See the method in our 'madness'
End a war so full of sadness
There can be no disputing
We were the birthplace of computing
We hope that you can see
This is the Bletchley legacy
At least two years.

It was Frank's turn now to step forward and sing the next verse. He was still dressed as Churchill and was still holding his massive cigar as he sang his lines with all of Churchill's mannerisms and emphasis, and once he had finished everyone joined in once more with the chorus.

Churchill: *Few armies went to battle better briefed.*
North Africa to European lands.
Ultra proved so crucial, more than priceless some would say,
Allowed commanders to be sure of battle plans.

ALL: *At least two years*
That's what historians will say
At least two years
Of death and pain were taken from the war
At least two years
Were saved for your and my today
At least two years
Some studies say it could be even more

Saving countless lives on both sides
We look back now with such pride
At those endless hours of working on the codes
Using our imagination
Our insight, dedication

Two Years

Maths and logic led the trek down Bletchley's road.
At least two years,
Two years, two years, at least two years
See the method in our 'madness'
End a war so full of sadness
There can be no disputing
We were the birthplace of computing
We hope that you can see
This is the Bletchley legacy
At least two years, years, years!

The song had finished, the stage was full, and every single member of the cast had their arms raised out toward all their friends and colleagues in the hall who had instantly jumped to their feet and were cheering, whistling, clapping and stamping their feet in joyous approval.

The cast now arranged themselves into three rows across the stage, with Dilly and his girls centre front, and all held hands and took their bows.

They all then stretched their arms out down toward Jo and the band. The band all stood up, many still holding their instruments, and turned to the audience and bowed as the cast clapped behind them.

Keith found himself at the front of the stage but right over to one side, and he just took a moment to look across at his friends who were still being cheered by the audience and who were clearly so excited and happy that the show had gone so well and had been received in such a wonderful way.

Frank was still hamming it up as Churchill, waving at the crowd and blowing kisses to the ladies on the front few rows. Nigel was surrounded by the cottage girls, who were hugging and teasing him, and Keith smiled at Nigel's slightly bewildered face as he could see that the Park's deputy commander was struggling to quite know how to react to all this female attention. Denniston was with Barbara and the Admiral, and he could see Mair, who had moved everyone with her singing in the first act, talking to her old boss Welchman. Hugh was still resplendent in his Scottish regalia and was dancing a little jig at the back of the stage with several other members of the cast. It all made for such a happy scene.

As Keith turned his gaze back to the front of the stage there was Mavis looking across at him, his beautiful wife with her beaming smile and her pretty rosy cheeks. Their eyes met just for a moment before Margaret threw her arms around her codebreaking partner and best friend, lifting her off her feet and spinning her around.

'Excuse me, Mr Batey, sir.'

Keith looked around to see one of the stagehands trying to squeeze past, carrying what looked like an oversized rotary desktop pencil sharpener mounted on a pole. Keith chuckled to himself, knowing what was to come next.

'Here let me give you a hand,' Keith offered, and the two men positioned the device upright on the edge of the stage.

The stagehand signalled to Jo down with the band, who herself then leant forward and made a signal to a group of American servicemen who had been watching the show sat down in the front section of each of the hall's wings. The GIs, all resplendent in their sharp uniforms, began to pull cases out from under their seats and retrieve cases from over by the walls. Latches were thrown and various brass and stringed musical instruments appeared. Meanwhile, Jo's musicians all retook their seats and made ready with their instruments too.

By now the audience had realised that something was afoot and they too all began to sit back down in their seats.

Back up on the stage the stagehand with the giant 'pencil sharpener' grinned at Keith, gave him a wink, and then began to turn the handle. The device on the pole was a miniature version of an air raid siren, and as the handle turned the hall was filled with that unmistakable but terrifying drone which was so familiar to everyone. Everyone on the stage reacted with mock alarm and began to move back and off the stage and out into the wings.

The hall lights dimmed and the spotlights began to sweep around the building, down onto the audience and up on the ceiling.

Down with the band Jo had taken her seat too and had handed over the control of the music to a young US Lieutenant who was now standing right in front of the stage and was signalling to all the musicians, both the Bletchley players and the US bandsmen and women.

The siren suddenly stopped, and the young American serviceman counted the musicians in. As he called out 'three!' the hall was suddenly filled with yet another unmistakable sound. This time it was the sound of wartime US military swing!

The audience instantly jumped up on their feet, while up on the stage Dilly's Girls – Claire, Margaret, Mavis, Betty, Joyce, Flo and Jean – ran back out, waving to a huge cheer.

As the introduction to the song played-out the girls danced, skipped and gyrated, holding hands and spinning each other around.

Then Claire stepped forward to begin the singing.

The Bletchleyette Boogie

(to Roll Over Beethoven)

Claire: *Just fifty miles from London there's*
a place worth taking a look
They call it Bletchley Park;
you'll even find it in the Doomsday Book
If you are good at puzzles then they'll
get you there by hook or by crook

Margaret: *It was purchased by an Admiral*
in the spring of 1938
As a place for cracking secrets he could
see that it would really be great
Included in his money was a mansion,
grounds, garden and lake

Mavis: *It's right by Bletchley station sitting*
neatly on the West Coast line
They started building huts there back
in August 1939

The Bletchleyette Boogie

They were soon recruiting ladies, come on,
girls, this is our time!

ALL: *We're the Bletchley ladies*
Grads and Wrens
Dilly's Fillies
All good friends
We're the Bletchleyettes
Cryptographic operators, yeah!
Making our mark
Here at Bletchley Park!

It's the Government code
And cipher school
Mavis Lever
She's no fool
We're the Bletchleyettes
Cryptographic operators, yeah!

Getting it done
But having some fun
Boffins and Debs
Using our heads
Making our mark
Here at Bletchley Park!

Betty: *When people see us ladies all they*
think about are dresses and frills
Joyce: *But we've got something special, boys,*
lateral thinking skills
Flo: *All those codes we broke proved*
to everyone we fitted the bill!

Margaret: *Three quarters of the staff are*
women taken from the middle class

Dilly's Girls

Mavis: *University degrees in engineering,*
science, physics and maths
Claire: *We're rockin' into Bletchley with our*
skills, brains, glamour and sass!

ALL: *Given entry*
Into STEM
Due to Britain's
Lack of men
We're the Bletchleyettes
Cryptographic operators, yeah!
Making our mark
Here at Bletchley Park!

Oxford Cambridge
Double first
We've got 15 Shillings
In our purse
We're the Bletchleyettes
Cryptographic operators, yeah!

Getting it done
But having some fun
Boffins and Debs
Using our heads
Making our mark
Here at Bletchley Park!

Well if you're feeling like I want to stretch me
Then get yourself off down to Bletchley
And sign up to the – secrets pact
And join our family – in the act of
Breaking codes and ciphers
Here at Bletchley Park!

At this point Jean stepped forward and threw everything she had into her final rockin' solo break.

The Bletchleyette Boogie

Jean: *We're the Debutantes and Wrens,*
with a country to defend,
so don't you step on our cipher drive!
Working that text here at Station X,
these girls are ready to strive
Breaking codes at Bletchley
H.M.S. Pembroke Five

ALL: *Code breaking at Bletchley*
Code breaking at Bletchley
Code breaking at Bletchley
Code breaking at Bletchley
We're making our mark
Here at Bletchley Park!

Once again the stage filled with all members of the cast who joined in with the joyful singing.

Code breaking at Bletchley
Code breaking at Bletchley
Code breaking at Bletchley
Code breaking at Bletchley
We're making our mark
Here at Bletchley Park!

Code breaking at Bletchley
Code breaking at Bletchley
Code breaking at Bletchley
Code breaking at Bletchley
We're making our mark
Here at Bletchley Park!

End

PART THREE

Dilly's Girls

AN HISTORICAL OVERVIEW

Prologue

• • • • • • • • • • • • • • • •

'Frank Birch took a moment to peek out into the Assembly Hall from the side of the stage'

Frank Birch first met Dilly at Cambridge in 1909, when he arrived at the University as a history undergraduate just as Dilly returned as a Fellow. The two men very quickly became firm friends.

In 1915 Frank also became a Fellow of King's College and would remain one until 1934.

Frank and Dilly were to work together at the Admiralty as codebreakers in Room-40 and then at ID25 during World War One, and then again at Bletchley Park during the Second World War. Together they wrote a satirical history of ID25 at the end of the Great War – 'A Codebreaking Parody of Alice's Adventures in Wonderland' – which was performed by way of a celebration for the end of the First World War at Frank's house in Chelsea. Frank wrote the script and Dilly all the poems.

When Dilly and Olive were first married, they moved in with Frank and his wife Vera at Number 14 Edith Grove in Chelsea.

After the war Frank decided to head back to Cambridge, where he became a lecturer in History.

But Frank had always had a love of the theatre, and left Cambridge University at the start of the 1930s to pursue a career on the stage, which

Frank Birch

included an appearance as Widow Twankey in pantomime. Throughout the 1930s he appeared on the stage, in films, and in a television production at the BBC.

Frank and Dilly remained good friends between the wars, and Frank was a popular visitor at Courns Wood, where he would always delight and entertain Dilly's boys with his impressions.

At the outbreak of the Second World War Frank rejoined many of his old codebreaking colleagues at Bletchley, where he worked in the Naval Enigma Section.

....

'A lady appeared on the side of the stage in front of the curtain. She was dressed smartly in typical late 1930s attire and was carrying a large black Kodak camera. It was Barbara Abernethy.'

The famous picture of the members of 'Captain Ridley's Shooting Party' all gathered in front of the Bletchley mansion was taken in September 1938. The photographer was Barbara Abernethy, who had joined GC&CS in August 1937 aged just 16. Barbara was fluent in French and German, and was working at the Foreign Office when Denniston, the leader of GC&CS, asked for a new typist.

....

'The highly eccentric Alfred Dillwyn 'Dilly' Knox who was (as he always was) puffing on his pipe'

Dilly is the central character in our story. He was the Chief Cryptographer at Bletchley, head of the Enigma Research section in the cottage, and perhaps the most eccentric of all the codebreakers.

Some of the other male codebreakers wrote in the years after the war that they felt that Dilly's often eccentric behaviour was contrived, but Dilly's team of highly intelligent young ladies would not have stood for any nonsense had they thought that his behaviour was in any way false and not completely natural for his character.

Dilly (pre-Bletchley).

Prologue

In her biography of her uncle and his brothers, Dilly's niece Penelope Fitzgerald describes how many of Dilly's eccentricities developed very early on in his life. Particularly of how he would suddenly stand stock still as if in a trance, lost in deep thought. There are also the stories of him being regularly found in his office at ID25 during the First World War stood staring at running water in the bathtub as he pondered the latest cryptology conundrums.

Much has also been made of Dilly allegedly having a ferocious temper, and this is mentioned in several books about Bletchley in which he is described as 'irritable', 'ill tempered', and 'irascible'.

Ms Fitzgerald also touches on this subject in her book, writing that all four Knox brothers did indeed have tempers, but then she quickly qualifies this by saying that none of them ever raised their voices in anger. She makes a special mention of Dilly in this respect and wrote that he had such a love of the truth that it was only any perceived dishonesty or 'uppishness' in others which would trigger an angry response, but that this would just take the form of a cutting or 'brusque' remark.

She wrote that Dilly 'hated dishonesty and any kind of meanness' and added that her uncle was 'totally honest' and 'modest'.

Dilly could be very direct, which was often taken by those that did not know him well as rudeness.

Perhaps so much is made in books about Dilly's alleged fierce temper because of the content of some of the letters he wrote to his old friend and commander at Bletchley, Alistair Denniston. 'Brusque' would certainly be the perfect word to describe some of the wording within many of these letters, but context is needed here before conclusions are drawn. For example, Dilly had very strong views on how the different sections at Bletchley should interact, which differed from his commander. More often than not there was merit in both views, but in some cases Dilly's determination to fight his corner proved critical to the war effort. Just take Matapan, for example, where Dilly had to fight to have the Italian Naval intercepts treated as Ultra, and this treatment of the Italian Enigma intelligence was pivotal in paving the way for the decisive Royal Navy victory in the Mediterranean.

Remember also that Denniston's office was in the mansion just a few hundred yards from the cottage, and yet rather than hammer fists on a desk, Dilly simply wrote his commander letters. This alone would suggest that any anger was very controlled, vented not by shouting and temper, but in Dilly's case just by writing his frustrations down.

There is also Denniston's diary account of the Warsaw meeting in July 1939, in which Dilly is described as having been furious at the end of the first day, declaring in temper that the journey had been a complete waste of time. This is one occasion where he almost certainly did vocally explode! But the Warsaw trip needs some context too. A month earlier there had been a meeting in Paris of the British, French and Polish cryptography teams. Dilly had demonstrated his methods for breaking Enigma, but there had been nothing of any substance from either the French or Polish contingents, leaving Dilly to conclude that neither had made any progress. Yet a month later the Poles had insisted that Dilly come to Warsaw, and despite having just had his first operation for cancer, and not only this but also being very sick with the flu, he made the long trip, only at the end of the first day to have still not been shown anything of any use or to have met anyone who had been working closely on the Enigma problem. Under these circumstances Dilly was probably more than entitled to have been absolutely furious and be excused for venting his anger.

The two books that give the biggest insight into Dilly's character were written by ladies that knew him well. 'The Knox Brothers' is the biography written by his niece and already mentioned, and then there is the wonderful book written by Mavis, 'Dilly: The man who broke Enigmas'.

While she was away at school Dilly's niece described him as 'the kindest of her visiting uncles', and within his niece's book Dilly's sister also remembered him as 'kind beyond belief in one's troubles' and that Dilly was always there for her when she needed him.

Such sentiments were echoed by the girls in the cottage at Bletchley, and Dilly was clearly respected and loved by his team. It is doubtful they would have shown such loyalty or remembered him with such love and fondness if he were prone to losing his temper and shouting at them all the time.

From an early age Dilly had had a passion for the books of Lewis Carroll, and he loved to bring the world of Alice into the daily cottage life by giving wonderfully odd Carrollian names to his ingenious methods and ideas. While the male codebreakers looked on all of this with a certain scepticism and cynicism, the girls totally bought into Dilly's world, and found Dilly's approach completely inspirational.

It is perhaps this positive reaction by the ladies to his methods and his approach to breaking codes in the early days at Bletchley that led him to insist that he only wanted ladies on his team when the cottage was reopened, and Dilly's research section re-established.

The suggestion that Dilly would prowl the grounds of Bletchley Park looking for the prettiest girls to join his team is completely refuted by Mavis in her book, and she is very clear that all the girls recruited for the cottage were interviewed in the same way and were selected on ability alone.

Dilly is perhaps best described as 'loyal', 'loved by his team', 'exceptional' though 'absent-minded', and a man 'whose brilliance has only rarely been acknowledged'.

....

'One is Oliver Strachey'

It is fitting that in the famous 'Shooting Party' picture Dilly and Oliver can be seen standing talking to each other a little way away from the main group since between them they were to break the German intelligence ciphers known as Abwher.

Oliver headed up the Abwher hand cipher section which was given the name ISOS (Illicit Services Oliver Strachey) at Bletchley.

Dilly was to take on the challenge of the Abwher Enigma, which was broken for the first time by Mavis Lever when looking for Dilly's 'lobsters'. As Abwher Enigma traffic grew, the ISK section was formed (Intelligence Services Knox).

Dilly and Oliver were also old friends.

Oliver had been chief cryptographer at MI1b during WW1, which was the Army intelligence unit. Dilly had worked for the Admiralty in what was known as 'Room-40' and then ID25. These two organisations merged after the War in 1919 to form the Government Code & Cipher School – GC&CS – under Admiral Hugh Sinclair who had recently replaced Captain Reginald 'Blinker' Hall as Director of Naval Intelligence.

• • • • • • • • • • • • • • • • •

'The Ministry wouldn't give Sinclair a penny toward relocating us'

Admiral Hugh Sinclair was known as 'C' as the head of the Secret Intelligence Service, after the initial of the first head of SIS Commander Mansfield Cumming. Sinclair was the overall director of the GC&CS and it was Sinclair who was responsible for Bletchley Park becoming the centre of code breaking during the Second World War.

Sinclair knew that war was inevitable, and he had seen the devastating impact of mass aerial bombing during the Spanish Civil War, so he knew that a safer place away from London needed to be found to house his codebreakers.

Bletchley Park was up for sale and the Admiral saw that this would be the perfect place. It was close enough to London to facilitate good communication links and its train station sat at a crossroad of north-south and east-west rail routes. The Park had a large mansion and ample grounds to facilitate any expansion that might be needed, and so it was that in June 1938 Sinclair approached the Foreign Office to ask for the £7,500 needed to purchase the Bletchley Park estate.

The Foreign Office told him that the war effort was nothing to do with them and that he should take his request to the War Office. In turn the War Office told Sinclair that since he was the former head of Naval Intelligence, he should take his request to the Admiralty. The Admiralty simply reminded him that he now worked for the Foreign Office. You just could not make this up, and so, exasperated, Sinclair bought the Park with his own money.

• • • • • • • • • • • • • • • • •

'Denniston has chosen Lady Leon's morning room'

Rather like Dilly, Commander Alistair Denniston is another key character from war time Bletchley who does not get the recognition he deserves, not to mention being completely mis-portrayed by Hollywood in the film 'The Imitation Game'. He was responsible for overseeing the transformation of the park from a collection of highly skilled codebreakers into a code breaking production line, only to be unceremoniously pushed aside midway through the war.

Denniston, like Dilly, had been recruited in the very early days of Room-40, when he had been teaching languages at the Royal Naval College on the Isle of Wight. Being quite short he became known to colleagues as 'The Little Man'.

It was Winston Churchill, then Secretary of State for War, who insisted that Denniston be put in charge of the codebreakers when GC&CS was first formed. Churchill had worked closely with the Admiralty's codebreakers in Room-40 during the Great War, and he knew Denniston well.

Denniston had huge respect for Dilly and his unique codebreaking abilities, and crucially knew how to handle his old friend.

Dilly and Denniston often disagreed over matters of how the GC&CS organisation should be run, and there were merits in both views. Dilly was adamant that a codebreaker should be able to see any breakthrough right the way through to how the resulting intelligence was used, whereas Denniston strongly believed in the approach of once a code is broken it should be passed on for analysis and distribution by others.

Dilly would often vent his frustration at various high-level decisions by writing letters to Denniston, which would invariably include a threat of resignation.

It was probably the content of these letters that has led some historians to portray Dilly as having a vicious temper, but fortunately Denniston knew his old friend only too well and would always respond in a calming way.

....

'Old 'Nobby' Clarke's picked the library for his naval section'

When Room-40 was first set up at the beginning of World War One, 'Blinker' Hall appointed Commander Herbert Hope to take charge, and he brought in William 'Nobby' Clarke.

Clarke knew German and his talent was for analysing the content of any messages rather than actual codebreaking. He later joined GC&CS in

1921 and three years later set up its Naval Section, which he was to run until 1941.

....

'Tiltman's bagged the dining room'

John Tiltman, like Dilly, was a talented cryptographer, and also like Dilly, was able to successfully make the transfer from the manual ciphers of the First World War through to the mechanical ciphers of World War Two.

Whereas Dilly broke Enigma machines, Tiltman was to play a vital role in the breaking of the other German mechanical cipher, the Lorenz.

It was the work on Lorenz which was to ultimately lead to the development of Colossus, the world's first fully digital and programmable computer.

....

'Cooper has got his air section in the drawing room'

Josh Cooper was perhaps even more eccentric than Dilly, so much so in fact that many workers at Bletchley remember finding Cooper a somewhat terrifying character when they first met him.

Cooper had joined GC&CS in 1925, and he was respected as a hugely talented codebreaker.

He was well known for his unusual thinking stance of wrapping his right arm around the back of his head and scratching his left ear.

Of all the Bletchley Park anecdotes one of the funniest involved Cooper, and it was when he was asked to be part of a team interviewing a captured German Luftwaffe officer. Cooper and his colleagues were seated behind a trellis table at the end of the room when the German pilot was marched in. The officer was in full Nazi uniform as he came to attention in front of the table, clicked his heels and offered a crisp Nazi salute with a loud 'Heil Hilter'!

Cooper's reaction was instinctive. He jumped to his feet and returned the greeting, only to instantly realise his mistake and quickly sit back down again. Unfortunately, he had pushed his chair back when standing up and with no seat under him anymore Cooper disappeared under the table.

We can only imagine what the German officer must have been thinking.

. . . .

'Captain Ridley's Shooting Party'

It was September 1938 when the codebreakers of GC&CS descended on Bletchley Park for the first time, and it was during this first visit when Barbara's famous photograph was taken. This was to be a rehearsal of the move from London should war with Germany become inevitable.

To the Bletchley locals, the sudden arrival of this very strange looking group of people in their town caused some interest. A large collection of middle-aged professor types accompanied by much younger women had booked themselves in at local hotels and were calling themselves 'Captain Ridley's Shooting Party'.

Captain W.H.W. Ridley was a Secret Intelligence Service (SIS) administrative officer who had been tasked with organising this trial run.

Jean's Arrival

JEAN ARRIVES AT BLETCHLEY full of hope singing about her dream to be able to help the war effort.

....

'I'm here for a job. Oh, my name is Jean.'

Jean was the first of Dilly's Girls that I read anything about. Having just watched my son's production of the play 'Breaking the Code', I entered Dilly's name into an Internet search engine and up popped a newspaper article about his team of ladies who were known at Bletchley as 'Dilly's Girls'.

The journalist who had written the article had interviewed several of the ladies who had worked with Dilly at Bletchley Park, and Jean was the first one interviewed. I decided there and then that Jean would be the character around whom Frank's musical would revolve.

Jean became part of Dilly's team as a teenager, and like all the other young women who worked at the Park during the war she arrived at Bletchley with little knowledge of what she would be doing. Having arrived at Bletchley she was immediately made to sign the Official Secrets Act, swearing not to tell anybody about what happened at Bletchley for 30 years. This included family, boyfriends and even the other people working at Bletchley.

Work was never discussed when the ladies were off duty, and Jean remembered that they did not even chat about it amongst themselves.

Everyone had signed the Official Secrets Act and as she said, 'that was that'.

Jean had just finished school and had applied to join the Women's Royal Naval Service – the Wrens – but had been rejected because she was too young. Jean recalls: 'I always thought that if I had joined the Wrens, I would have ended up at Bletchley anyway, doing something far less interesting than I was'.

Although our story begins with Jean arriving at Bletchley Park to be interviewed, she was in fact interviewed at home. Jean lived in Wendover, which was about ten miles north of Dilly's home Courns Wood, and so when her name was put forward by a friend of her family already working at the Park, Dilly decided to stop off one day on his way in to work to meet her.

Jean was interviewed by Dilly when she was just seventeen and remembered it as 'a bit of a farce'. She had not been well and was still in bed when Dilly arrived. Dilly asked Jean if she knew any German words and when she said that she did not Dilly offered that it might be useful if she knew a few, but she remembers Dilly spending most of the interview telling her about the other girls that worked in the Cottage. Jean also remembered noting just how poorly Dilly looked.

Taking Dilly's advice, Jean did then return to school to learn some German before she joined Dilly's newly created ISK section. In the article she vividly remembered how she and the others would use Dilly's rods – the coloured strips of card with the letters of the alphabet on them which the girls called 'sticks'. She recalls it as being an amazing system, one that would work more often than not, and one that she proudly remembers being very good at.

Unlike the more senior ladies like Mavis and Margaret, Jean never understood how or why Dilly's rods worked, but she knew that they did, and tellingly she remembers enjoying her work. These mundane tasks were brought to life by Dilly's wonderfully eccentric descriptions and names he was always giving to his ideas, tricks, and methods.

In her free time Jean loved to play tennis on the courts next to the cottage and always looked forward to the monthly dances held in the Assembly Hall.

Despite the fact that Jean didn't arrive at Bletchley for her interview, bag in hand, so many others did, walking down the lane which ran directly from the train station, often late at night, to be met by sentries on duty by the gate. One can only imagine how daunting that must have been: to arrive at a strange station, seemingly in the middle of nowhere, to make your way down a dark country lane, high wire fences topped with barbed wire running along either side of you, to be met by soldiers on guard, and then finally to be escorted to a large country mansion to sign the Official Secrets Act, all of this while not having a clue what you might be letting yourself in for.

Jean

Dilly's Girls (Part 1)

WE ARE INTRODUCED TO DILLY, the girls and the cottage in this full-on upbeat song.

....

'Alfred Dillwyn "Dilly" Knox grew up in Kibworth'

Dilly was born on the 23rd July 1884 in Oxford, the second son of Edmund and Ellen Knox. Dilly's father was the sub-warden of Oxford University Merton College. There were four Knox brothers in all: Eddie (the eldest), then Dilly, Wilfred and Ronnie. Two sisters, Ethel and Winifred, completed the family.

Only Ethel, Eddie, Winifred and Dilly were born in Oxford, since a year after Dilly arrived on the scene, the family moved to Kibworth in Leicestershire where Edmund was to be the clergyman there at St Wilfred's church.

The Knox children adored their time growing up at the rectory. The large house with its big garden was surrounded by fields and this provided the perfect setting for the fondest childhood memories. Not only that, but a railway line ran not far from the bottom of their garden and Dilly and his brothers and sisters soon had the timetable memorised and loved to wave at the steam trains as they thundered down the tracks. The Knox siblings really were the original railway children.

In 1891 the family moved to Aston on the outskirts of Birmingham. Just a year later young Dilly's world was shattered when his mother was taken ill and died of influenza. With his father unable to cope by himself, Dilly and his sisters were sent to live with a great aunt in Eastbourne.

Happily, the family was reunited two years later when Edmund was offered the Parish of St Paul's in Birmingham. Their father also remarried, and his new bride Ethel was immediately impressed by the Knox children, and they by her, and she told the children she was to be known as 'Mrs K' since she in no way wanted to take the place of their mother's memory.

Dilly loved books, poetry and puzzles. Lewis Carroll was a particular favourite, teasing the reader with his famous 'chopped logic' in his Alice stories. What seemed to the reader like nonsense could always be unravelled by logic. The Knox boys were devoted to Punch, a weekly magazine packed with humour, satire and cartoons. Eddie would later become its editor. They wrote a letter to Arthur Conan Doyle, pointing out the plot errors in his Sherlock Holmes stories, and were disappointed when he did not reply. The brothers invented games for teaching logic, and so it seems the young Dilly was already honing his skills as a future codebreaker even at this young age.

. . . .

'To Eton was the place he headed next'

There was no money available for private education and so scholarships would need to be won. With this in mind Dilly was sent to Summer Fields Preparatory School in North Oxford where he only needed a single year's tutoring to win himself a place at Eton in 1897.

His work at Eton was described as untidy, unintelligible, and illegible, but his genius was recognised early on.

In her biography of the Knox brothers, Dilly's niece describes how it was while at Eton that Dilly became a 'ferocious agnostic', which caused him to do much soul searching since he had been raised in a devoutly Christian environment.

Dilly's Girls (Part 1)

. . . .

'And finally to the college King's in Cambridge'

In 1903 Edmund became the Bishop of Manchester and in that same year Dilly started at King's College Cambridge reading Classics.

Dilly had submitted two quite brilliant papers as part of his Cambridge entrance exam, one on Mathematics and the other on Greek Verse. He did not bother to finish the other papers he took, but his potential was clear, and a King's Classics scholarship was secured.

Because Dilly had been at Eton, when he arrived at King's College he was readily accepted into the 'included' group of undergraduates, though his niece wrote that this 'was of singularly little importance to him'.

At Cambridge Dilly was quite the sportsman. He swam and rowed on the river Cam, and excelled at cricket where he was famed for his slow and unplayable spin bowling. He was prolific with the bat as well.

Dilly also became a popular and much in demand speaker at the various college societies, even though years earlier he had been given the nickname 'Erm' by his brothers due to his hesitations when speaking.

It was also while he was at King's College that Dilly acquired his motorbike.

. . . .

'So the first code Dilly faced was not Enigma'

Dilly graduated from King's in 1907 having won the Chancellors Classical Medal and set out on a career in education, teaching Classics and Ancient History at St Paul's School, Hammersmith, 'where he made no attempt to keep order in the classroom and was loved by all'.

In 1909 King's College Cambridge contacted Dilly with the offer of a Fellowship.

It was on his return to Cambridge that Dilly met and befriended Frank Birch. Frank was a new History undergraduate at King's and someone that was to remain a close friend of Dilly's for the rest of his life. Frank was to also work with Dilly as a codebreaker during both world wars.

When Dilly went back to Cambridge, he inherited his old tutor's work on Herodas, an ancient Greek writer and poet who lived during the 3rd Century BC. Dilly was tasked with translating Herodas' Mimes, which were a collection of scenes from popular life in Alexandria written in 'the language of the people'.

Here, the Mimes in question was a worm-eaten piece of ancient papyrus, about five inches high, and written by a copyist at around AD100. This piece of history had laid buried beneath the Saharan sands for nearly two thousand years, only to be finally uncovered during an excavation of the Ancient Egyptian city of Oxyrhynchus, about two hundred miles south of Cairo in 1889.

Dilly was faced with the same sort of problems he would come up against later when breaking enemy codes during the two world wars. Parts of the old papyrus were missing or had been misaligned by the archaeologists, in the same way as some Morse intercepts and messages were later found to be incomplete. The Egyptian copyist had also made errors, just as lazy German signallers and Enigma operators would in later years.

Dilly had no admiration for Herodas as a writer, but saw the translation as a challenge, a game where all the rules were missing, and one that he intended to win!

Dilly did successfully break the Herodas code, but not before normal life was shook to the core by the outbreak of The Great War in 1914.

• • • • • • • • • • • • • • • •

'In World War I recruited by the Navy'

When war was declared in 1914, Dilly tried to enlist as a motorcycle dispatch rider, but poor eyesight and even poorer motorbike riding skills let him down. But as luck would have it, another King's Fellow was on the lookout for talented people to join the Navy's newly formed Naval Intelligence Division, and Dilly was recruited in 1915. Winston Churchill was also involved in those early days, and as The First Lord of the Admiralty he took it upon himself to personally draft the charter for this new intelligence section.

Premises were found in Room 40 of the Old Admiralty Buildings and, while most of the new recruits were assigned translation tasks, Dilly was put on the team dealing with codes and cipher keys. Codes replaced words, ciphers replaced letters, and the settings of a cipher became known as the key.

With so many similarities between solving unreadable ancient Greek texts and breaking enemy codes, Dilly took to his new task like a duck to water. Using inspired guesswork and cribs – pieces of text that were predicted to be in messages – Dilly set about his new challenge with enthusiasm.

•••••••••••••••••

'He broke the German telegram that brought in Uncle Sam to the last war and ensured our victory!'

The one piece of code breaking that undoubtedly had the biggest impact on the outcome of the First World War was the breaking of the Zimmermann telegram which ultimately resulted in America joining the conflict.

Arthur Zimmermann was the German Foreign Secretary at the time, and on 16th January 1917 he sent an enciphered telegram to the German ambassador in Mexico which was to prove to be the political turning point of the Great War. Crucially the telegram was sent first to the German ambassador in Washington, Johann von Bernstorff, before retransmission on to Mexico. The message was intercepted since the underwater cables touched on British soil just off Land's End, and the message quickly found its way to Room-40, landing on Dilly's desk.

Dilly was able to break enough of the code that even with his limited knowledge of German he knew straight away that the contents of this message needed urgent attention. Dilly took the partially decoded message to a colleague, Nigel de Grey, who was able to translate the German text in full.

It took the two men all morning to fully decode and translate the telegram. The message had been sent in the high-grade diplomatic code called '7500', which Room-40 had only just started being able to solve.

Not all the 7500 code groups were known at the time, and Dilly had to use all his experience of looking for repeated patterns to derive the missing sections of the message.

Dilly and de Grey had uncovered an audacious proposal from the Germans to Mexico which suggested the Mexican government should form a military alliance against the United States in exchange for the return of Texas, New Mexico and Arizona, which had been lost by Mexico to America in the 1846-8 war between the two countries.

De Grey then took the decoded message straight to his superior, Captain Reginald 'Blinker' Hall.

From that point on Dilly had no further role in proceedings, but he was full of admiration in the way that the British handled this 'diplomatic dynamite'. The need to bring America into the war, which this telegram almost certainly would, had to be weighed against letting the Germans know that their code had been broken. This was the classic cryptologist conundrum.

Hall came up with a quite brilliant solution. He rightly guessed that the message would be transmitted on from Washington to Mexico by von Bernstorff using an older lower-grade diplomatic code known as '13040', which the British had been successfully breaking since 1915. So, Hall had the message restructured using this older code and it was this version of the message that they presented to the Americans.

The restructured message was taken to the American embassy, where de Grey was tasked with showing the Americans how Room-40 had decoded the message and to prove that it was genuine. However, even at this last vital stage it was all so close to going wrong, because on leaving Room-40 de Grey had grabbed his own '13040' code book by mistake. His book was incomplete and did not contain all the '13040' codes. It was only when he opened it in front of the Americans that he realised his error.

Thinking quickly on his feet de Grey knew that if he asked for his book to be swapped the Americans would suspect foul play, and so he just focused on demonstrating the decoding of parts of the telegram that carried codes in his book, hoping that this would be enough.

It was, and the rest, as they say, is history.

Dilly's Girls (Part 1)

. . . .

'Where they say he did his best work in the bath!'

Room-40 expended into a set of rooms nearby and became known as Section 25 of Naval Intelligence Division (ID25) in May 1917.

Dilly's office in ID25 was Room 53. It was only a small room, but it had its own bath. Dilly found that lying in the water or just watching the water run from the taps helped him concentrate his mind.

It was also around about this time that Dilly was assigned a secretary, Miss Olive Roddam. Olive was later to become his wife.

Toward the end of the war the tracking of German U-Boats became critical, just as it would 25 years later, and great alarm swept through ID25 when it was realised that the Germans had introduced a new codebook. But Dilly broke the new code and was able to find a way into the new key system, causing great celebrations in the section, and he did it because he spotted that a small message had a pattern.

Dilly spotted that the pattern in the message had the rhythm of a poem. Why would there be a poem in a message? He suspected that this may well be a romantic poem. Dilly deduced that any romantic poem would more than likely include the word 'Roses'. With all this in mind Dilly took his ideas to the linguists, who confirmed that he was right. He now had the key and was able to work back to compile the complete new codebook from scratch.

By the end of the war more than twenty thousand messages had been decoded by Room-40/ID25.

. . . .

'Between the wars he continued his code breaking'

After the war Dilly considered returning to King's but in the end decided to become part of the new Government Code & Cipher School – GC&CS – which was established in 1919.

Dilly had not given up on Herodas and hoped to be able to finish his work on the translation in his spare time. Identifying the errors made by the copyists was just like codebreaking, and Dilly made use of the best-preserved pieces of the old papyrus as his cribs.

GC&CS was a merger of the Navy (the Admiralty's ID25) and the Army (the War Office's MI1b) cryptological departments into a new section, in new offices at Watergate House, and under a new commander, Commander Alistair Denniston.

Dilly and Olive married in 1920, and in his absent-minded way Dilly forgot to invite two of his brothers to the wedding!

Olive loved and desperately missed the countryside and when Dilly was left a legacy in 1921 he and Olive bought Courns Wood, a beautiful country house in 40 acres of Chiltern woodlands, just a few miles from High Wycombe. It was at Courns Wood where Dilly would develop a passion for tree planting.

Each day Dilly would travel by train to London, using this travel time to continue work on his old Greek foe, laying out copies of the Mimes across his knees, the seats, and on the floor of the carriage. Dilly completed Herodas in 1922, and now with no need for a train to work on his challenge from Ancient Greece he took to making the journey on his motorbike.

Also in 1922 the Foreign Office took control of GC&CS, and in 1925 the GC&CS offices moved to 54 Broadway Buildings.

With the Germans defeated, GC&CS had turned its attention to other countries. Dilly broke the Hungarian codes, learning the language at the same time, but it was soon that the Russian Bolshevik communications became the focus of his codebreaking work. Russian expert John Tiltman was recalled from India in 1929 to form a new military GC&CS section, and he and Dilly worked together and had soon broken the latest Russian codes.

Dilly's motorcycle would last until 1931 when he badly broke his leg in an accident. No longer able to ride his motorbike, Dilly bought himself a car, a Baby Austin Seven.

• • • • • • • • • • • • • • • •

'Soon after that he purchased an Enigma'

The new Enigma electro-mechanical cipher machine was exhibited by its German inventor Arthur Scherbius for the first time in 1924 at the

International Postal Union Congress held in Sweden. A year later Dilly purchased an Enigma machine during a visit to Vienna.

GC&CS had appointed Edward Travis, Alistair Denniston's deputy, to take charge of all aspects of British Government communications security, and when Scherbius applied for a British patent for his Enigma machine in 1927, Travis asked Hugh Foss, a GC&CS employee since 1924 and someone with previous exposure to an earlier version of Enigma, to investigate and report on its suitability as a secure cipher machine. Foss produced his report in 1928, which concluded that Enigma could be broken.

In his report Foss referred to the Enigma as the 'Reciprocal Enigma' since its mechanism included a reflector known as the 'Umkehrwalze'. This meant that if 'A' mapped to 'B' then 'B' would map to 'A', and crucially that any letter could never map to itself.

Dilly quickly realised that this meant that he could approach the Enigma problem textually.

....

'He worked out how to break it with his Rods'

Dilly knew that he had to invent a process that could reproduce the action of an Enigma machine and he invented a manual method for breaking the early Enigma machines which he named 'Rodding'.

Dilly's 'Rods' were in fact strips of card. Three sets of rods were needed, one for each rotating wheel in the Enigma machine. Each set was colour-coded and consisted of 26 individual rods, one for each letter on the wheel.

Rodding still required a crib to start the process off, and this method would only produce a fragmented sequence of characters from the text. The codebreakers still needed all their intuition and skills to fill the gaps, working the problem like a crossword puzzle. But each correct guess would extend the crib, allowing the process to continue.

Rodding worked from a table, which had to be constructed before the process could begin, and here too Dilly created a procedure for creating the first column of each rodding table, which he named 'Buttoning-up'. Once the first column in the table had been worked out, then the rest of the table could be extrapolated by the codebreaker.

In October 1935 Mussolini's fascist forces invaded Abyssinia, threatening British controlled Egypt, and pushing Italy ever closer to an alliance with Nazi Germany. Dilly joined 'Nobby' Clarke's Naval Section and set about breaking the Italian codebooks.

Then, during the Spanish Civil War in 1936, the Germans sold the Spanish and the Italians a version of the commercial Enigma machine for wartime use.

Dilly quickly realised that this was a new model, which became known as the 'K' model, and began work on finding a way into the secrets of this new machine. He knew that operator errors were the things to look out for, and in his mischievously unique way labelled these 'Boils'. The breakthrough came in 1937 when 20 contiguous Italian messages were sent out using the same Enigma settings, and Dilly was able to establish the wiring of this new machine using his buttoning-up method.

Dilly soon found that the Spanish were using the same 'K' Enigma, as were the volunteer German Luftwaffe units that flew missions for Franco during the Spanish war.

So Dilly had successfully broken Italian, Spanish and German Enigma traffic. These successes led to interest from and some cooperation with the French.

....

'A new German one upgraded with a Stecker'

Gustave Bertrand was an intelligence officer in charge of the French cipher department within the French equivalent of GC&CS, the Services de Renseignement. He had learned as early as 1926 that the Germans had introduced a new 'unbreakable' Enigma machine.

The French had been intercepting these new German Enigma messages via stations close to the France-Germany border for some time, but they had had no success in breaking them. So, Bertrand decided that espionage was the only route to breaking the new German codes and installed himself in the French embassy in Berlin.

Then, one day in 1931, Hans Schmidt, an official from the German cipher office, walked into the embassy and offered to sell top secret German documents about Enigma to the French.

Schmidt was given the codename 'Asche', and Bertrand took Asche's offer – of secret documents in exchange for ten thousand German marks – to his superiors back in France. However, the French cryptologists took one look at the samples and declared them to be of little use, and so Bertrand turned to the British, and a week later approached Wilfred 'Biffy' Dunderdale who was the SIS station chief in Paris.

Sadly, GC&CS was not consulted, and it was left to politicians to decide that this was not a spending priority and the British refused to pay. There is little doubt that Dunderdale would have copied and passed on those initial sample documents, but from that moment on the British had cut themselves off from all the rest of Asche's priceless Enigma secrets.

Dilly did learn, however, that the Germans had added a plug-board – or 'Steckerboard' – to their Enigma design. This plug-board connected pairs of letters together and effectively switched them over. The Germans generally made use of ten plug-board connections, which had the effect of multiplying the number of ways an Enigma could be set up by 150 million million times.

Unlike the Poles and French, GC&CS received virtually no German Enigma traffic to analyse, and so all Dilly could do was use his intuition. It would be another four years before GC&CS encountered its first steckered Enigma message, which was during the Spanish civil war when the German navy was on manoeuvres in Spanish waters. The Italians and Spanish used separate codebooks for indicator settings, but the Germans included the indicator settings at the beginning of each message, and this presented Dilly with a possible new way in to breaking the code.

Dilly had already worked out a theoretical approach to the challenge of the stecker, where it could be treated as a separate 'super-encipherment' layer, which could be stripped off, allowing Dilly's un-steckered methods to be applied.

Although Denniston felt Dilly was making good progress in his work on Enigma, he was also keen to establish better inter-security relations with the French, and as a result Bertrand was invited to London for a meeting in November 1938.

Bertrand was impressed by Dilly's methods and a deal was struck whereby the British promised Bertrand a regular supply of British de-codes in exchange for Asche's secrets. Before the end of the year Bertrand finally handed over the German Enigma user's manual, which included a genuine stream of enciphered text along with the associated key settings. This was the same manual he had passed on to the Polish codebreakers six years earlier.

Dilly immediately dived into applying his stecker-adapted methods on this new information, but he just could not get it to work, and it dawned on him that the Germans must have changed the 'Qwertzu'!

....

'How the keyboard mapped he really
should have guessed'

The keyboard on an Enigma machine had its keys laid out in the continental 'QWERTZU' order rather than the more familiar 'QWERTY' layout.

The way in which each letter key was wired within the machine to what was called the 'entry-plate' was one of the crucial pieces of information needed to crack Enigma.

Dilly had worked out that on the early un-steckered machines the keys were wired as they were laid out, i.e. that 'Q' went to input one, 'W' to two, 'E' to input three, and so on.

He called this the 'diagonal' or in more usual Dilly speak he named it the 'Qwertzu'. But Dilly soon realised that the diagonal on these new German steckered machines did not follow this mapping.

Dilly knew that mixing up the diagonal was an obvious step to make any Enigma machine even more difficult to break, and it looked like the Germans had finally had the good sense to make maximum use of this obvious and easily built-in cipher option.

At this time German wireless traffic was being transmitted at low power on medium frequencies which made it difficult to intercept back in the UK, and Dilly knew that without any more German messages to work on, finding a way to work out the new entry-plate wiring would be all but impossible.

However, the answer lay in Poland.

Dilly's Girls (Part 1)

• • • • • • • • • • • • • • • • •

'When he found out from his Polish friends near Warsaw'

After Bertrand's 1932 approach to the British had been rejected, Bertrand had turned to the Poles and their response to his offer of these priceless German Enigma secrets was completely different to that of the French and British. It was one of excitement and joy!

Polish relations with Germany had been poor since the end of the First World War and the threat to Poland from Nazi Germany was very real indeed.

With Poland being right on the German border, Polish intelligence had no problem intercepting the German wireless traffic and they were desperate to track the movements and plans of their potentially dangerous neighbour.

Marian Rejewski, Jerzy Rozycki and Henryk Zygalski were three brilliant young mathematicians straight out of university who had been recruited by the Polish cipher department. Rejewski approached the problem of Enigma from a purely mathematical perspective and using something called Permutation Theory he developed six complex equations which would solve Enigma. Each equation had three unknown parameters, or variables: the stecker, the diagonal, and the wiring of the right-hand wheel.

Part of the intelligence the Poles retrieved from Asche was a full set of key settings for the months of September and October 1932, and this information would prove crucial as it allowed Rejewski to derive the stecker.

Rejewski then made an inspired – but in hindsight an obvious – guess at to what the diagonal might be, and was amazed to find that it was simply 'ABCDE', i.e. that 'A' mapped to input one, 'B' to input two and so on.

With the above two pieces of information, Rejewski's equations now gave him the wiring for the first wheel, and because he had a full set of keys for two different months he was also able to resolve the wiring of the other two wheels and the reflector.

By the end of 1932 Rejewski had solved the Wehrmacht Enigma!

It was vital that the Germans did not find out that Enigma had been broken and the Poles told nobody, not even Bertrand, who continued to supply them with Asche's secrets in exchange for payment.

But Rejewski's equations would only work while the Germans were operating with a fixed Grundstellung – starting position – and the Poles too ran into difficulties during April 1938 when the Germans changed their indicating system.

With war with Germany now imminent and Enigma messages once more unreadable, the Polish authorities asked Bertrand to arrange a meeting with the British and French, and a meeting was set up for January 1939 in Paris.

However, the January meeting was not a total success. The Poles did not fully trust the British following the apparent appeasement of Hitler at Munich in September 1938 and so did not send any codebreakers. Denniston took three of his: Dilly, Tiltman and Foss.

Dilly was exasperated that no one seemed to have any answers at the meeting, especially regarding his 'Qwertzu' question. Despite extravagant claims to the contrary it was clear to Dilly that the French had achieved very little, and he suspected much the same for the Poles.

Dilly gave a demonstration of his rodding method, and Denniston wrote in his diary that everyone was most impressed with the progress that Dilly had made. But based on their showing at that meeting in Paris, Dilly was convinced that neither the French nor the Poles had managed to break Enigma.

It was during this first meeting, however, that it became clear to the British contingent that the Poles had employed mathematicians in their quest to break Enigma, and on his return to the UK, Denniston also set out to find skilled mathematicians to join the British team code breaking team. Two of the mathematicians approached were Alan Turing and Peter Twinn.

With war with Germany sadly now certain, the Poles decided that the time had come to hand over their Enigma secrets, and a second meeting was arranged for July in Warsaw. A special request was made that Dilly should attend.

Dilly's Girls (Part 1)

....

'Lately he's been looking really poorly'

By July Dilly had fallen ill, very ill. Not only had he recently been diagnosed with lymphatic cancer and had just had his first operation, but he was also suffering badly with the flu. But despite all of this he was determined to go to Warsaw and dragged himself out of his sick bed to make the journey to Poland.

Once again, just as in Paris, the first day was a huge disappointment with none of the Polish codebreakers in attendance, although it did become clear that they had broken Enigma when Denniston and Dilly were shown the models of the Enigma built by the Poles and the electro-mechanical 'Bomby' they had built to decipher them.

Much has been made by historians of Dilly's anger during that first day, but who can blame him? Despite being so very ill, he had still made the long journey only to once again be frustrated by not being introduced to anyone with any detailed Enigma knowledge.

But fortunately, the second day was a totally different story. Dilly was taken to the Polish cipher room where he met Rejewski and his colleagues, and with their mutual Enigma affinity they bonded immediately.

Of course, Dilly's first question was 'Quel est le Qwertzu?' Can you imagine what he thought when he was told it was as simple as 'ABC'?

Some historians, and indeed some fellow Bletchley codebreakers, later wrote of Dilly's jealously of the Poles in that that they were the first to break the Whermacht Enigma, but nothing could be further from the truth. This simply was not in Dilly's character. Knox and Rejewski became firm friends, and on returning to London Dilly sent his Polish counterpart a set of his rods and a silk scarf showing a horse winning the Derby, a gift that was treasured by the Polish mathematician for the rest of his life.

....

'Dilly's methods once again could do the rest!'

Arrangements were made to have the Polish Enigma collection of documentation, models and 'Bomby' shipped back to the UK.

As soon as Peter Twinn, a recent addition to Dilly's team, received the Qwertzu information, he was able to confirm within two hours that the sample message inside Bertrand's operator's manual was authentic and that Dilly's methods worked.

The first thing Dilly did on his return to the UK was to contact Alan Turing, a Cambridge mathematician who had been approached by Denniston earlier in the year. He needed to talk to him urgently about those electro-mechanical 'Bomby' machines he had seen in Warsaw.

Quod Erat Demonstandum

MAVIS AND KEITH WERE the classic Bletchley Park love story, and it is a story that I can really relate to, having also met my wife at work. In my case it was at the futuristic IBM UK head office in Portsmouth, and, like Keith, I graduated with a mathematics degree, though not to the level of a Cambridge first!

In this song Mavis sings of her love for Keith and how frustrated she is that he has not asked her out yet. That is not quite how it happened, of course, but theirs really is a wonderful story.

Mavis had originally been sent to work for GC&CS at Broadway Buildings in January 1940 as a linguist, having studied German at university in London and Zurich. She had wanted to train as a nurse for the war effort but was told that she must use her German skills and was sent to the Foreign Office where she was interviewed by a formidable lady called Miss Moore.

Once installed in the Foreign Office, Mavis worked on commercial codes delivered in Morse and she soon found herself in a team trying to track down somewhere called St Goch, a place which had appeared in an intercepted message, and which no one was able to locate. What she did next was typical Knox and would have made her future boss smile. Just like in Dilly's favourite book, 'Alice's Adventures in Wonderland', it so often pays to ask what many would consider the obvious question, and Mavis asked if Morse code could distinguish capital letters. Having been told this was not possible, she switched the capitals and undid the assumption that had been made, and came up with the abbreviation StgoCh, for Santiago in Chile. Mavis had found the mysterious secret location!

This clearly had impressed the powers that be, and very soon after this Mavis found herself on a train up to Bletchley, where after an interview with Commander Denniston, she was escorted by his secretary Barbara Abernethy to the cottage where she met Dilly.

Meanwhile, Keith had just taken his maths finals at Cambridge in May 1940 and had headed back to his home in Carlisle when he received a letter from Gordon Welchman inviting him to join his team at Bletchley.

Welchman wrote after the war that he considered that you did not need to be a mathematician to be good at codebreaking, but that mathematicians tended to be good at it. So, he had contacted some of the students he had known from his days at Cambridge, and Keith had been one of these.

Much to Mavis's amusement, Dilly playfully labelled all Welchman's Cambridge maths recruits as 'Wranglergoves', which was yet another Carrollian reference based on the 'Borogoves' mentioned in the Jabberwocky poem in 'Alice through the Looking Glass'. Of course, Dilly was not comparing Keith to a thin, shabby looking fictional bird, but this was a nod to the Cambridge term of 'Wrangler' which was given to any maths student who has completed the third year with a first class honours degree.

Keith arrived at Bletchley where he was greeted at the Registry and was straight away given a quick lecture on the German wireless network, though he says he was far too distracted by all the young ladies he could see through the window wandering around the Park to take much notice. Then Hugh Alexander came in and gave a talk about Enigma, using a machine that did not work. Welcome to Bletchley!

Mavis and Keith first met when Mavis brought a message in to Hut 3 one night where Keith was working. Both recalled that first meeting, so clearly each made an impression on the other.

However, it was to be over a year before their paths crossed again, which just illustrates how little the different sections at Bletchley Park interacted with one other. Keith said later that inter-hut discussions were forbidden, and that he had assumed that if caught you would 'simply be shot'!

It was during the spring of 1941 when their paths would cross again.

The cottage was now busy working on Italian Enigma traffic, and although the girls had successfully established that they were still using the old pre-war 'K' machine, the Italians had introduced two new rotors with unknown wiring.

Mavis was working late one night and was all alone in the cottage, when she spotted a message that did not contain a single letter 'L'. She quickly worked out that an Italian operator had sent a test message by simply repeatedly pressing the letter 'L', which was the key at the bottom right of the Enigma keyboard. This lazy Italian soldier had unwittingly just provided Mavis with the ultimate crib.

It was a dreadful night, absolutely pouring down with rain, and she needed some help to work out the unknown rotor wirings based on the discovery she had just found. Mavis rushed out into the darkness and rain, running over to Hut 6, where Keith was also working late, and seeing Mavis he immediately offered to help. Back at the cottage the two intrepid codebreakers sat drying out and drinking coffee, working on Mavis's discovery which they hoped would give them the answers they needed to solve the Enigma's settings and wiring.

Mavis thought that Keith was 'very nice' and decided that she would test him by accidentally-on-purpose dropping her pencil on the floor to see how he would react. Years later Keith said he knew exactly what she was up to but chose to completely ignore it, leaving Mavis to recover the pencil herself!

By morning they had resolved the wiring of the two new Italian Enigma rotors.

Keith was later transferred to work full time in the cottage, and this is when the two young cryptologists started dating.

As the war went on Keith began to feel that he should be taking a more active role in the war effort, clearly struggling to reconcile his life at Bletchley Park with his many friends who were overseas with their lives constantly on the line. So, he approached Welchman to ask for a transfer to the Royal Air Force.

There was no way the authorities would ever risk having a leading codebreaker potentially fall into enemy hands, so a compromise was reached, and Keith was told he could join the Fleet Air Arm. If he was going to crash then they had better make sure it would be into the sea where it's likely that no one would ever find him.

Keith joined the Fleet Air Arm in June 1942 and proposed to Mavis before he left. Dilly warned Mavis that mathematicians are normally very unimaginative, but Mavis reassured him that hers was just fine.

Keith's training was not without its moments, and on landing his first solo flight he came in so low that his examiners had to dive for cover! His training was to be completed in Canada during November, so Keith and Mavis were married before he left at Marylebone Registry Office with Margaret Rock as Mavis' Maid of Honour and Peter Twinn as Keith's Best Man. Dilly and Olive's wedding present to the couple was a silver condiment set engraved with the initials ISK.

The newlyweds managed a three-day honeymoon in the Lake District before Keith was due to leave for Canada, and Mavis was most annoyed when Keith's brother Herbert turned up and the two brothers spent a whole precious day playing chess together!

With German U-Boats rife an Atlantic crossing was a very risky business, and Mavis relied on the girls in the Naval Section to keep her informed of Keith's ship's progress.

After the war Mavis and Margaret went to Eastcote with the newly formed GCHQ to work on Russian codes.

In 1947 Mavis left GCHQ to start a family and went with Keith to Ottawa when he was appointed to a post in the High Commission. They had two daughters and a son, and Mavis stayed at home to raise the children.

In the 1960s Keith became Secretary of the Chest – the Chief Financial Officer – at Oxford University.

They lived in a house in the grounds of the University, which was owned by the Nuneham Courtenay Estate, and here Mavis set to work on the restoration of the eighteenth century gardens. Mavis went on to serve as Honorary Secretary, and then President, of the Garden History Society for almost 30 years, and she was a leading figure in the movement to protect historic designed landscapes, helping to ensure the survival of many important gardens and parks for the future.

Mavis always maintained that it was Dilly's insistence that 'nothing is impossible' that gave her the drive and confidence to tackle such large projects, and that it was his love of his own Naphill Wood that cemented her love of nature, allowing her to play such a key role in the recovery and protection of these beautiful historic gardens and parks.

So how perfectly poetic it was to find out during my research that the Nuneham Courtenay Estate gardens had been the inspiration for several chapters of Lewis Carroll's 'Through the Looking Glass' and 'Alice in Wonderland'. Dilly would most certainly have approved!

In 2020 the Science Museum in London put on a special exhibition to mark 100 years of codebreaking in the UK, from the earliest days in Room-40 through to GCHQ today. It was a wonderful exhibition, one not to be missed. As we made our way around the exhibits, we arrived at the area dedicated to Bletchley. There were just three photographs of codebreakers in that section, Alan Turing, Dilly and Mavis. I would say that if the organisers had to limit this section to just three pictures, they had most certainly picked the right ones.

Keith & Mavis Batey

My Beautiful Enigma

DURING HER INTERVIEW Jean asks Dilly about the Enigma. Cue Arthur Scherbius and his Bavarian assistants and Nazi Stormtroopers, who proudly show off and tell us all about his 'beautiful' invention!

....

'I registered a patent for a ciphering machine'

Some sources credit Dutchman Hugo Alexander Koch of being the first to design a 'secret writing machine' based on rotors, but Scherbius developed his idea quite independently, and although Koch filed for his rotor machine patent in 1919 no machine was ever built from his designs and in 1927 he assigned all rights to Scherbius, the inventor of the Enigma machine. Scherbius had filed for his patent back in 1918.

....

'And he'd invented his beautiful Enigma!'

Enigma was a cipher machine and was used to encipher and decipher individual letters in a message.

It was not capable of transmitting or receiving messages. This was done via Morse code completely separately from the Enigma machine.

An Enigma was not capable of printing messages out, so the operators had to write everything down.

Typically two soldiers would work together when operating an Enigma machine.

First, the machine would be set up based on instructions for the given day and then attention could be turned to the message that needed sending.

Let us imagine that a message contained the word 'weather', which in German is 'wetter'.

The Enigma operator would type the letter 'W' and the machine would light up the enciphered result, possibly 'Q', which would be written down by their colleague. They would then type the rest of the word which may encipher as 'XAHBS'.

The enciphered message (which would include our enciphered word wetter 'QXAHBS') would then be transmitted via Morse code.

The soldiers at the receiving end would also have an Enigma machine, which crucially would have been set up in the same way as the sending machine. They would receive and write down the Morse message.

The Enigma operator would type each letter in the received message in turn. When they get to our example word, weather, 'Q' would light up 'W', 'X' would decipher to 'E', 'A' to 'T', and so on.

The operator's partner would be writing the translated letters down, ending up with the word 'WETTER'. The message had been successfully received and deciphered!

....

'But then the Nazis come to power,
and they took it in their ranks'

Enigma was adopted by the German Navy in 1926, the German Army in 1928 and finally the German Air Force in 1935. It was also used by Abwehr and other German government departments.

• • • • • • • • • • • • • • • •

'It has a keyboard'

The Enigma machine had the appearance of an old typewriter. It had a keyboard of 26 letters laid out in the pattern of a standard continental keyboard:

QWERTZUIO
ASDFGHJK
PYXCVBNML

There were no keys for numbers or punctuation.

• • • • • • • • • • • • • • • •

'The letters lit by lights'

Just above the keyboard there was a lamp board which consisted of 26 small circular back-lit windows. Each window showed a letter, and these windows were laid out in the same sequence as the keyboard. Each press of a key on the keyboard would light up one of the letters on the lamp board.

• • • • • • • • • • • • • • • •

'Press a key it turns a rotor,
this is 'stepping' there you see'

Behind the lamp board is where you would find the heart of Enigma, the scrambler unit, which consisted of five wheels lined up in a row. Each wheel had 26 positions, one for each letter of the alphabet.

The outer wheels were fixed on most Enigma models, but the three central wheels would turn, and were often referred to as the rotors. The three rotors were removable and interchangeable. Each time the Enigma was set up, three rotors would be selected from a separate box of five available rotors. Each of these five rotors was wired differently, so each one offered a different ciphering fingerprint. A codebook would tell the

Enigma operator which three rotors to select on any given day, and the order in which to load them into the machine.

The Enigma was an electro-mechanical device. The action of pressing a key on the keyboard would cause two things to happen. First, mechanical connections would always cause the right-hand rotor, and sometimes the centre and left-hand rotors, to move on one position. Second, electrical connections would then cause one of the letters on the lamp board to light up, powered either via an internal 4.5V battery or the Enigma machine could be connected to an external power source.

The right-hand rotor would move on one position every time one of the keys on the keyboard was pressed. On one of its 26 moves it would move the centre rotor on one position, which in turn would move the left rotor on one position on one of its 26 moves, rather like an odometer in a car. These rotor moves were known by the codebreakers at Bletchley as 'turnovers' or 'stepping'.

The turnover process was not exactly the same as an odometer in a car, however, as Enigma on occasion would give rise to what was known as 'double-stepping', where the centre rotor could advance on two consecutive key presses.

Each individual rotor consisted of several core circular parts – or rings – of varying sizes, that all came together around a central hub. The central hub contained the wiring of the Enigma rotor, and this internal wiring would connect 26 spring-loaded contact 'pins' on the right-hand side of the rotor to 26 small circular flat contact 'plates' on the left-hand side. These terminals would then form the electrical contacts between the rotors and the two fixed outer wheels. The right-hand side of the central hub of each rotor would also be stamped with a Roman numeral to identify the rotor's internal wiring (i.e. I, II, III, IV or V).

The largest part of a rotor was the 'finger ring', or 'roller ring', which was the only part of each of the three rotors that would protrude through the metal case of the Enigma machine once the rotors had been fitted and the lid closed (not the outer wooden box lid, but the metal lid of the actual Enigma machine). The operator could then move each rotor to its correct starting position by rolling this ring with their finger.

On the right-hand side of the 'finger ring' you would find the 'ratchet ring'. This ring carried 26 angled teeth, which would drive the turnover process when the rotor was at its turnover position.

On the left-hand side of the 'finger ring' there were three more key parts to each rotor. A spring loaded 'ring adjustment lever' allowed the operator to set the required turnover position for the rotor. Next there was the 'alphabet ring', or 'alphabet tyre', which simply displayed the 26 letters of the alphabet, or on some Enigma models the numbers '01' through to '26'. The 'alphabet ring' could be viewed by the operator through a small window in the lid of the Enigma machine. Finally, there was the 'turnover ring'. This ring carried a single notch, which could be positioned against any of the 26 letters (or numbers) via the 'ring adjustment lever'. Adjusting this ring would allow the operator to position the turnover notch next to any of the letters. The position of this ring was usually adjusted once a day, and the setting of this ring was known as the 'Ringstellung'.

Each spring-loaded terminal on the right side of a rotor was wired (connected) to a flat circular terminal on the other side of the rotor, and this wheel wiring was the first way in which the letters were scrambled, e.g. the letter 'A' spring-pin might be wired to the flat circular 'G' terminal-plate on the other side of the rotor. This rotor wiring was unique to each of the five available rotors, three of which would be loaded into the Enigma as part of the setup process.

Each time a key was pressed at least one of the rotors moved on one position, changing the internal electrical connections, thus causing the wiring of keyboard to lamp board to change. This meant that pressing the same letter twice in a row would light up two different letters on the lamp board.

Deep within the mechanics of the Enigma machine, pressing a key on the keyboard caused small 'arms' to lift up between the rotors, which were looking for the notches on the turnover rings.

The right-hand rotor arm would always find a turnover notch, causing the right rotor to advance on every key press.

The left and centre rotor arms only had one notch each to look for. The centre arm looked for the turnover notch on the right-hand rotor and when detected would move the centre rotor on one position. The left-hand arm looked for the turnover notch on the centre rotor, and when detected would move the left-hand rotor on one position.

'Double-stepping' was caused by the fact that the rotors were mechanically linked when turnovers were detected, causing the left-hand rotor to drag the centre rotor along with it when it moved on. The centre rotor would also drag the right-hand rotor in the same way when it turned, but since the right-hand rotor always advanced anyway, this was not a noticeable issue.

Either side of the three moving rotors were the fixed outer wheels. There was the fixed 'entry' wheel (or plate) on the right-hand side which was known as the 'Eintrittwalze', and the fixed 'reversing' wheel (or 'reflecting' wheel) on the left-hand side which was known as the 'Umkehrwalze'.

Each key on the keyboard was connected to one of the terminals on the 'entry' wheel, and it is these wiring connections that Dilly referred to as the 'Qwertzu' or the 'diagonal'. This wiring itself presented the Germans with another very easy opportunity to scramble the letters, and Dilly was shocked to find out that the wiring was simply A to A, B to B etc.

The 'reversing' wheel further scrambled the electric current and sent it back through the rotors now following a different route.

. . . .

'Plug connections pair the letters via the Steckerbrett at the front'

The early versions of Enigma were enhanced by the Germans with the addition of the 'Steckerbrett', a plug-board positioned at the front of the machine which allowed the operator to further scramble the letters by linking pairs of letters via plugs – known as 'steckers' – and cables.

The plug-board had 26 pairs of sockets, again laid out in the 'QWERTZU' pattern, which could be connected by twin cable leads.

Ten cables were normally used, leaving six sockets unused (or 'self-steckered').

. . . .

'Encryption at a pace'

On pressing a key, mechanical connections would cause one or more of the rotors to move on one position, and then electrical current would flow from the key terminal, via the plug-board, to the entry wheel, through the three rotors, to the reversing wheel, back through the three rotors, out through the entry wheel, back through the plug-board, and finally to the lamp-board. All of this would happen in an instant.

The sequence of the rotor combinations would only repeat after 16,900 key presses (26x26x25), i.e. when the position of the three rotors would return to its starting point, and each message was limited to just 250 characters to avoid this ever getting close to happening.

Since the operator could choose three rotors from a set of five to put into the Enigma machine, this meant that there were 60 possible rotor orders (5x4x3).

Once the rotors were loaded there were now 17,576 different possible wiring routes through these rotors as they continually turned (26x26x26).

There were also 17,576 different ring (turnover) settings possible (the turnover ring could be positioned at 26 different points on each of the three rotors).

The plug-board then added over 150 million million stecker pairings (allowing for six self-steckered letters).

All of this meant that there were about 159 million million million possible daily keys!

. . . .

'And now they're using
my beautiful Enigma'

Each morning the Enigma operator would reach for their settings book which would give the following setup instructions for the day:

1. The rotor order (the 'Walzenlage'), i.e. which three rotors to use and the order to fit them.

2. The ring settings (the 'Ringstellung'), i.e. the turnover point for each of the rotors.
3. The cross-plugging needed for the plug-board (the 'Steckerverbindungen').

Next, having set the Enigma as per the daily instructions above, the operator would make a number of random decisions.

Using the rotor 'roller' wheels, the operator would turn each of the three rotors to a random starting position known as the 'indicator setting'. For example, the left rotor might be set to 'D', the centre rotor to 'J' and the right-hand rotor to 'D'. This combination of three letters has now been chosen by the operator as the indicator setting.

The operator would then key in another three randomly selected letters which would represent the 'text setting'. These would be typed into the Enigma machine twice. For example, the operator might select the letters 'AXB' as the 'text setting' and would therefore key in 'AXBAXB'.

The Enigma machine would then encipher these six letters, perhaps giving the result 'VADTYE'. This sequence of six letters is the 'indicator'.

The operator would then set the three rotors to the chosen text setting, i.e. to 'A', 'X' and 'B' in our example, and then would type in the letters of the message, with the second operator noting down the enciphered letters as they light up on the lamp-board. The resulting scrambled message would be passed to the Morse code signaller.

The Morse code signaller would then transmit the message.

Each transmitted message would have four elements as follows:

a) The 'preamble'. This would be transmitted as 'clear text' before the actual message itself and would include the call sign, time, the number of letters in the message and crucially the Enigma operator's chosen 'indicator setting', i.e. 'DJD' in our example.
b) A group of five letters which would indicate which set of keys from the operator's instructions were being used.
c) The six indicator letters, i.e. 'VADTYE' in our example.
d) Finally, the enciphered text of the message, transmitted in five letter groups.

On the receiving end, a Morse operator would listen to all the dots and dashes and write down the transmitted message which would be passed on to the local Enigma operators. They would already have set their Enigma machine based on the same 'settings book' (steps 1-3 above).

The 'preamble' in the received message tells the operator to move the three rotors to positions 'D', 'J' and 'D'.

The operator would then key in the transmitted six indicator letters, i.e. 'VADTYE' in our example, which would light up 'AXBAXB' on the lamp board.

The operator would then reset the three rotors to positions 'A', 'X' and 'B', and begin to decipher the text.

Note: After 1940 the 'text setting' letters ('AXB' in our example) were only keyed in once.

•••••••••••••••••

'No one will ever be able to beat my Enigma'

It would seem that 159 million million million possible daily keys would make Enigma impossible to break; however, this doesn't factor in some crucial flaws which were to play a major part in the code breaking successes at Bletchley Park.

Because the left-hand-side fixed wheel was a reflector, ensuring that Enigma was self-reciprocal, this meant that encryption was the same as decryption.

However, this reflector also gave Enigma the property that no letter could ever encrypt to itself.

Also, if 'A' encrypted to 'B' this meant that 'B' encrypted to 'A'.

These two flaws would offer the codebreakers a chink of light.

On the Team!

JEAN IS OVERJOYED to have been given the job and skips out of the Mansion in full song. She bumps into the rest of Dilly's Girls and they all hit it off!

. . . .

'The sun is dancing on the lake, now that's a sight!'

In our story Jean is interviewed in the Mansion, and on walking out afterwards she would have looked out across the lawns and caught sight of the lake through the trees.

. . . .

'Can't tell anybody what I do!'

All new recruits were made to sign the Official Secrets Act on arrival at Bletchley, and everyone took their responsibilities in this area very seriously.

Keith Batey was to say many years later that most just assumed that if you were caught speaking about your work you would be shot!

Even friends working in different parts of the Park would not discuss their different roles.

Bletchley veterans would keep their secrets for years after the War, having parents die not ever knowing what a vital role their son or daughter had played in Britain's victory over Nazi Germany.

It was only when Winterbotham's book 'The Ultra Secret' was published in 1974 that public discussion on the achievements at Bletchley during the War became possible, and even then, many who had worked there still refused to speak openly about it.

Welcome to The Cottage

THE TEAM TAKE JEAN back to the cottage where they tell her a bit about her new boss and offer an explanation as to why he just has ladies working for him.

. . . .

'So how is it that you all work in here, at The Cottage?'

Dilly had earmarked the former groom's cottage for his Enigma Research section during the 'Captain Ridley's Shooting Party' rehearsal in September 1938. He had probably chosen the cottage to keep as far away as possible from the daily administrative hassles of the Mansion, and not to mention the prying eyes of the top brass.

That first visit to Bletchley was an undoubted success, but our intrepid codebreakers were to return to London as the likelihood of war seemed to fade just a little with Prime Minister Neville Chamberlain's declaration of 'Peace for our Time' at the end of the month.

During the first half of 1939, however, it became clear that a war with Germany was inevitable, and so on 15th August 1939 GC&CS permanently relocated to Bletchley Park and Dilly set up his section in the cottage.

All of this was very much a new experience for Dilly since he had never run a section before, and organisation was not something that Dilly was known for. In those early days Dilly's Enigma Research team consisted just of himself, Tony Kendrick, Peter Twinn, and a career civil servant clerk allocated to him called Joyce Fox-Mail.

Kendrick had been working on the German Services Enigma as Dilly's assistant for some time. He had been crippled by polio as a child and was a very private man. He was courteous and kind to all and had a good sense of humour. Just like Dilly his dress sense was somewhat lacking – whereas Dilly's clothes just had the appearance of being several sizes too small, Kendrick's were just shabby – and the two men had always gotten on well.

Peter Twinn had joined Dilly and Tony in February 1939, when GC&CS decided to bring in some mathematicians after the meeting with the French and Poles in Paris at the beginning of the year. Twinn had become the first British cryptographer to read a German Wehrmacht Enigma message when Dilly messaged back from Warsaw that the unknown 'diagonal' – the wiring of the keyboard to the entry plate – was simply ABCD. Twinn readily admitted, however, that all he had done was apply Dilly's methods. He later wrote how he wished that he had thought to try the obvious and that if he had how he could have made a real name for himself on joining GC&CS!

The cottage numbers were then bolstered when the other Oxbridge 'Professor Types' as Dilly called them, who had been previously picked out and placed on stand-by, arrived in the cottage on 3rd September. They were Alan Turing, Gordon Welchman and John Jeffreys.

Dilly had already spent some time with Turing working on Enigma, having had him stay at Courns Wood, and had grown to like and respect the young Cambridge maths genius. But Dilly knew little of Welchman and Jeffreys.

Commander Denniston then found Dilly two more recruits for the Cottage in the shape of daughters of friends of his from his local golf club, Elizabeth Granger and Claire Harding.

In a meeting on 1st November 1939 Dilly, Twinn, Jeffreys, Turing and Welchman set out their list of requirements, which included punches, cyclometers – two unsteckered Enigmas wired together which was a technique demonstrated to Dilly by the Poles – and a British version of the Polish 'Bomby'.

The Polish 'Bomby' were machines which had been used successfully by the Poles to identify repeated letters in Enigma keys, which were known as 'females'. These machines were used in conjunction with a grid system invented by Zygalski, one of the Polish codebreaking mathematicians. This grid system made use of what were known as Zygalski sheets, and these sheets were lettered sheets of paper with holes carefully punched to help identify the all-important 'females'.

On moving into the cottage Dilly's priority was to fulfil his promise of contacting and cooperating with his new Polish friends, who by October 1939 were now based near Paris, and who had had to destroy all their equipment and documents before fleeing Poland.

Dilly had wanted Rejewski and his team to come to Bletchley, but this had been blocked by the French. As far as the French were concerned, the Polish cryptographers would have to stay in France, since France was paying for the Polish Army.

A new Polish/French signals intelligence centre known as PC Bruno had been set up near Paris in October under Major Bertrand's command. It was located at the Château de Vignolles in Gretz-Armainvilliers, about 40 kilometres southeast of Paris, and it was here that the Polish team found themselves based.

PC Bruno's chief cryptographer Henri Braquenie, who Dilly had met at the Paris conference, came over to Bletchley and worked with Dilly in the cottage for a week early in December. During his visit he stayed with Dilly and his family at Courns Wood, and the two men worked together to set up a daily communication of keys between Bletchley and PC Bruno.

Not wanting to risk the exposure of the new British Typex cipher machines, they set on a wonderfully ironic solution, whereby the replica Enigma machines built by the Poles would be used to facilitate communication between the two allied cipher centres. So, the daily keys to codes needed to break German Enigma were to be sent via Enigma ciphers, and these messages were always closed with a 'Heil Hitler!'

The Poles needed Zygalski sheets and Dilly was determined to deliver them. Sixty sets of 26 sheets had to be made, with many of the sheets containing one thousand precisely positioned holes. Dilly was no organiser, and so Jeffreys was put in charge of the planning of what Dilly had by now labelled the 'sex statistics'.

Each of the sheets represented a possible sequence for the insertion of the rotors, and each sheet had 26 × 26 letters around the edge, with the holes punched to represent certain combinations. These sheets were cumbersome and very time consuming to use, but offered a chance to determine an Enigma machine's ring setting.

Braquenie took the first batch of sheets with him when he returned to France.

Meanwhile, with every surface in the cottage taken up by this mass production of the hole-punched Zygalski sheets, Turing took himself off up into the loft of a nearby stable to work on German Naval Enigma, and Welchman and Kendrick relocated to Elmers School, which was next to the Park and had just been acquired by GC&CS, to begin the planning for turning Bletchley Park into a code breaking production line.

As work continued on Zygalski sheet production, Dilly continued to work on Enigma, and it was around this time that he came up with what was to become another key code breaking tool, the use of 'cillies'.

A 'cilly' was yet another Dilly discovery and this was all to do with operator errors that would help the codebreakers unravel Enigma. A 'cilly' was a combination of two different mistakes by Enigma operators. First Dilly noticed that operators often used the final position of the three rotors at the end of a message as the indicator setting for the next message. This was often followed either by a keyboard 'slide', when the operator would type letters that sat next to each other on the keyboard, or would use 'pronounceables', where perhaps the first three letters of a name were used. It was a reoccurrence of the three letters 'CIL' from the same German operator that Dilly first guessed was the beginning of a girlfriend's name, giving Dilly the idea for his name for this new technique.

Another key Dilly discovery soon followed when he noticed yet another operator procedural error in weather messages, where someone in Germany had the idea to set the stecker connections based on a substitution from the daily settings. So, every day the Germans would change the letters in the code in a way that gave away the stecker settings!

Knowing the stecker settings meant that Dilly's 'rodding' method could be used.

Dilly always gave each one of his code breaking discoveries and ideas a name, so as well as 'cillies' the cottage was soon full of talk about 'snakes', 'alligators', 'slugs', 'grass skirts', 'starfish' and 'beetles'.

Despite all his discoveries, Dilly began to notice that Commander Denniston and his deputy Edward Travis, nicknamed 'Jumbo', were taking more and more interest in the activities of the cottage and had begun to question Dilly's priorities. Travis was another organiser and had already made progress in the expansion of Bletchley and the construction of Huts to facilitate the vast amounts of traffic they were expecting to have to handle once Enigma was broken, and he was a great admirer of Welchman and his ability for planning.

Both Denniston and Travis began to question the work being done at the cottage, in particular the need to generate the Zygalski sheets and have the Polish cyclometers. The cyclometer was essential for the testing of 'females' and consisted of two un-steckered Enigma machines wired together so that the outputs of one machine fed the inputs of the other.

In the end Dilly had to ask Jeffreys to go against direct orders so that more resources could be put on this work for the Poles, and finally as more pressure was applied from the commanders, Dilly had to write one of his many letters threatening to resign if he was not able to keep his promise to Rejewski.

Denniston gave in and allowed Dilly to fulfil his promise, and the sheets were completed and were taken to Paris by Alan Turing on 17th January 1940.

Alan returned from Paris with a lot more than just thanks. He came back with corrected information from the Polish codebreakers regarding the two new rotors (rotors four & five) introduced in 1938. They had inadvertently given wrong wiring details for these new wheels during the original meeting in Warsaw.

Back with this corrected rotor information it was quickly proven that this was why Dilly's 'cillies' had not worked better before, since the theory completely depended on turnover matches.

Dilly's 'cillies' were then used to break the first wartime German Enigma message at Bletchley Park, which was greeted with a huge cheer in the cottage!

Dilly's genius had been proven once again, and his loyalty to his Polish friends had reaped the ultimate dividend.

But Dilly's code breaking world was about to crumble around him.

It was February 1940 and Hut 6 production was now in full swing with Gordon Welchman in charge and he had taken over responsibility for German Army Enigma. Turing, Kendrick and Twinn had been relocated to Hut 4 to look after German Naval Enigma, reporting to Dilly's old friend Frank Birch.

Denniston and Travis had decided that there was no longer any need for Dilly's Enigma Research section, and to make matters even worse the cottage was closed due to security fears since it shared an attic with the cottage next door, which was occupied by an estate worker. Dilly was told to make his office in Bletchley's old plum shed.

....

'And moved Dilly's office into
Bletchley's old plum shed'

A few weeks after setting up the cottage Dilly got permission from Denniston to use an old plum store shed in the stable yard as an experimental workshop. Here Dilly could work with Alan Turing on their ideas for the British version of the Polish 'Bomby' machines.

Alan was an accomplished mechanical and electrical engineer as well as being a truly exceptional mathematician, and Dilly wanted him to have somewhere where he could experiment with his ideas and fashion metal parts and build electrical circuits.

Now with his section and the cottage closed down, Dilly found himself working all alone in the plum shed, though his friends Turing, Jeffreys and Twinn often popped in to see him.

Dilly of course was still very interested in the happenings of Hut 6, but he desperately resented having to pass his ideas on to others to take forward and not being allowed to see things through to completion himself. His name did live on in Hut 6, however, where 'Dillyismus' was the term used there for Dilly's technique for determining the stecker settings when the rest of the message was known.

Another one of Dilly's famous resignation letters was duly despatched to Denniston, though as always Dilly must have been certain that his resignation would not be accepted.

While Denniston's decision to restructure Bletchley as a code breaking production line was ultimately the correct one, he probably realised that Dilly had been treated badly and that things could have been handled better. The commander once again demonstrated his wonderful ability to handle and appease his brilliant but eccentric old friend and made moves to put things right.

Dilly was given back the title of Chief Cryptographer that he had enjoyed in the Room-40 days during the First World War but which he had lost when GC&CS was formed, and arrangements were made for Dilly to return to a revamped and bigger stable yard cottage. The estate worker had been relocated and the two conjoined old cottage buildings had been merged into one.

. . . .

'All Dilly needed now was an entourage'

Denniston was happy for Dilly to select his own team, and Dilly insisted that his new Enigma Research unit in the cottage was to be an all-female team.

Why did Dilly decide that his new team was to be made up entirely of ladies?

The reason was quite straight forward. Dilly simply found women easier to talk to, to work with, and probably to trust as well. He had just seen a number of talented, but very ambitious, young men arrive at Bletchley and with the necessary restructure of code breaking activities at the Park, these men were now running the Enigma sections and were in charge of decisions relating to Enigma.

Even more crucially, in the early months of the cottage, Dilly had been impressed with the way in which the girls had worked tirelessly, often through the night and crossing over shifts, while still maintaining complete accuracy with the endless punching of holes, to get the Zygalski sheets completed on time.

The ladies had also responded to his penchant for naming all his cryptology discoveries and ideas, something that seemed to make the often-dull world of cryptology just that bit more exciting and magical.

Quite simply, Dilly just got on better with women.

Mavis

In her book about Dilly, 'Dilly; The man who broke Enigmas', Mavis describes how Turing was to write a manual for newcomers to Huts 6 and 8, which became known as the 'Prof's Treatise on Enigma'. It covered Dilly's breaking of the un-steckered Enigma machines right through to the latest German Army, Navy and Air Force variations. In this manual, examples were given of the techniques that Dilly had invented, such as 'rodding', but none of Dilly's names were used. 'Beetles' and 'starfish' had been relabelled 'direct-clicks' and 'cross-clicks'. 'Buttoning-up' became simply 'adding up'. 'Probability' replaced 'serendipity'. Mavis commented that it all seemed very 'heavy' compared to Dilly's treatment of the Enigma puzzles, and she wrote that the manual was never used in the cottage.

Mavis also commented on how Alan's manual did not mention Dilly. This was not surprising, since the manual was not intended as a history of the breaking of Enigma, but with all the secrecy that has surrounded Enigma and the events at Bletchley for years after the war, Mavis did wonder if this manual inadvertently contributed to the general misunderstanding by many today that the breaking of Enigma was all down to Turing.

There were just eight other ladies working with Dilly in the cottage when Mavis joined his team in May 1940. Among them were Margaret Rock and Claire Harding, who was back working with Dilly as the Section Manager, responsible for allocating the daily tasks to the team.

....

'This is Margaret, she's his rock'

Margaret Rock was a little older than the other girls at 36 years of age when she joined Dilly's Enigma Research section. She had studied at Bedford Collage University of London before becoming a statistician. Margaret had just the sort of ordered mind needed to complement all of Dilly's mad-cap ideas, and she had joined Dilly's section in the cottage just before Mavis in April.

Margaret was born in Hammersmith London in 1903. The family relocated to Portsmouth in 1917 as her father was in the Royal Navy. He was sadly killed when his ship was sunk off the coast of Ireland when it hit mines laid by a German U-Boat.

Margaret

Recruited by GC&CS and then assigned to work with Dilly in the cottage, she really did become Dilly's 'rock' and when Dilly became forced to work at home due to illness it was Margaret who went with him to Courns Wood, where she worked with Dilly on Russian codes right up until his death.

Margaret and Mavis became close friends, and Margaret was Mavis's lady-in-waiting when she married Keith. Margaret was to never marry and remained a close family friend of the Bateys and was godmother to their daughter.

After the war she remained with GC&CS as the organisation relocated to Eastcote, and then to Cheltenham as GCHQ, where she worked up to her retirement in 1963. Margaret was awarded the MBE.

....

'And here's Betty, Joyce and Flo'

There was a speech therapist, Joyce Mitchell, and there were three actresses.

All the girls loved their boss, finding him endearingly eccentric and someone who was always concerned for their welfare. Dilly would sleep over at the cottage during the week, always working late into the night, and surviving for the large part on just black coffee and chocolate.

Dilly described the job of the cottage as being one 'to retrieve the misses of Hut 6 and to look for new lines of attack'.

In her early days in the cottage, Mavis found herself endlessly putting dots in squares for frequency counts or building catalogues that Dilly had called 'corsets' where they attempted to find the word EINS in text. Sometimes the girls were tasked with making 'snakes' which were alphabets for 'cillies'.

But it was not long after Mavis joined the team that the so-called Phoney War was to come to an end, as the British Expeditionary Force in Europe found itself pushed right back to the coast at the northern French town of Dunkirk at the end of May.

The miracle that saw so many soldiers successfully evacuated meant that trains stopping at Bletchley station were suddenly rammed full of exhausted troops and Dilly's Girls all jumped at the chance to help in the canteen between shifts in the cottage as Bletchley did what it could to provide food for the men.

Britain stood alone and it was time for its leader to make his legendary speech.

Dear Mr Churchill

WHEN DILLY RETURNED FROM the Warsaw conference of July 1939 he reported that the Polish methods of breaking Enigma all depended on the Germans continuing to use the method of double enciphering the indicators, and he knew that this could change at any time. It was in May 1940 when the Germans did finally make this change.

After that conference Dilly had also reported that although the Polish methods were neat, they did reply heavily on the use of machines which they had called 'Bomby' (Bomby was the plural, Bomba the singular).

Some historians have written that the Poles named their machines 'Bomby' because they ticked like a bomb when they ran. Others suggest that Rejewski had chosen the name based on his favourite ice cream dessert! Perhaps it was a combination of the two.

Seeing the machines that the Poles had built had planted an idea in Dilly's mind of a different type of mechanical device to use in the battle with Enigma, and as soon as Dilly got back from the conference he met up with Alan Turing at Courns Wood to discuss his ideas. Dilly believed that it should be possible to develop a machine to check for standard beginnings of encoded texts and indicator settings.

When Alan eventually joined Dilly and the others in the cottage, he already had a full understanding of the history of breaking Enigma, having studied it during the summer back at Cambridge, where he had been working on the ideas for a mechanical solution to cryptology after that meeting with Dilly at Courns Wood. The drawings and plans of the

Polish 'Bomby' had been sent over to Bletchley and were now available in the cottage for Alan to study.

Turing took himself away into the loft of a nearby stable to design the British 'Bombe', a new style electro-mechanical machine, which would be able to run through all the possibilities of rotor choice, rotor order, ring position and machine settings.

Even Alan did not escape Dilly's passion for naming things and people based on the Lewis Carroll books, and Dilly would refer to Turing as his 'Bombe-ish Boy' which was a nod once again to the Jabberwocky poem and the 'Beamish Boy'.

....

'Dear Mr Churchill, we're writing with a plea'

On delivering some papers to Dilly's office, our story has Mavis and Jean finding Dilly deep in discussion with Alan Turing, Gordon Welchman, Hugh Alexander and Keith Batey. They are discussing the need to raise money so that Alan can build the machine he has designed to break the latest version of Enigma. They listen to Winston Churchill's famous 'Beaches' speech on the radio, remark on how the Prime Minister had praised the work at Bletchley on his recent visit, and then Jean suggests they write to the PM and ask him for the required funds directly. Dilly then dictates a letter to Jean.

This scene is a fabrication, although it does refer to several events that did occur.

It was immediately after Dunkirk, on June 4th 1940, that Churchill made that legendary speech, and so the timing of this fits perfectly to our story.

Churchill did indeed pay a visit to Bletchley Park during the war, but that was over a year later, on 6th September 1941.

Travis took him on a tour around the park, visiting a few of the huts, and then the Prime Minister addressed some of the Bletchley workers who were free at the time and able to gather. Churchill stood and spoke on top of a pile of rubble just by the mansion.

There was a letter sent to Churchill, not long after his visit, but this did not involve Dilly, Mavis, Jean or Keith, and neither was it a request for funding to build the first of Alan's Bombe machines.

During 1941, as the Park had to deal with more and more intelligence traffic, it became clear that Bletchley needed more resources. More new recruits were desperately needed, as was more equipment. Denniston had tried, but his appeals for more funding from Whitehall had so far fallen on deaf ears. So, following Churchill's successful visit in September, Alan Turing, Gordon Welchman, Hugh Alexander and Stuart Milner-Barry decided to write to Churchill directly on 21st October 1941.

Alexander and Milner-Barry were two more of Welchman's 'Wranglergoves', mathematicians recruited by Welchman from Cambridge.

Stuart Milner-Barry was the 33-year-old chess correspondent from The Times, who had been a fellow student with Welchman at Trinity College Cambridge.

Alexander had been in Argentina representing his country at an international chess tournament with Milner-Barry when the call came from Bletchley. He had studied maths at Trinity College Cambridge.

By October 1941 Welchman was in charge of Hut 6 with Milner-Barry his deputy. Turing was in charge of German Naval Enigma in Hut 8 and had Alexander as his number two. To all the junior staff these four were known as the 'Wicked Uncles'.

A letter to the Prime Minister was penned but fearing that it may never reach Churchill if it were sent via Denniston they decided to deliver it themselves and Milner-Barry headed down to London hoping to be able to give the letter to the Prime Minister in person.

Although Milner-Barry did get inside Number Ten Downing Street he was not allowed to hand over the letter directly to Churchill himself. But the letter was passed on to Churchill, and on reading it Churchill made his famous 'Action this day!' instruction.

Endless Hours

LIFE AT BLETCHLEY was tough, with the code-breakers working 'Endless Hours' often in dim and airless conditions.

....

'Hello, I'm Mair'

Enter the name Mair Russell-Jones into the Internet and click on images and you will be greeted by the beaming face of a dear old lady in a bright pink coat. She is sitting in her garden, eyes glinting through her glasses, looking very proud, and so she should be!

Her name is Mair, and she spent four years working in Hut 6 at Bletchley Park during the war, and in the picture she is shown proudly wearing the Bletchley Park Commemorative Badge, which was presented by the Government to all surviving Bletchley Park workers in 2009.

The badge is headed 'GC&CS' with the words 'BLETCHLEY PARK AND ITS OUTSTATIONS' appearing along the lower edge. More poignantly on the rear of the medal it states, 'WE ALSO SERVED'.

Finally official recognition for the ten-thousand or so men and women who served their country during World War Two, and who were then sworn to secrecy, never to tell a soul about what it was that they did, not even husbands, wives, parents or children.

I first encountered Mair when I purchased the book 'My Secret Life in Hut Six'. This book is Mair's story, beautifully and tenderly written by her son Gethin, and includes large sections written in Mair's own words.

It is a wonderfully captivating story, perhaps typical of many of the ladies that worked at Bletchley, but as well as telling her story the book also opened my eyes to the stark reality of life at the Park. Many of the workers became very ill, and some even died, due to the conditions they faced, and any musical about Bletchley needs to touch on this harsh reality. Thus, the song 'Endless Hours' has its place.

Her son Gethin knew next to nothing of his mother's activities during the war, only that she had worked in a place known as Bletchley Park, but in 1999 he and his wife found themselves living in Milton Keynes, not far from his mother's old wartime haunt, and so a visit to the Park was arranged.

The Bletchley Park Trust has done, and continues to do, a wonderful job in the restoration and maintenance of this old wartime base. It is a marvellous family day out, and just as we did when we went, Gethin and his family took in a guided tour of the Park.

As they approached Hut 6 Gethin mentioned to the guide the fact that his mother was one of the original Hut 6 workers, but even when introduced to the others on the tour by the guide Mair told everyone that she could not reveal a thing. The guide smiled and explained to everyone that Mair's response was common among old Bletchley workers even all these years after the end of the war. Mair had carefully protected her secret from the age of 24 to 82 and was not going to break her promise now!

Not long after that visit to Bletchley Mair was taken very ill when she suffered a stroke after surgery. In hospital she was then struck down by the dreadful blood poisoning disease septicaemia, the same disease that caused the death of my father, also aged 82, and also while in hospital but in his case suffering with kidney and liver problems.

Not for the first time in her life Mair found herself fighting a terrible illness that threatened her life but fight it she did. However, her recovery was long and hard, and when she began to suffer with very heavily laboured breathing a tracheostomy had to be performed, making verbal communication almost impossible.

In the preface to his book, Gethin describes two moments that ignited the spark that led him to write the life story of his mother. He paints such a loving picture of a sunny Sunday afternoon in the park near to the care home where Mair was still recovering. This was one of her first outings since the stroke. She was wheelchair bound, well wrapped up in a coat and blanket, and her neck was still bandaged. Now able to speak just a few whispered words, she sat listening to a brass band that was playing in the park, and when the band finished their set by playing some of the old favourites from the 1940s, she leant toward her son and he heard her quietly say that this reminded her of her time at Bletchley.

Then, just a few weeks later, Gethin picked up a book about Bletchley which had been given to his mother. Flicking through the pages he noticed some photographs in the middle, one of which was labelled 'Workers in Hut 6'. There in that black and white photograph was Mair. Can you imagine how he must have felt? There, in that book about Bletchley Park was a picture of his mother, hard at work, poring over that day's Enigma codes!

At that point he knew the time had come to tell his mother's story.

Mair was born in a small village at the head of the Garw Valley in South Wales called Pontycymer. She began piano lessons at the age of five and was soon excelling and it was her love for music that eventually led her to Cardiff University in the autumn of 1937 to study music, with German and history as her subsidiary subjects.

In 1940 Mair was in her last academic year at the university when she met Dora, an old university friend who was home on leave, and who mentioned to her that she was working at a place called Bletchley Park, though beyond that she was unable to say any more. Mair thought nothing more of the name Bletchley and returned to her studies. However, it would seem likely that her friend must have mentioned Mair to her superiors because not long after that meeting Mair had an unexpected visitor.

It was now February 1941 and Mair was hard at work in the university library when she felt a tap on her shoulder and turned to see a very official looking gentleman stood by her. He introduced himself as a representative of the Foreign Office and asked Mair if she would consider serving her country by doing some very secret and very important work which was critical to the war effort. If interested, she must write to the Foreign Office and he left an address in London. Then, with no further words, he was gone.

Mair decided that this was something she must do and a letter to Whitehall was duly written and posted. Within a week she received a reply, and an invitation to attend an interview with a Miss Moore, the very same 'formidable' Miss Moore that had interviewed Mavis and most of the other girls working in the cottage with Dilly.

The interview clearly went well and Mair was offered the job there and then but was warned that if she agreed she would immediately be required to sign the Official Secrets Act. Mair accepted the offer and was taken to another room where three Army officers witnessed her signing.

Mair

Returning to Cardiff, Mair was allowed to complete her final exams but would not get the opportunity to graduate and although she was told that she had passed, she never did find out what level of degree she had achieved.

It was August 1941 when Mair headed to Bletchley by train.

It was a grey, rainy evening when Mair arrived at Bletchley Station. She was under instructions to head straight to her lodgings, which were in a place called New Bradwell, a short train ride away on a local line.

The next morning Mair caught the Bletchley Park staff bus into work, where she was allocated to her new team. Mair could so easily have ended up being one of Dilly's Girls, but instead she and three of the other new starters were allocated to Gordon Welchman's team in Hut 6.

....

'These huts are so dark'

When Mair arrived at Bletchley there were six operational huts. Huts 3 and 6 were where Enigma messages sent by the German Army and Air Force were decrypted, translated and analysed for vital intelligence during the war. Decryption took place in Hut 6 and then translation in Hut 3, which unbeknown to Mair was where her friend Dora was working.

Mair remembers Hut 6 being very gloomy inside. The heavy blackout curtains kept out any natural sunlight and the rooms inside were lit by fluorescent tube lights that hung from the ceiling casting a hazy glow throughout.

Mair also described the hut as being filled with tobacco smoke. She did not smoke, but almost everyone else was constantly puffing away on either a cigarette or a pipe.

The huts had bare concrete floors simply covered by a coating of red tile paint. The huts did have heating, but it was totally inadequate for the cold winters. The wind would blow down into the fire causing long flames to reach out into the room, or it would simply put the fire out altogether causing the old stoves to belch out huge clouds of thick black smoke. All the girls wore extra layers of clothes but still shivered their way through their shifts most days.

During summer it was the opposite, with the heavy curtains trapping the heat in the room and making for stifling conditions to work in.

In the spring of 1943 new purpose-built concrete blocks were opened to accommodate the increased workforce, with now over 10,000 personnel working at Bletchley, and everyone transferred from the old wooden huts to the new blocks. The names remained, however, so Mair's new block was still known as 'Hut 6'.

Mair hated these new concrete buildings. Even though the old wooden huts were far from ideal they were at the very least 'homely and familiar'. The whitewashed concrete block walls soon turned a brownish yellow from the nicotine in the air. The heaters in the blocks were even worse than the ones in the old wooden huts, giving out chemical smelling sulphurous toxic fumes. As per the old huts the blocks were also dimly lit by those same tubular lights, and to Mair the whole place just felt so 'cheerless'. She felt the old comradery had been lost and it now just seemed like they were all working in a soulless factory.

• • • • • • • • • • • • • • • • •

'We take it in turns at 3 shifts a day'

The huts were operational 24 hours a day and operated a shift pattern of 8am to 4pm, 4pm to Midnight, Midnight to 8am. Each shift included a half hour meal break, when almost everyone headed for the canteen.

Mair remembers mealtime fondly, the food was good and there were lots of it! There was always lots of meat and vegetables and always some lovely stodgy pudding to follow. However, the food was always the same whichever shift you happened to be working and Mair remembered finding the heavy portions difficult to manage in the middle of the night.

In her book, Mair recalls how on her first day she found herself sitting next to an over-talkative Scottish lady who was telling her all about a Bletchley 'legend' called Mavis and the amazing things she had done in the cottage. Knowing how work talk was very much frowned upon, Mair decided to avoid her new Scottish friend in future.

Endless Hours

• • • • • • • • • • • • • • • • •

'Don't understand, can't understand, what everything means'

Mair found Gordon Welchman 'friendly enough' but he was so involved in his work he had little time for the team under him.

This paints an interesting comparison to life in the cottage, where Dilly and his team worked very closely together, and where Mair's respect for her boss contrasts with a genuine love that Mavis and all the rest of Dilly's Girls had for theirs.

Mair writes in her book that nothing was ever explained properly, and that at the start of a shift she and the others would often sit down feeling completely 'helpless and inadequate'. She did not understand the machines she had to use and found the work dreadfully tedious.

You have to wonder how different her Bletchley experience could have been if her name had been picked out and allocated to work with Dilly in the cottage rather than with Welchman in Hut 6.

Days would have been spent looking for 'beetles' and 'starfish' rather than 'direct clicks' or 'cross clicks', having to 'button up' rather than simply 'add', all the same sort of work, of course, but just somehow made magical by Dilly's eccentric and inventive imagination. Not to mention the hours spent searching for Dilly's lost glasses, which he was always leaving hidden under piles of paper in the relaxed and sometimes chaotic environment that was daily life on Dilly's team in the cottage!

Welchman was an organiser. Everything had to be in its place and all aspects of work in Hut 6 were taken very seriously indeed. Of course, breaking Enigma was a serious job, and there is no doubt that Dilly and his girls knew that and took what they did very seriously too, but it does not hurt to make the daily grind a little more interesting and perhaps more importantly, more inspiring. After all, inspiration was the key to beating Enigma!

Mair also makes another very interesting comment in her book, and that was that Welchman and Dilly 'really disliked one another'.

The likelihood is that Mair never ever actually met Dilly and so her statement must be based on things she heard within Hut 6, perhaps conversations between Welchman and his deputy Stuart Milner-Barry, or maybe gossip from other members of the Hut 6 team.

It is certainly true that Milner-Barry held Dilly with little regard, since in his memoirs he wrote that Knox 'had been defeated by Enigma' and that all credit, other than the Poles, should go to Turing and Welchman.

This statement, of course, is simply not true. The Enigma was not a single entity but was a family of machines; there were many variations in use before and during the War.

Dilly specialised in solving Enigma, and no one at Bletchley knew more about the internal working of this machine than Dilly. Before any message could be broken, the complex wiring and workings of the Enigma and its rotors had to be solved, and this was Dilly's speciality.

Dilly broke all the early commercial versions of Enigma, the Italian Naval machine, and then his finest hour was the breaking of all versions of the Abwher Enigma after Hut 6 had been defeated by this particular challenge.

In total, Dilly and his girls were responsible for the breaking of over ten different variations of Enigma, making Milner-Barry's statement look somewhat ridiculous.

But what about Dilly himself, did he share a similar loathing of Welchman? Well, this very matter is directly referenced in the book Mavis wrote about her boss, 'Dilly: The man who broke Enigmas'.

Very soon after joining Dilly's team in the cottage, Welchman was sent with Tony Kendrick over to Elmer's school which had recently been acquired by GC&CS and which sat right next door to Bletchley Park.

Welchman had been tasked with planning the reorganisation of the Park so that it would be able to deal with the huge amount of traffic that would undoubtedly be coming their way as the war progressed, and with every surface in the cottage covered in the Zygalski sheets being punched and prepared for Dilly's Polish friends now based at PC Bruno near Paris, the school would be the ideal place to lay out plans and drawings.

But Welchman was very clear in his book that he felt that he had been 'banished' from the cottage, writing that 'During my first week or so at Bletchley I got the impression that he (Dilly) didn't like me. Very soon after my arrival I was turned out of the cottage and sent to Elmer's School'.

But Mavis writes in her book that Welchman was not moved out to the school because Dilly did not like him. She relates that when Dilly was told about Welchman's perception, he said apologetically: 'Hadn't one said the right thing?' to which the response was 'You haven't said anything; you haven't spoken to him at all for two weeks!'

So, it would seem that any dislike that may or may not have existed between the two men was based on early perceptions and possible misunderstandings.

....

'The Bletchley Park 'Rattle', coughs everywhere'

Its no surprise that so many of the workers in the huts and blocks at Bletchley suffered with continual coughs and illness given the smoky conditions and uncomfortable temperatures they had to endure for what so often must have seemed like endless hours.

Having to concentrate so hard for hours on end in dimly lit rooms, working at rickety wooden trellis tables, sat on very basic, hard, wooden fold up chairs with a single wooden bar across your back for hour after hour is just hard to imagine these days in our air-conditioned offices, sat on our ergonomically designed chairs.

But the final straw for so many was the lack of any decent rest and sleep between shifts. An all-consuming tiredness in the above mix would just be too much for the strongest will to fight against.

Many workers were lucky and were allocated billets with friendly and helpful families, some even found themselves roomed in local country houses, but for others, like Mair, their assigned lodgings proved to be a nightmare.

....

'She had to sleep on a board which she had to fit on the bath every night'

On arriving at Bletchley Mair went straight to her lodgings, which was to be with a Mr and Mrs Hill who lived in the railway works town of New Bradwell. Sadly, they were to prove far from welcoming.

Mrs Hill was just plain nasty and treated Mair terribly, and although Mr Hill at first seemed more approachable and willing to talk to Mair, he soon displayed a more sinister side. He constantly badgered Mair about what it was she was doing at work and when she kept refusing to tell him he told her that one night she would talk in her sleep and that he would be there when she did, sitting outside her room listening out for her to reveal something.

Whether Mr Hill actually meant this or not, Mair became terrified of falling asleep and would lie awake for hours and hours wondering if Mr Hill was sat listening just the other side of her bedroom door.

Then one day Mrs Hill announced that their daughter-in-law was visiting and that Mair would have to give up her room and sleep in the bathroom instead, on a board placed over the bath which was just covered by a single sheet. Just to make matters worse she was not allowed to lock the door just in case someone needed the toilet in the middle of the night.

All of this caused Mair to become withdrawn, always feeling so tired, and within six weeks of starting work at Bletchley she developed a bad cough.

Everything came to a head during an evening shift when despite feeling cold and shivering, she began to sweat; her teeth were chattering, and her head was throbbing.

Mair fainted and was rushed to the sick bay where concerned doctors quickly diagnosed the flu and signed her off for six weeks' leave to recover.

While the doctors were checking her over, Mair broke down and told the doctors all about the Hills and they promised her there and then that new digs would be found for her when she came back.

. . . .

'We've lost some good friends here'

Mair returned to Bletchley in October 1941 and quickly made a new friend, and the two of them agreed to share digs in a house belonging to a very kind and friendly Mrs Wallers.

Mair remembered the following years at Bletchley Park as some of the happiest times of her life, but the working conditions were still as hard as ever and many of the ladies working in the huts became very ill.

Endless Hours

It was just after D-Day, June 6th 1944, when Mair bumped into her old friend Dora and was shocked to see her looking so poorly with grey coloured skin and a terrible hacking cough.

After the summer, two of Mair's Hut 6 colleagues fell ill and were sent home. Then very sad news arrived in Hut 6 when everyone was told that one of the girls had died of pneumonia.

As 1944 drew to a close, Mair herself fell ill. After a short spell in the Bletchley Park sickbay, she was rushed to Aylesbury General Hospital also with suspected pneumonia where for several weeks Mair was quite literally fighting for her life.

But fight she did and finally after three months Mair was discharged from hospital and she headed back to her home in Wales to complete her recovery.

Mair was never to make it back to Bletchley Park since in May 1945 she received her discharge letter.

Mair's war was finally over.

Our Green and Pleasant Land!

JEAN IS ON HER HALF-HOUR BREAK and takes us to her favourite part of the Park, the Lake. She is lost in the beauty of Bletchley Park, and sings of the wildlife and colours. She hears a Spitfire flying over and as she waves the pilot rocks his wings back and does a fly past much to her delight. Jean, Mavis and Margaret then take the audience on a tour of Bletchley Park in song!

. . . .

'When I get some time alone I like to head down to the lake'

The lake at Bletchley Park is very much the focal point of the estate's grounds and was popular among the codebreakers as somewhere to visit on their breaks.

Some would take a rowboat out on the water, only more often than not to be chased back to dry land by madly flapping and very annoyed geese! Others just enjoyed sitting on the grass around its edge, taking in the sun and watching the birds and other wildlife while trying to dodge the frogs.

The wartime winters were extremely cold, and the lake completely froze over on a couple of occasions, allowing many of the Bletchley workers to enthusiastically take to the ice on their skates.

On a sunny summer day the mansion could be seen peeking through the trees, reflected in the sparkling water, making for the perfect place to come and relax between shifts in the huts.

The lake lay across the lawns in front of the mansion, a little more than midway between the house and Bletchley Railway Station.

To visualise Bletchley Park before the start of the war, imagine a simple 3x3 grid – like the side of a Rubik Cube – with each of the nine sections covering approximately 350 square metres, laid over a map with the lake in the centre section.

The mansion, stable yard and cottages lay in the centre-left section, across the lawns immediately to the west of the lake.

In the grid section south of the mansion, so the bottom-left square, you can see St. Mary's Church, Elmers School and the Rectory.

A mass of railway lines sweeps down the three right hand side sections of our grid, running north-south, and into Bletchley Station which is in our lower right-hand-side section, i.e. the south-east part of our map. Back in the 1940s the station was far bigger than it is today, with its eight platforms and huge engine sheds almost filling that bottom right section of our map.

Finally, visualise a long straight pathway that runs from the station up to the mansion. This was the path that so many of the workers took when they first arrived at the station and headed on up past the lake to the mansion.

• • • • • • • • • • • • • • • •

'Oh there's a sound I've come to know,
an RAF air fighter'

Although there is little doubt that British aircraft would be seen regularly overhead, it is unlikely that one ever flew down and buzzed the lake to impress a lady codebreaker!

The lake is relatively small and the surrounding trees would have made this a far too risky manoeuvre.

But this does make for a wonderful scene in our story and is also a nod to the heroics of the RAF fighter pilots of the Battle of Britain fought during July, August and September 1940.

The markings on our Spitfire make it part of 19 Squadron based at RAF Duxford, which was located just south of Cambridge and about 40 miles east of Bletchley.

. . . .

'The mansion is the centre piece
and is the place to start'

Almost without fail the mansion at Bletchley Park has been described by historians, authors and the codebreakers who worked there during the war alike, in less than favourable terms as far as aesthetics are concerned.

The somewhat unusual design of this old house is all down to the eclectic tastes of its owner during the later part of the 19th century and the early part of the 20th century, Sir Herbert Leon, a successful stockbroker and then later politician, who bought the grounds and property in 1883.

The first thing that everyone notices is the large bell-shaped green copper dome that forms part of the roof on one corner of the mansion. Not only this, but the way in which the dome has been fitted, looking almost as if it has been spliced into an existing open gable roof, makes it look even more out of place.

Sections of the roof present a mixture of fascias: ornamental brickwork, stone battlements, complex wooden lattice work, and simple wooden beams.

Windows are in all different styles and sizes around the mansion, and there is a mixture of stone and wooden archways.

The above features all combine to give the most unusual and eccentric of stately home designs, but equally a design that just seems so perfect for the collection of brilliant, unusual, varied and often very eccentric people that worked there during the war.

As far as I am concerned, the mansion is perfect!

Our Green and Pleasant Land!

. . . .

'Offices through every door, even Dilly he has one'

Dilly did not have an office in the main house and, apart from a brief spell when the cottage was closed and he was moved into Bletchley's old plum shed, Dilly was based almost exclusively in the cottage.

But having Dilly interview Jean in the mansion allows for a neat split of the stage in our production, and the chance for Jean to walk across the park on her way to meet the rest of the girls.

. . . .

'Upstairs is where you'll find the spies,
the home of MI6!'

When the staff of GC&CS first moved to Bletchley Park they weren't alone, and the first floor of the mansion was reserved for members of MI6.

The naval, military and air sections of GC&CS were spread around the ground floor of the mansion.

It was described by codebreakers as 'total chaos' in the mansion during those early days and Dilly must have allowed himself a smile of satisfaction that he had dodged all of this by selecting the cottage for his Enigma research section.

The cramped conditions in the mansion eventually led to Denniston writing to Stewart Menzies, suggesting that MI6 be relocated elsewhere. Menzies, who had taken over as the head of SIS, MI6 and Bletchley Park when Admiral Sinclair sadly died of cancer just after the outbreak of the war, agreed and MI6 soon began to move out.

. . . .

'My favourite is the wireless room
that's in the water tower!'

'Station X' was the first name given to Bletchley Park in its new war time intelligence role, and this was because of its wireless room which had been constructed in the mansion's water tower.

Admiral Sinclair knew that he had to upgrade the security surrounding all the SIS communication facilities and with this in mind he created a new division of SIS which would focus solely on all aspects of communications.

Representatives of this new division arrived at Bletchley as soon as Sinclair had purchased the estate and were also there throughout Captain Ridley's visit in August 1938 and were still there when GC&CS later moved in for real.

Engineers got to work in building a radiotelegraphy station in the mansion's tower which would duplicate and then eventually replace the existing SIS wireless station at Barnes in west London which was known as 'Station X'.

Bletchley's grounds were full of huge mature conifers and one such tree on the front lawn was used to support the wireless station's aerial.

The 'X' in the name 'Station X' conjures up wonderful ideas of secrecy and espionage, but its name was stamped with an 'X' simply because it was the tenth such wireless facility.

. . . .

'Behind the house are garages,
they smell of gasoline'

Immediately behind the mansion there are several garages and a yard, and then off to the right of these – due north – is the entrance to the stable yard where you will find Dilly's cottage.

The stables, some bungalows and the cottages enclose the stable yard, which is accessed via a wonderful archway with its cross-gabled roof displaying an ornamental clock and topped with a weathervane.

After Dunkirk, Dilly joined the Home Guard and they regularly drilled in the stable yard. Alan also joined, but only so that he could learn how to fire a rifle. Despite his terrible eyesight Dilly was reportedly a very good shot.

On one occasion a bomb landed in the stable yard while Dilly and Mavis were working in the cottage, but thankfully it failed to explode.

Our Green and Pleasant Land!

. . . .

'And beyond are all the wooden huts
and purpose-built brick blocks'

It was clear from the start that the mansion alone would not be big enough to cope with the needs of GC&CS during the war and so the construction of a series of wooden huts was quickly begun.

Hut 1 was the first hut built in 1939 just by the tennis courts which were next to the cottages.

The first section to move to a hut was the Naval Section in November 1939, when they moved into what was to be known as Hut 4. Hut 4 was constructed alongside the south side of the mansion.

Huts continued to spring up around the back and side of the cottages. Huts 3, 6 and then 8 wrapped themselves around Hut 1 and down toward the lake.

New buildings were appearing to the south of the mansion too. Hut 12 close to Hut 4 and then alongside the Rectory a large canteen was erected.

The Assembly Hall, where our production is taking place, was constructed behind the canteen and on the road that ran down to the Eight Bells Inn, which sat on the main road into Bletchley from the station just south of our grid map described earlier.

The concrete blocks were not opened until the spring of 1943, so they would not have been there at the time Jean sings her song, but have been included to paint the full Bletchley wartime picture.

Described by most as functional but grim, these blocks extended east to the north of the lake, and beyond.

Using our 'Rubik Cube' map grid once again as a reference, the new blocks filled the north-west and centre-north sections, and in fact spread further north even than that, filling those same two sections on a new row added to the top of our imagined map.

Bletchley Park had truly transformed into a huge and fully functional and organised code-breaking facility.

....

'The station is just down the road and the sky's now full of steam'

Bletchley Railway Station was perfectly located on both the national North–South West-Coast Main Line – then known as the London and Birmingham Railway – and the East–West Cambridge–Oxford Varsity Line.

Sadly, little if anything remains of the original station following its redevelopment in the 1970s, but just imagine the perfect model railway layout with a setting back in the middle of the last century and you will probably conjure up an image very close to that of Bletchley's station during the war.

Old aerial photographs from the time show a mass of rail tracks running from the north and south and into eight long straight platforms. Platform canopies extend out down the platforms at both ends of the main terminus that spanned all the tracks.

The main station building itself oozes character in its two brick stories with gabled roofs and ornamental frontages. It is such a shame that all of this had to be demolished in the 1970s.

A large rectangular signal box sits at the north end of the central platform controlling dozens of signals which sit atop supports that extend over the tracks at various points. A huge engine shed runs up to the main station buildings on the west side of the lines, and smaller goods sheds are fed by several sidings packed with trucks over on the east side.

As a boy I can remember listening to the steam trains shunting trucks across from the docks, over a swing bridge and to the yards in my hometown. All this was about half a mile away from where I lived so much the same distance as the Bletchley Park mansion was to the station, so the sounds from the station would have been easily heard by the codebreakers hard at work.

Whistles from the trains and guards, the hissing and puffing of the steam engines, the clatter of the wagons and coaches, even possibly the clunking of slamming doors would have easily carried across the gardens and lake to the huts, especially in the evenings carried on an easterly breeze.

Our Green and Pleasant Land!

Since the station was the way in which most of the workers first arrived at Bletchley Park it deserved a mention in our musical, and what a wonderful way to fill the stage at the end of Act I!

Dilly's Girls (Part 2)

JEAN AND THE GIRLS in the cottage are asked to make an extra effort to try and de-code some intercepted messages from the Italian Navy. Thanks to Mavis they are successful and the intelligence they glean leads to a crushing British victory as the Italian Navy is decimated by the Royal Navy at the Battle of Cape Matapan. The victorious Admiral Cunningham then visits the girls to personally thank them!

. . . .

'There's been an increase in Italian signals'

Benito Mussolini, dictator of Italy, declared war on France and Great Britain on 10th June 1940, and this announcement was to have a sudden and dramatic impact on daily life in the cottage.

Dilly had been glad to get his section back up and running in the cottage but there was a distinct feeling amongst the girls that they were now very much the bottom of the pile when it came to Enigma at Bletchley, and that they were just working on odds and ends for Dilly that could be passed onto Welchman's team in Hut 6.

Outwardly Dilly was as enthusiastic as ever, declaring that the mission of his section was 'to retrieve the misses by Hut 6 and to discover new lines of attack!', but the girls knew that deep down inside he must have been hurting.

But now, with Italy part of what was to formally become known as the Axis, Italian signals were suddenly a priority, and in particular Italian Navy Enigma messages. Hut 6 declared that they did not have the time or resources to handle this new workload, and so Italian traffic was tasked to the cottage and to Dilly and the girls.

Now the cottage had a real purpose, and everyone was buzzing with excitement when the first Italian Navy intercepts arrived.

Dilly had already broken the Enigma that had been used by the Italians during the Spanish Civil War, but the big question was whether the Italians were still using this same 'K' model of machine. The only way to find out was to test their existing 'cribs' using Dilly's 'rodding' method.

Rodding had proved very successful in the past, but it took a huge amount of concentration and lots of patience. There were 78 different rod tests to do in order to verify all 26 positions of each of the three Enigma rotors.

Even though many of the girls never actually grasped the mechanics and inner workings of an Enigma machine, they all became very skilful 'rodders'. Dilly had made rodding into a word game which even someone with no experience of Enigma could follow.

Dilly's rules were to use pencil for guesses and ink for 'clicks', where a click was a confirmed single letter in a potential crib. There were two types of click. The most important type was when both letters of a crib appeared side by side on the same rod, which was known as a 'beetle' in the cottage. The second type was where the two letters were on different rods and this was known as a 'starfish'.

Early signs were not good, however, and after several weeks of testing the old cribs there had been no success, leading to real fears that the Italians were indeed now working with rewired wheels and a new version of Enigma.

It was Mavis that was to make the crucial breakthrough, late one night in September 1940.

An example of an old crib was 'PERXCOMANDANTE', where the 'X' represented a space in the middle of the text 'For Commandant'. Since this crib had not returned any success in any of the intercepts received so far, Mavis set about looking for just the beginning of the crib, 'PERX'. This was not ideal since it held fewer letters, but it might just prove to be a way in.

While looking for 'PERX' Mavis came across 'PERS' and then she made the inspired guess that this may be for the word 'PERSONALE', giving her five extra crib letters to work with.

Suddenly Mavis realised that her rodding tests were giving her results on her message!

She had been working an evening shift and Dilly had already left, so she decided to work on alone all through the night. Armed with her little Italian pocket dictionary, she was determined to get past the turnover on the right-hand side rotor and onto the middle one.

When Dilly arrived at the cottage the next morning, he could not believe his eyes when Mavis handed him the fully deciphered message. The Italians were still using the 'K' Enigma, and the cottage was back in business!

....

'Dilly took our Mavis out one night to dinner,
to the Fountain Inn on Stony Stratford Road'

In our show the girls sing about Mavis and Dilly going out to dinner after the Battle of Matapan, but it was after Mavis broke into that first wartime Italian navy message that Dilly took her out to the Fountain Inn at Stony Stratford to say a big 'thank you'.

Dilly drove her to Stony Stratford, just to the north-west of Bletchley, in his Baby Austin and this was Mavis's first experience of Dilly's infamous driving. She would later marvel at how he had somehow managed to avoid hitting any of the tank traps laid out of the old Watling Road as they sped along at top speed with Dilly barely ever looking at the road ahead and rarely having either hand on the steering wheel!

Mavis fondly remembers that evening and how Dilly took great interest in what she hoped might be a career after the war in journalism, offering to put her in touch with his brother who was a national editor.

Back at Bletchley, Dilly managed to get Mavis promoted up a grade, from a backroom girl to the front room as a machine cryptographer, which came with a very welcome pay rise since two-thirds of her weekly 35 shillings was going on her billet.

So, there you have why it was the girls all loved their boss so much. He always made sure credit was given where it was due, and Dilly was never slow to show his appreciation for their work. He always showed a great interest in his team, genuinely caring for each and every one of them, and Dilly wasn't shy of fighting to get his girls moved up through the pay grades, which back at Bletchley during the war wasn't always an easy thing to achieve.

After Mavis's breakthrough, the cottage knew that the Italians were still using the 'K' model of the Enigma and that Dilly's rodding method would work. However, every message still had to be broken separately since the indicating system was still an unknown, and it was assumed that these settings were being taken from a codebook.

The Italians did also introduce a couple of new rotors with unknown wiring, and it was to be Mavis once again who made the critical breakthrough to resolve these.

Once more she was working late in the cottage all alone when she spotted a message that did not contain a single letter 'L' and realised that the operator must have been sending some sort of test message where he had simply pressed the same letter 'L' over and over again, giving her a massive crib to work from. The repetitive nature of the message meant that Dilly's buttoning up method was proving tricky to manage, but Mavis was able to enlist the help of Keith who was also working late in Hut 6 and the two of them resolved the wiring of the new rotors together.

Finally, the Italians themselves went some way to helping the girls in the cottage by the fact that their Enigma procedures insisted on the encoding of full stops in messages which always appeared as 'XALTX' and the final one was always padded with additional 'X's to ensure every message contained letters in groups of five. Dilly's click-sheets of 'starfish' and 'beetles' were duly extended to include every possible 'XALTX' combination.

It would now not be long before the name of Mavis Lever and the team of Dilly's Girls would be cemented forever into British code breaking folklore.

....

'This all led to our boys defeating their ships in battle at the Cape of Matapan'

The total destruction of the Italian Navy at Matapan was described by Churchill as the greatest sea battle since Trafalgar, and its success was in no small part down to the intelligence that came out of the cottage.

The breaking of the enemy codes was of course important, but how that information was then used and distributed was just as critical, and this fact was recognised early on by the head of the SIS Air Intelligence Section, Group Captain Fredrick Winterbotham.

From the very early days, any decrypted Luftwaffe messages coming out of Hut 6 were passed on to Hut 3 for processing.

Winterbotham devised a system where three RAF officers were assigned to Hut 3 to take responsibility for these German Air Force intercepts and to ensure that the intelligence was used in an operationally effective way. They would manage translations, prioritise the messages, determine who the information should be distributed to, and most importantly ensure that the intelligence remained secure.

At first this information was distributed onward under the codeword 'BONIFACE', implying that it had been obtained from an agent in Berlin. It would be a little later in 1941 when the more famous codeword 'ULTRA' was introduced and adopted.

Soon after Winterbotham had set up his process for Luftwaffe intercepts, the Army introduced a similar processing method also within Hut 3.

But the Admiralty insisted that all naval messages be sent direct to them from Nobby Clarke's section in Hut 4, and Dilly was told that the cottage was to be treated as a subsidiary of Clarke's Naval Section, meaning that all cottage intercepts were also to be sent direct to the Admiralty.

Dilly was furious. He knew that the processes implemented by Winterbotham were critical and insisted that the Italian naval messages coming out of the cottage should be treated in the same way, and that he be able to play a part in how this information was dealt with. One of his infamous letters to Denniston was duly dispatched, which included of course his usual threat to resign.

Denniston did not agree with Dilly, but fortunately Clarke was on Dilly's side in this matter and was more than happy to have Dilly's Italian Enigma messages dealt with in what was to become the Ultra way.

Clarke arranged to have a naval commander, Charles O'Callaghan, brought in to work in Hut 3 as the Italian expert and liaison officer. All Italian Enigma breaks would route direct to Hut 3 from the cottage and Dilly would be granted full access to O'Callaghan. This arrangement was to prove vital to the success of Matapan, and once again would show that Dilly had been correct to insist that his team's Italian naval intercepts be treated as Ultra.

....

'So all of us are frantic at the Cottage,
we must explain this high activity!'

On 28th October 1940 the Italian Army invaded Greece after its previous successful campaign in Albania during the spring of 1939. However, this time Mussolini was faced with a determined Greek army, entrenched fortifications and a mountainous terrain, and the invasion was halted just inside the border. Not only was the invasion halted, but it was not long before the Italians were being forced back as the Greeks began a counter-offensive, but by February 1941 the Front became bogged down and had become static.

Churchill was determined to support his Greek allies and ordered Operation Lustre which was to see Allied troops shipped to Greece from Egypt, and the movement of troops began on the 4th March 1941.

Regular convoys sailed between Alexandria in Egypt and Piraeus (Athens) in Greece at three-day intervals, escorted by Royal Navy Warships under the command of Admiral Cunningham, Commander-in-Chief, Mediterranean. Almost immediately German High Command made it clear to Mussolini that the Italians were expected to do something to hinder this British operation.

It was on 21st March that Hut 3 received a decoded Afrika Korps Luftwaffe message which reported that German fighters were being flown to Sicily to provide cover for some sort of special action, and Hut 3 alerted Dilly to be on the lookout for any messages that might relate to this. It was crucial to establish the day on which this 'special action' was to take place and it was not long before the cottage found it.

Four days after that initial warning the girls broke a message that simply said, 'Today is X-3' and the cottage erupted with excitement! Even such a short message had been sent with three full stops in it, allowing the new 'XALTX' click charts to work their magic. None of the girls left the cottage over the next three days.

Everyday Enigma messages were being sent with different key settings meaning that every message still had to be broken individually. The work was hard and tiring, but the girls would all sing out together 'Today is X-2' and then 'X-1' to remind themselves just how important their work was.

Claire Harding's organisational skills came to the fore as she kept order in the frantically busy cottage, making sure all the girls knew their respective jobs for the day and keeping all the rods and other tools tidied away in their respective jam jars and tins when not being used.

Hour after hour, and then day after day, Dilly's Girls worked on their rods in the cottage, never thinking once to leave their posts.

It is very unlikely that any of the messages processed in the cottage were those sent direct to the Italian fleet, but fortunately all the relevant messages were being repeated via Enigma for sending to the Italian commander on Rhodes, the Greek island occupied by Italy since 1912. The commander's official title, EGEOMIL, became a crucial crib during these hectic three days.

'X-0' day finally arrived and there was nothing more any of them could do now but hope that their deciphered messages had reached the people that really needed to know, and so the girls headed back to their lodgings.

Mavis arrived at Bletchley Station late that night, on her way back to Leighton Buzzard where she was billeted, only to find that there were no trains running her way until the 'milk train' early the next morning. So, she curled up on a platform bench and fell asleep exhausted.

Mavis fell asleep exhausted.

• • • • • • • • • • • • • • • • •

'It's the Admiral of the British Royal Navy'

The cottage need not have worried because the messages had reached the people that needed to know, and none more important than Admiral Cunningham himself.

Despite having previously made a bet of ten shillings with his staff officer that they would see nothing of the Italian fleet, Cunningham was satisfied of the authenticity of the intelligence being provided and perfectly understood the rules of Ultra.

As soon as he received the 'X-3' message for the 28th March Cunningham was convinced that there was indeed going to be an Italian attack on the Lustre convoys. The Admiral immediately cancelled the next convoy due to set sail from Greece back to Egypt and instructed the convoy currently on its way to Greece to continue north as planned so as not to arouse suspicions, but ordered it to turn back at dusk on the 27th March.

The Royal Navy 'B-Force' currently based at Piraeus under the command of Vice Admiral Pridham-Wippell would sail from Greek waters to a position south of Crete on the 27th and Cunningham would set sail from Alexandria on the same day, where they would endeavour to make the enemy strike where they believed the British convoy would have been on the 28th.

Another Ultra message on the 27th March confirmed the high likelihood of an Italian naval engagement, and Cunningham put his plan into action.

To throw local enemy agents off his trail, in particular the Japanese Counsel in Alexandria who Cunningham knew was reporting back to Mussolini, Cunningham booked himself into the local golf hotel, and arrived complete with clubs and luggage looking for all the world as if he was planning a golfing break for a few days. However, during the night, he snuck away and headed back to his flagship, HMS Warspite.

The Warspite, the aircraft carrier Formidable, and battleships Barham and Valiant, all set sail from Alexandria, and knowing how important it was not to reveal the true source of the intelligence, Cunningham made the sailing sound like it was his own impromptu decision and signalled that he was sailing because of reports he had received from aerial reconnaïssance.

Meanwhile the Italian force under the command of Admiral Iachino included Mussolini's pride and joy, the flagship Vittorio Veneto, which was being screened by several destroyers, and most of the Italian heavy cruiser force.

Cunningham realised that an air attack would weaken the Italian force and so early on the 28th March he ordered an attack by HMS Formidable's torpedo bombers. The Vittorio Veneto was hit, and the Italian ships were ordered to pull back. However, the air attack had also disabled the Italian cruiser Pola, and unaware that the British were still in pursuit Iachino ordered a squadron of cruisers and destroyers to return to protect the Pola.

It was shortly after 10pm in the evening that the British force made their decisive move.

The Italians did not anticipate any night-time action, and none of their gun batteries were prepared for firing. Also, crucially, the Italians did not have radar and so were completely unaware as the British ships moved in.

The Warspite, Barham and Valiant all opened fire as their searchlights lit up the enemy ships. Midshipman Philip Mountbatten – later HRH Prince Philip, Duke of Edinburgh – took charge of the searchlights on board HMS Valiant. Just 3,800 yards away from their targets, effectively point-blank in naval terms, the huge British guns pounded the Italian ships, and it took just five minutes to destroy the Italian force. Three Italian heavy cruisers and two destroyers were sunk in those few minutes.

The tragic statistic of such a wartime encounter was that over 2,300 Italian sailors lost their lives. The only British casualties were the three crew members of a single torpedo bomber that had been shot down by the Vittorio Veneto earlier that day.

Cunningham immediately ordered the rescue of survivors, and during the night over a thousand Italian sailors were successfully recovered from the sea and the stricken ships, but as dawn arrived the Admiral knew he must pull back due to the threat of an attack from the air. He did, however, order the sending of a signal broadcasting the position of the battle and granting safe passage to any hospital ship able to continue the rescue of the remaining Italian crewmen, and later that day another 160 men were rescued by such an Italian ship.

Italy's flagship Vittorio Veneto did manage to limp back to port, but neither it nor any other remaining ship in the Italian fleet would threaten again at sea during the war.

Back in Britain Cunningham's victory was just the morale boosting news that was needed. This was the first British naval victory of the war, Admiral Cunningham was hailed as a hero and the 'new Nelson', and a few somewhat bewildered airmen were given a much-publicised award for their part in spotting the enemy and alerting the British fleet!

. . . .

'And he's here to thank you
for our victory!'

The next day a message arrived at Bletchley Park from the Director of Naval Intelligence at the Admiralty, Admiral John Henry Godfrey, which simply read '*Tell Dilly we have had a great victory in the Mediterranean and it is entirely due to him and his girls*'. Such direct acknowledgment was unheard of, and naturally caused great excitement back in the cottage.

Dilly would laugh as he repeatedly referred to 'the cottage aeroplane' in reference to the official account of how Cunningham knew to put his ships to sea due to aerial reconnaissance, and to honour his team in the cottage he wrote a poem, in which every verse began with the words 'When Cunningham won at Matapan, by the grace of God and' followed by the name of one of the girls. Every girl had her own verse, and even the tea lady Mrs Balance was included. A final verse fittingly also paid tribute to the two people that had made the Ultra treatment possible, Nobby Clarke and Admiral Godfrey.

Excitement levels in the cottage lifted even higher when it was announced that Godfrey was bringing Admiral Cunningham to Bletchley and the cottage to thank Dilly and the girls in person.

When the day arrived some bottles of wine were purchased from the Eight Bells pub at the end of the road, and the Admiral was as thrilled to meet the team as they were him. It was a day none of them would ever forget.

Nobby Clarke would later add one final verse to Dilly's Matapan poem in honour of Dilly himself, which simply read:

When Cunningham won at Matapan
By the grace of God and Dilly
He was the brains behind them all
And should ne'er be forgotten. Will he?

The Golf, Chess and Cheese Society

•••••••••••••••••

'Bletchley's not all work, you know, sometimes we do have fun.'

The daily codebreaking shifts were long, intense, hard work, and often uncomfortable, but life could be fun at Bletchley too. The Bletchley workers organised many extracurricular activities to maintain morale at the park.

In honour of the Government Code & Cipher School (GC&CS) they coined a collective term for all their various clubs and activities as the 'Golf, Cheese & Chess Society'.

Given that many of the codebreakers had university backgrounds it was no surprise that so many societies were formed, and even those with no background in higher education loved to join in.

After 'endless hours' sat focused and concentrating, often in less-than-ideal conditions, it was so important that the workers had some way to unwind for the sake of both their physical and their mental wellbeing.

The Park itself offered an instant escape, with the lovely grounds and the lake at its centre. Just sitting on the grass and relaxing in the sun provided the perfect antidote to those dimly lit and smoke-filled huts. Row boats could be taken out onto the lake and skating on the frozen water became possible during the cold winters of the war.

Physical exercise was very important, and one of the earliest and most popular activities at Bletchley was a game of rounders, often played on the lawn in front of the mansion using a cut-down broom handle with a strap for the bat and an old tennis ball. These games often drew a large collection of spectators which sometimes included some of Bletchley's 'top brass' such as Denniston.

While watching a match, the Oxbridge professor types would discuss and debate the finer points of a game of rounders with as much intensity and detail as they often applied to breaking the enemy codes, and care was taken to get all rules agreed and written down, but always in Latin of course.

Tennis was also very popular at the Park with the codebreakers taking advantage of the two grass courts just next to Dilly's cottage.

There was a book club, language courses, a film club, a choral society, fencing club, various chess clubs, an athletics club, and a classical music appreciation society which made the best use it could of the limited records available.

....

'If Scottish dancing is your thing
then Hugh Foss is your man.'

All varieties of dance class were held in the mansion's ballroom, and twice weekly dances were organised, many of them with a fancy-dress theme in the local school hall. A particular favourite of the dance gatherings was the Scottish Dancing Society, which was run by the exuberant and highly skilled Scottish dancer Hugh Foss.

Hugh had been born in Japan to a missionary family and became fluent in Japanese from a very early age. After graduating from Christ's College Cambridge he had joined GC&CS in 1924 where he became a pre-war cipher machine specialist, and when Dilly returned from a trip to Vienna with an early commercial version of the Enigma machine tucked under his arm, it had been Hugh that had been tasked with the job of testing this new electro-mechanical cipher marvel to see if it was as secure as its designers were claiming.

It did not take Foss long to identify the two critical shortcomings of Enigma: that no letter could encrypt to itself, and that if 'A' mapped to 'B', then 'B' would map to 'A'. Based on his findings he wrote a paper entitled 'The Reciprocal Enigma', in which he determined that if the rotor wiring was known and if reliable cribs were available, then Enigma could be broken. Because of this work Dilly had insisted that Hugh accompany him and Denniston when they travelled to Paris for that first meeting with the Polish codebreakers in January 1939.

....

'The drama scene at Bletchley runs productions by the score.'

But the extracurricular activity that Bletchley Park is most famous for was its long list of shows, plays and musical productions, most of which were held at the newly constructed Assembly Hall behind the canteen on the edge of the Park. It was a wonderful facility, with a large stage and plenty of room for a band just in front of the stage, and room for a large and always very enthusiastic audience.

The annual Christmas revue was always the highlight of the festive period, which was produced every year by Bill Marchant, the deputy head of Hut 3, and his wife. There were also midsummer revues and other grand productions. Musical performances, plays and films took place regularly in the Assembly Hall. Many of the codebreakers contributed with the writing, and the university background and calibre of these people meant that the songs, comic sketches and skits were of the highest quality. Not only was the standard of writing high, but there were several professional actors and musicians working at Bletchley during the war, and all threw themselves wholeheartedly into the drama scene. All the shows were elaborately staged with impressive sets and wonderful costumes.

These productions were not just popular with the Bletchley staff. Travis, the Station Commander at Bletchley during the second half of the war, would invite many senior officers to Bletchley to watch the shows as a way of improving relations between Bletchley and Whitehall.

The shows were also very popular with many of the locals too, and although no one living locally knew what was going on at Bletchley Park during the war, many said that they missed the wonderful productions that were put on in the Assembly Hall after the war ended and the codebreakers had left.

Lobsters and Crabs

....

'I spy, with my little eye,
an Enigma beginning with 'A''

Abwehr was the German military intelligence service which had been established in 1920 despite being forbidden under the Treaty of Versailles.

Early Abwehr messages began to be intercepted by what was at first just a collection of largely amateur radio enthusiasts that became known as the Radio Security Service, or the RSS.

Initially they were intercepting messages that had been encrypted on the more old fashioned and much smaller hand ciphers. Enigma machines were not really the most suitable piece of equipment for spies to be carrying around with them and so much smaller ciphers were being used. Can you imagine a German agent having to parachute into enemy territory while having to carry something that resembled a typewriter!

These Abwher radio messages became known to the British sections as 'Intelligence Sections' or 'Illicit Services'. This non-Enigma Abwher traffic was given to Dilly's good friend Oliver Strachey to process, and in March 1940 a new section at Bletchley was set up in Elmers School to research these hand ciphers. This new section became known as 'Illicit Services Oliver Strachey', or ISOS.

By December that year ISOS had broken the main hand cipher being used by Abwher, giving MI5 advance warning of almost all German spy movements in the UK. All operational spies in the UK were soon rounded up and 'persuaded' to become double agents and to work for the British instead. They proved a huge success and German High Command suspected nothing as they still fed controlled intelligence back to Berlin. Hitler was so pleased with one of the spies that he personally awarded him the Iron Cross!

During 1941 there was a sudden increase in the number of non-military services messages which all carried the unique stamp of having eight letters separate from the main message text. The main message text continued to present itself in the usual Enigma form of groups of five letters. By August and September that year this unknown traffic had increased to more than 20 messages a day.

These messages were clearly being ciphered via an as yet unknown Abwher Enigma machine.

....

'An answer Hut 6 could not find'

The new Abwher Enigma traffic was initially sent to Welchman, but when he could make no headway with it and Hut 6 was unable to crack the German Intelligence Abwher Enigma code, it was passed on to Dilly and his team in the cottage as 'unknown Enigma research'.

Dilly's view was always that cryptography and intelligence were inseparable, and his first step was to spend time with Strachey in the school to find out as much as he could about the various Abwher communication channels and networks, and the work that ISOS had been doing on the hand ciphers.

This did not go down well with Denniston, who hated the idea of the different sections at Bletchley sharing information due to security fears, and Dilly was told in no uncertain terms that these visits to the school must cease immediately.

Exasperated with this decision, Dilly penned another one of his infamous letters to his old friend, boss and sparring partner, which naturally included the usual threat to resign. Dilly firmly believed that in order to break into this new intelligence Enigma, he must be given access to all existing Abwher progress and knowledge. Dilly argued that relying on someone else passing on relevant data to his team in the cottage was just not good enough; after all, he did not know if anything was useful until he had seen it. Fortunately, in this case Dilly's argument was indisputable and Denniston gave way.

• • • • • • • • • • • • • • • •

'Four rotors not the normal three
are used to mix the text'

Dilly was able to find a way to break into the new Abwher Enigma without using any actual text cribs.

Instead of three letter key indicators as per the services Enigma messages, Abwher had four letter indicators, which told Dilly that this new machine had a 'settable' reflector wheel. He devised a plan which involved finding two days of messages where the same wheel order had been selected, and such that the start positions on one of these days could be found by rotating each wheel and the reflector through the same number of places. This would then double the number of indicators on the key block. Having hatched his plan, Dilly called into Hut 7 to enlist the help of the card sorting and tabulating section to gather the evidence.

• • • • • • • • • • • • • • • •

'Night after night, Dilly's working,
surviving just on tea'

Armed with the information he needed, Dilly hunkered down in the cottage, working day after day, night after night, but was unable to find the two related days he wanted. The girls made sure that at least one of them was always with him to make the black coffee and to help find things such as his pipe and glasses, which he was forever putting down and then losing.

• • • • • • • • • • • • • • • •

*'It isn't right, Dilly's hurting,
he needs to let it be!'*

In his letter to Denniston, Dilly had also apologised for being away from Bletchley for a period, which he wrote was due to a 'minor ailment'. This minor ailment was in fact second degree cancer, lymphoma, but few at Bletchley at this time were aware of just how ill he was.

• • • • • • • • • • • • • • • •

'To solve this there's a plan I have evolved'

Although Dilly was unable to find the two related days that he had hoped for, when studying the results he found what he was looking for on just a single day's setting.

From an early age all the Knox brothers had had a great ability for words and were particularly addicted to the 'chopped logic' made famous by Lewis Carroll. 'Chopped logic' was the sort of nonsense based on the ambiguity of words used by the Mad Hatter in Alice's Adventures in Wonderland or found in the Jabberwocky poem.

Lewis Carroll liked to tease his readers and would often take them on a journey through the most complicated twists and turns of reasoning to a conclusion that finished up meaning the exact opposite of what they thought they had initially read! This was also a favourite game of Dilly's. He would often say that 'Nonsense could always be unravelled by logic'. The 'clock question' mentioned in this song was one of Dilly's favourite puzzles which he would often pose to visitors to the cottage.

Throughout his code breaking career, Dilly had always loved to use rhyme and meter in verses as a way of prompting trains of thought, and the girls loved him for it and found that it inspired them in their work. It made the hours and hours of poring over the daily Enigma riddles far more interesting. Dilly's approach to the Abwher Enigma was to be no different.

Dilly knew that the Abwher indicator settings were defined in a key-block of eight letters, and he set about devising a procedure to break this 'unknown' Enigma. He formed chains of the letters within the key-block as 1-5, 2-6, 3-7 and 4-8. Dilly was looking for a day when the letter chains in adjacent positions were related, and when he found such an occurrence, he announced that this was to be called a 'crab' on the account that 'things moved sideways' through the chains.

This 'crab' had told him that in a single day's key-block – or indicator settings – all three wheels and the reflector had turned over between the first two letters of the key and again in its repeat position, and from this Dilly was able to deduce a number of things: that the Abwher Enigma had three wheels and a rotating reflector, that sometimes all four turned at the same time producing a 'crab', that the wheels had many turnover positions (else 'crabs' would be rare), and that it had a 'QWERTZU' diagonal (otherwise Dilly's chains would have failed).

Dilly now knew that he was dealing with a multi-turnover Enigma machine, i.e. one where any of the wheels and reflector could turn at any time, and where sometimes all four would turn together. The fact that the wheels had multiple turnover triggers rather than just one was potentially the biggest problem to overcome.

Fortunately, the Abwher Enigma did not employ a plug-board, and it was always a mystery to Dilly as to why the Germans had not included this additional level of security, but it was a big relief that they had not.

....

'A lonely crab's our lobster and the key!'

Dilly knew that it must be possible for the three wheels and the reflector to rotate without the same event happening four positions later, and this he decided was half a 'crab', or named in its own right, a 'lobster'. He realised that this isolated turnover event would be the key to breaking Abwher Enigma and so everyone in the cottage was sent on a 'lobster' hunt.

In our song the girls sing about the cottage becoming their 'Wonderland' in tribute to Dilly and his love of Lewis Carroll as they go on the search to find Dilly his 'lobster'. Mavis later wrote in her biography of Dilly that 'it was a real Wonderland situation when lobsters, starfish and beetles could all be coaxed to join the dance!'

. . . .

'Mavis has cracked it, she broke a message, and from then on we were in!'

The wiring of the wheels was discovered via Dilly's 'lobstering' method, and the first Abwher Enigma message was broken on the 8th December 1941 by Mavis, which was coincidentally the day the Americans joined the war.

Mavis had spotted a repeated sequence across several messages and made a great guess that one of the Abwher operators had a girlfriend called Rosa and that he liked to use her name as the indicator settings.

A rewired Abwher was then broken by Margaret when she spotted that a short message was being sent at the same time every day and that it was a weather report.

All the girls in the cottage were to play a crucial role in the Abwher success, and Dilly stressed this in his report to Denniston after that first message was broken by Mavis.

The message that Denniston dictates to Menzies in our show was the actual text of the message sent to MI6 after the Abwher breakthrough.

. . . .

'ISK was now THE brand'

When Mavis broke that first Abwher Enigma message, Dilly's Enigma research section in the cottage consisted of Dilly and 17 girls, only two of whom were linguists. Their success in breaking Abwher Enigma led to a new section being formed at Bletchley on Christmas Day 1941 which would be known as 'Intelligence Services Knox', or ISK.

By the spring of 1942 MI6 knew that it now controlled all German agents currently operating in Britain, and the Abwher messages confirmed that German High Command believed the controlled intelligence that these double agents were feeding back.

By the end of the war ISK had more than 100 staff, had moved to its own hut, and had deciphered more than 140,800 messages.

The official history of the Abwher Enigma and the encryption methods used to break it was recorded in a paper later written by Mavis, Keith,

Margaret and Peter Twinn, which was then published under authors 'Batey, Batey, Rock and Twinn'. There was a long running joke at GCHQ that this sounded like a firm of solicitors from the Home Counties!

The Abwher Enigma would be for evermore known as the 'Lobster Enigma'.

Dilly's Girls (Part 3)

. . . .

'A note has just come in from the Commander,
it says here that our Dilly's taken ill'

The Cottage receives word that Dilly is ill and will not be coming to Bletchley any time soon. Dilly had been diagnosed with lymphatic cancer just before the Warsaw conference back in July 1939.

. . . .

'He'll continue working from his home'

By the time Abwher Enigma had been broken and ISK had been set up, Dilly's failing health was clear for everyone to see, and soon he had no choice but to stay at Courns Wood and work from home, with just the occasional visit to Bletchley.

. . . .

'Margaret's gone to work with him at Courns Wood'

Margaret herself was taken very ill in January and was away from work for several months, but apart from this period she was to spend the remainder of Dilly's life working with him on Russian codes and other intelligence at Courns Wood.

. . . .

'Mavis is now in charge here at the cottage'

In February 1942 Denniston was replaced as the head of Bletchley Park by Edward 'Jumbo' Travis.

Denniston's fate was probably sealed by the letter sent to Churchill the previous October by Turing, Welchman, Alexander and Milner-Barry. Churchill had known Denniston since the Room-40 days and had personally requested him as head of GC&CS, but it must have been impossible to overlook the fact that the four codebreakers had felt the need to go behind Denniston's back and write to the Prime Minister directly. Given Churchill's 'action this day' response, poor Denniston's position at Bletchley Park was now untenable.

On 13th February 1942 Peter Twinn was told to regard himself as in charge of the ISK section and the cottage until Dilly's return, and John Tiltman was made Bletchley's Chief Cryptographer replacing Dilly in this position.

Atlantic Convoy

DILLY AND MARGARET HAVE come back to Bletchley to visit the team in the cottage, and to show them the code books that were recovered by HMS Petard which everyone hopes will allow Alan Turing and his team to break into the German Naval Enigma known as 'Shark'.

This is, of course, an imagined scene. However, any musical about the codebreakers at Bletchley Park must include an account of the development of Turing's Bombe machines and the important role they played in the daily breaking of Enigma keys, and in particular how they were used to eventually break German Naval Enigma traffic and secure victory in the Battle of the Atlantic.

Today, Bletchley Park has a special display dedicated to the recovery of the codebooks by three sailors from HMS Petard. It was a story that struck me more than any other when I first visited Bletchley Park. I had never heard this account before and was in total awe of the bravery and sacrifice of these men. There must be countless such acts of heroism that happened throughout the war, many of which went unrecorded. I wanted their story told in this Bletchley-based musical.

. . . .

'Not planes, but ships, this one was fought at sea'

Churchill would write years later that the Battle of the Atlantic was the only campaign of the war that truly gave him sleepless nights. Of course, this was written after the war, and he was known for the odd exaggeration to make his point, but he knew at the time that Britain's survival depended on victory in the Atlantic.

The convoys from America were our lifeline, bringing food, oil, steel, armaments, and other critical supplies without which Britain would have starved and been unable to continue the fight against Nazism. Apart from this trans-Atlantic supply chain, Britain was truly alone in 1940.

Twelve months earlier the US Ambassador in London, Joseph Kennedy, had argued strongly against the US providing economic and military aid to the British, telling his president that in his opinion the British Isles were lost and that 'democracy was finished in the United Kingdom'. Fortunately, these views were out of step with President Roosevelt's policies, and for the time being at least the convoys continued.

. . . .

'Alan Turing'

It was during the first conference with the Polish codebreakers in Paris that Commander Denniston realised the important role that mathematicians would come to play in the breaking of the Enigma code. The achievements of the three Polish mathematicians had been truly remarkable.

On returning from Paris Denniston set off on a GC&CS recruitment drive during which he visited many of the Oxford and Cambridge colleges, where he spoke to many of his former colleagues while on the lookout for new talent, not only in the humanities subjects but also in mathematics.

It is fair to say that Alan Turing, like many of the other top mathematicians, was particularly attracted to the complexities and challenge of the Enigma problem, and he attended one of the first code and cipher training courses that Denniston had organised. After the course he was added to an emergency list to be contacted in the event of war breaking out.

Turing was also invited to visit Dilly's Enigma section, where the two men immediately hit it off and became friends.

On returning home from the Warsaw conference in July 1939 Dilly's first thought was to contact Turing, and Alan went to visit Dilly at his home Courns Wood. Dilly was an accomplished mathematician himself, and after seeing what the Polish mathematicians had achieved, he believed that the 'QWERTZU' problem could have been solved using maths. Rejewski had used Permutation Theory to develop their Enigma solution, but Dilly felt that this was not practical for code breaking going forward, and Turing agreed.

Both Dilly and Turing also agreed that the Polish electro-mechanical 'Bomby' machine was the way forward to facilitate the mass breaking of Enigma message keys, but that the Polish design could be improved upon.

Dilly allowed Turing to take a sample Enigma message back to King's in Cambridge so that he would be able to work on the problem during the summer. Turing locked himself away in his room and began his Enigma work back at King's until he was finally called to join Dilly's section in the cottage in September 1939.

Once at Bletchley Turing decided to take on the problem of the German Naval Enigma, mainly because no one else was dealing with it at the time and he liked to work alone. He took himself off to one of the stable lofts near the cottage where he would stay all day long, and the girls in the cottage would have to take him his lunch and send it up to him via a pulley system.

Turing began where the Poles had left off, and by this point he was armed with all the Polish 'Bomby' design drawings and documents that had arrived at Bletchley from Warsaw via France.

Frank Birch, Dilly's old friend, was in charge of the German Naval section at Bletchley. Dilly felt strongly that this section should have been given to Turing, but Alan was not concerned, and he spent the first months up in his stable loft or in Bletchley's old plum shed, which Dilly had organised for him to use as his workshop, working on his designs for a new improved version of the 'Bomby' and on techniques for solving the complex naval indicator system.

. . . .

'The German Navy Enigma was more complex than the rest'

At this early stage of the war the Germans had two daily settings for their Naval Enigma, one for home waters and one for foreign waters.

Since there was little or no traffic coming in for the latter, Turing focused his attention on the 'home' settings, which had been labelled 'Dolphin Enigma' at Bletchley.

It was during those last few months of 1939 that Turing managed to work out why the naval Dolphin Enigma was proving so hard to unravel, and this was because Dolphin operators encrypted the starting position of the wheels twice, once via Enigma and then again by hand via a bigram table.

Bigrams tables were issued to all naval Enigma operators and consisted of pages of letter pairings which were to be used in the encryption process, and which would often be valid for many months at a time.

In our previous Enigma example we had an indicator-setting of 'DJD', which represented the initial position of the three wheels.

With the three wheels positioned as per the indicator-setting, the chosen text-setting, 'AXB' for example, was then typed twice, which in our imagined example encrypted as 'VADTYE' and this was then transmitted as the indicator in the message.

Under Dolphin, however, the indicator would be further encrypted via the bigram tables. The three pairs of letters, 'VT', 'AY' and 'DE' would be translated via the bigram table.

By now the German naval section at Bletchley was operating in two parts. Frank Birch and his team were busy generating what they considered to be quality cribs, which were text strings that the codebreakers believed, would exist in the messages. Alan had been joined by Peter Twinn in Hut 4, but they knew that without a pinch of the bigram tables from the enemy there could be little progress on resolving the German Naval Enigma no matter how good any cribs may be.

Meanwhile, the development of Turing's version of the Polish 'Bomby', which he now called the 'Bombe', was going well.

His machine would test the encrypted Enigma messages against the cribs and would automatically narrow down the possibilities for the keys, the settings and the wheel orders. Menzies had agreed to the funding of £100,000 for the first Bombes to be made, and the contract for the manufacture of these was given to the British Tabulating Machinery Company, based in Letchworth.

Over the next year or so there followed a series of frustrations, breakthroughs, disappointments and lots of tension.

In December 1939 Turing was able to work out the indicator-settings for five days' worth of pre-war messages.

In February 1940 there was a key 'pinch' when U-Boat U33 was sunk, and two wartime naval Enigma wheels were captured.

In March 1940 the first Bombe arrived at Bletchley and was named 'Victory'.

On 26th April 1940 HMS Griffin captured a German Navy patrol boat and the crew were able to retrieve some Enigma cipher tables. Sadly, the patrol boat was looted by British sailors looking for trophies when it was brought back to port, and the resulting Enigma haul was much less fruitful than it could have been.

Turing now knew how the naval indicating system worked and with the captured tables and cribs for messages sent on the 25th and 26th April he was able to use Victory to find the keys. But it took the Bombe two weeks to return the answers.

Gordon Welchman devised an enhancement to speed up the Bombe, but his 'Diagonal' would not be introduced on new Bombes until August.

The whole second half of 1940 produced very little progress on the German Naval Enigma.

....

'Like hungry wolves they always operate in packs'

After the fall of France, the U-Boats now had bases all along the French Atlantic coast, making it even easier for them to wreak their havoc on allied shipping convoys. The U-Boats began to make use of the 'wolf-pack' tactic, which had been devised by their commander in chief, Admiral Karl Donitz.

. . . .

'They had broken all our codes, so it didn't take much time, before they were set ready to attack!'

To make matters even worse, the German Navy had broken the British Merchant Navy code and so knew the positions of all the British convoys.

. . . .

'German U-Boats all lined up, right along those shipping lines'

The U-Boats would all line up north-south along the shipping routes and as soon as contact was made with a British convoy a signal would be sent allowing U-Boats to group together and home-in on the target. Once all the U-Boats were assembled they would pounce.

In June 1940 Turing and Twinn moved into Hut 8, where they were soon joined by Tony Kendrick and Joan Clarke.

Between June and October 1940 hundreds of allied ships were sunk. Surviving ships could not stop to help sailors in the sea through fear of being hit themselves. Convoy veterans remember seeing ships hit by the U-Boats, and then the stricken crews having to throw themselves overboard to escape the carnage. Sailors in the sea were visible initially only by the small lights on their lifejackets as they rode the crest of a wave only to disappear back down into the swell.

These stranded sailors in the water would wave, shout out and cheer as the other ships approached, only for their cheers to turn to cries of despair as they watched them sail on past. The men on board could only stand and watch this desperate scene, knowing that they would now be haunted forever.

Bletchley had to break into Dolphin, and fast.

Birch's team continued to provide endless cribs, but Turing insisted that they needed more 'pinches' from the enemy, and that cribs alone were not enough. Tensions were rising between the huts at Bletchley.

Naval Intelligence Division was desperate to break into Dolphin, and its director, Rear-Admiral John Godfrey, set up an organisation to arrange pinches, which would be headed up by Lieutenant-Commander Ian Fleming of future James Bond fame.

Fleming devised an ingenious and daring plan which he named Operation Ruthless. A team would disguise themselves as a German bomber crew, and then using a captured German plane would fly up and join Luftwaffe bombing mission on its way home after a raid. It would then set an engine on fire and make a crash landing in the sea near a targeted enemy patrol boat. When the boat moved in to rescue the crew, the British team would overpower the German crew and sail the boat back to Britain, complete with all its code books. Sadly, for Bletchley, although a team was assembled and a plane was found, a suitable German patrol boat was never spotted, and the plan had to be shelved.

In August 1940 two new Bombes arrived at Bletchley, both with the Welchman 'diagonal' enhancement. But these were utilised by Hut 6 for German Air Force and Army traffic since there was little chance of breaking the naval code.

Month after month passed by, and it was not until March 1941 that the next breakthrough came, when British commandos captured the Dolphin key tables for February from a German armed trawler. This pinch enabled Hut 8 to read the February messages that were intercepted and some in April, but none were broken in real-time. However, it did enable the Hut 8 team to reconstruct the bigram tables that were in use at that time.

Meantime the RAF was roped in to trying to help via the introduction of a strategy known as 'gardening'. Planes would drop mines into specific parts of the North Sea which the Germans would locate and then report via Enigma. The locations were carefully chosen so that the grid references contained no numbers for which the Germans had more than one way of spelling. All this helped to generate cribs.

. . . .

'We prayed to get some luck, and then
it came with U-Boat U11—Zero!'

May and June 1941 saw three crucial pinches which enabled the codebreakers to break the Dolphin messages through June and July.

Early in May the weather ship Munchen was captured, giving up the settings for June. A few days later U-Boat U-110 was forced to surface off Iceland providing even more Enigma material. Then finally at the end of June a second weather ship, Lauenberg, was captured, giving Hut 8 the settings for July.

Having broken Dolphin for these months, Bletchley now had a huge library of solid cribs which allowed Dolphin to be broken right through to the end of the war.

Turing was still working on reducing the Bombe time needed to solve the daily keys. The Bombes could test all possible positions on a given single wheel in about 20 minutes, but to test all combinations of possible wheel orders would take nearly five days.

Turing devised a method of cutting down the number of possibilities for the wheel orders which was named 'Banburismus', after the long strips of paper involved in the procedure, which were printed in Banbury.

A Banburismus section was set up in Hut 8. Here the intercepted messages were punched into the Banbury sheets, which would then be compared, and the codebreakers would then look for points in a number of messages where the sequence of the Enigma machine repeated. This would indicate that the same German word had been encoded in both messages. The aim was to cut down the number of possible wheel orders from 336 to approximately 20, cutting Bombe time down to six hours and 40 minutes for each run.

Hut 8 was now divided into four sections, the registration room where traffic arrived and was sorted, the Banburismus room, the crib room, and the 'Big' room which housed the punch and Type-X machines.

The impact of Bletchley being able to break Dolphin was massive. Between March and June 1941 approximately 282,000 tons of shipping was sunk by the U-Boats every month. In July this dropped to 120,000 and by November it was just 62,000 tons.

. . . .

'But early on in '42, this all came to an end.
Shark replaced Dolphin, 3 rotors became 4'

Admiral Donitz was concerned that the Naval Enigma may have been broken and despite being assured that Enigma was unbreakable he insisted on a modification. This resulted in a new reflector being introduced which not only had different wiring but could also crucially be manually moved just like the existing three wheels. The Enigma effectively now had four rotors.

In February 1942, just as Denniston was being replaced by Travis and Dilly was resigned to having to work from home because of his cancer, the U-Boats introduced the new 4-wheel Enigma which became known at Bletchley as 'Shark'.

. . . .

'Convoys were at the mercy of
those submarines once more!'

With its additional wheel, Shark Enigma ruled out the use of Banburismus and the U-Boats could no longer be tracked. The convoys were once again at the mercy of the U-Boat wolf packs.

Fortunately for Britain, the spring of 1942 saw Donitz turn his attention to the eastern seaboard of the United States where, during three months alone, the U-Boats sank 1.25 million tons of shipping. However, when the US introduced a new submarine tracking system, he once again made the North Atlantic his target, and in August 1942 resumed attacks on the precious British convoys.

Eighty-six U-Boats, four times as many as before, located a third of the 63 convoys that sailed during August and September sinking more than 40 ships. More than 400,000 tons of shipping was sent to the bottom of the ocean during September, and another 620,000 tons in October.

The eventual Shark Enigma breakthrough was triggered by an event not in the Atlantic, but in the Mediterranean Sea. It involved a story of bravery and self sacrifice which I heard of for the first time when I visited Bletchley Park and saw the very moving tribute to the three sailors involved. I just had to include a song in the musical which recalled the events of 30th October 1942.

....

'Three hero sailors knew that this could be our chance!'

It was on 30th October 1942 that a Sunderland Flying Boat reported the sighting of a U-Boat about 70 miles north of the Egyptian city of Port Said.

HMS Petard, a P-class destroyer, was in the waters off Port Said on its way to relieve HMS Hero and was instructed to investigate the U-Boat sighting with another destroyer, HMS Pakenham, and two escort destroyers, Dulverton and Hurworth.

The U-Boat was located, and ten hours of ferocious depth charging followed. The U-Boat captain took every evasive measure he could think of, travelling more than 30 miles and diving down to suicidal depths to try and avoid the explosions. But the crew on Petard used an old trick of jamming soap into the aperture of the depth charge detonator to cause it to explode at a deeper depth, and the U-Boat was forced to the surface.

Once on the surface U-559 came under heavy fire from Petard, and the German crew had no choice but to abandon ship and began swimming over toward the British ships which had lowered nets to bring the stricken enemy sailors aboard.

....

'That night three men dived in the sea, and swam toward the enemy'

Meantime one of Petard's whaler row boats had been launched and was heading over toward the submarine. The British knew that the U-Boat captain would have ordered the opening of the seacocks and that it was only a matter of time before the submarine would sink. Wanting to get over as quickly as possible, two of Petard's men stripped off, dived into the sea, and swam over to the submarine.

First Lieutenant Anthony Fasson and Able Seaman Colin Grazier swam past the fleeing Germans and boarded the U-Boat. By the time they had swum the 60 yards to the submarine, only its conning tower was visible above the sea. The two men climbed down into the dark and waded through the rising water, making their way to the captain's cabin where they began the search for codebooks and documents. They smashed open cupboards with a machine gun and when they found a set of keys were able to open some of the locked drawers.

....

'Young Tommy Brown, was just sixteen years old'

They were soon followed by Tommy Brown who was able to step over to the submarine when the deck of the whaler, which had now reached the U-Boat, was level with the conning tower.

Tommy was just 16 years old and was a NAFFI canteen assistant aboard Petard. He climbed down the tower after his two friends.

....

'Three times in all young Tommy made this trip!'

Fasson and Grazier handed their priceless findings to Tommy and he made three trips back up the tower, passing the codebooks to the men on the rowboat.

....

'Then Tommy called down to his friends'

After his third trip back up the tower Tommy felt the U-Boat lurch and shudder and he turned to shout back down the tower to get out now!

....

'The sea rushed past him down the tower'

Tommy saw the faces of Fasson and Grazier appear at the bottom of the tower when there was a sudden flood of water over the bulkhead, and just as his shipmates had started to climb toward him the submarine went under.

. . . .

'Just like his friends he almost drowned'

Tommy was also pulled down under the water but somehow managed to kick his way back to the surface where he was dragged exhausted aboard the whaler. Fasson and Grazier were never seen again.

The codebooks, a Short Weather Cipher and a Short Signal Book, arrived at Bletchley Park on the 24th November 1942. These books provided Hut 8 with the information they needed to break Shark Enigma, meaning that the Atlantic convoy lifeline was assured.

Both Fasson and Grazier were awarded the George Cross medal, the highest possible award for bravery when not under direct enemy fire.

Young Tommy Brown was promoted to Senior Canteen Assistant immediately after the incident, but when his age was discovered, he was sent back home to North Shields. Tommy had lied about his age when he joined the NAFFI at the age of 15. He would later go back to sea on HMS Belfast.

Tommy sadly died in 1945 while trying to rescue his four-year-old sister from a house fire.

Tommy Brown's part in the recovery of those vital documents was also recognised when he was later awarded the George Medal for his bravery.

The secret nature of the work at Bletchley Park and of those documents snatched from the sinking U-Boat meant that nobody could know the real story behind the bravery of these three young men until many years later.

A wonderful memorial to the three sailors was unveiled in October 2002 to coincide with the 60th anniversary of that fateful night. It now stands proudly in Grazier's hometown of Tamworth and takes the form of three anchors linked by chains. Three shipmates now forever linked by their heroic actions.

The Bombe Song

MARGARET, MAVIS AND SOME of the other girls from the cottage are asked to help out in Hut 11 during the first attempt to decipher the latest German 'Shark' Enigma on Turing's Bombe machine. It takes a few false starts but then success!

....

'Oh it's our Bombe with an 'E',
Alan Turing's legacy'

Without a doubt the highlight of my first visit to Bletchley Park was the demonstration of a replica Bombe machine in Block B. I could only stand and marvel at the incredible achievement of the team that had managed to recreate this amazing machine. It had taken 12 years of work by a dedicated team of enthusiasts to build the Bombe based on thousands of drawings and documents that were released by GCHQ 40 years after the end of the war. At one point more than 60 volunteers were involved in the project. A few original parts were sourced but most had to be manufactured, including more than 200 drums.

Two Bletchley Park experts demonstrated each of the code breaking stages; from the working out of a crib through to the final Bombe 'stop'.

The Bombe had been positioned so that visitors could walk right around it as the drums clicked round, allowing all to marvel at the skill it must have taken to build this electro-mechanical wonder, and to also appreciate the genius of its design.

Turing's Bombe machines were originally built in Letchworth by the British Tabulating Machine Company, and credit must also be given to the engineering skills of a man call Harold Keen who was able to turn Turing's designs into a reality. Each Bombe stood encased in a bronze-coloured cabinet about eight feet high and seven feet wide. These were electro-mechanical machines with a mass of wires, cables, gears and electric connections complemented by an array of inter-connecting crankshafts, levers and other intricate moving parts.

• • • • • • • • • • • • • • • • •

'Watch closely what the Wrens do!'

The Bombe machines were mainly operated by members of the WRNS, the Women's Royal Naval Service, more commonly and officially known as the Wrens.

Many of the ladies had applied to become a Wren with dreams of a life at sea and of perhaps marrying a sailor. There is no doubt that the posters showing the girls in the smart, crisp, glamorous uniforms also appealed.

After enrolment, two weeks were spent at Naval College learning all about Royal Navy etiquette, the varied duties, endless drill and lots of marching.

Finally, posting assignments arrived, and many new recruits found themselves on trains heading for a place called Bletchley, which, they were soon to discover, was nowhere near the sea!

• • • • • • • • • • • • • • • • •

'A day of toil. The smell of oil. Suffering with the heat from the electric coils.'

Although the machines were serviced by RAF engineers, the Wrens were responsible for the maintenance of some parts; in particular they were responsible for ensuring that all the drums were correctly adjusted and that all the electrical connections were sound. This often involved making meticulous adjustments with a pair of tweezers.

Two requirements of the ladies working these machines were that they were tall and had excellent eyesight.

The machines were noisy when running and so there was little chance of conversation during the day. Hours were spent up on their feet and the levels of concentration needed were high when loading the drums and plugging the back of the Bombe before each run.

....

'It's another day of pressure on an 8-hour shift.'

The Bombe operators worked through a shift pattern which was similar to the shifts in other areas of the Park. For the Wrens, the shift operated over a four-week cycle or, in Royal Navy terms, a four week 'watch'.

During the first three weeks the girls worked a week of an 8am until 4pm shift, followed by a week of 4pm until midnight, and then a week of midnight until 8am.

The final week involved three frantic days of eight hours on, then eight hours off, and finally a desperately needed four-day break away from all the pressure and noise before the Bombe watch would start all over again.

....

'The process to identify potential initial positions for the rotor cores has begun'

The Bombe machines did not decipher Enigma messages. Work had to be done before the machines were started and then again after they stopped before intercepted messages could be read.

The Bombes established which of the Enigma wheels – rotors – had been selected by the German Enigma operator, and the order in which they had been loaded into the Enigma machine. They then found the starting position of each of the rotors by trying out each of the possible combinations in turn.

However, the Bombes only identified one of the plug-board settings. They did not establish the remaining nine plug-board settings.

When a Bombe stopped running – known as a 'stop' – it meant that it had found a potential start position for the rotors. Each potential result had to then be checked.

• • • • • • • • • • • • • • • •

'Each Bombe is set with coloured drums'

The Wrens would load the front of a Bombe with a number of coloured drums, each drum being about five inches in diameter and three inches deep. These drums replicated the internal wiring of the different Enigma rotors, and these different wirings were identified by the different colours of the Bombe drums. Two sets of wiring were built into each drum to imitate the effect of the reflector inside an Enigma machine, i.e. there were always two electrical routes through a drum just as current would flow through an Enigma rotor twice.

When fully loaded with drums the front of a Bombe was a mass of colour, as each machine could facilitate 36 sets of three drums and an additional set of three drums on the right-hand side which were known as the indicator drums. The indicator drums were read on a 'stop' to get the resulting Enigma indicator settings.

Each set of three drums replicated an Enigma machine. The three drums of each drum-set were loaded up one above the other on the front of the Bombe. These drum sets sat in three rows of 12 sets across the Bombe.

Around the edge of each drum were the letters of the alphabet, just as per the actual Enigma rotors (though some Enigma rotors did display numbers instead of letters).

It took about one second for the Bombe to spin the first drum in each set and test each letter. Once all 26 letters had been tested on the first drum the second drum in the set would click round one position, and so on.

. . . .

'Codebreakers try to find a crib,
that's text hidden in the message'

'Cribs' were the key to breaking Enigma and were the first step in the usage of Bombes to crack the enciphered messages. A crib was simply a codebreaker's guess at the content of a given message. The Bombe would then test the validity of this guess. Cribs would exploit the Enigma weakness that no letter could be enciphered as itself.

For example, the codebreaker might think that the text 'Nothing to report' – in German 'Nichts zu berichten' -–is in a particular message. Although this message is unlikely to be significant for its content, its importance might be that it is just the message the codebreakers need in order to discover that day's Enigma settings.

If this text were in the message then it would appear as follows, where Xs are used to mark the blank spaces:

Crib	N	I	C	H	T	S	X	Z	U	X

Crib	B	E	R	I	C	H	T	E	N

The codebreaker would line the crib up below the actual encoded text of the message to see if there is a position where it might fit. This is illustrated below where the bottom row represents the crib, the middle row the enciphered message, and the top row has been included simply as a position reference:

Posn	1	2	3	4	5	6	7	8	9	10
Msg	X	O	C	P	N	E	O	V	B	D
Crib	N	I	C	H	T	S	X	Z	U	X

Posn	11	12	13	14	15	16	17	18	19	
Msg	H	P	R	T	F	Z	R	O	S	T
Crib	B	E	R	I	C	H	T	E	N	

The above attempt is invalid because there are two places that break the reciprocal Enigma rule, i.e. that no letter can map to itself. In position '3' the letter 'C' appears mapping to itself, and the same for 'R' in position '13'.

So, the codebreaker would continue to slide the crib up and down the message text to see if there is anywhere that the guess might fit.

Sliding the crib one place to the right would line up the letters as below:

Posn		1	2	3	4	5	6	7	8	9	10
Msg	X	O	C	P	N	E	O	V	B	D	H
Crib		N	I	C	H	T	S	X	Z	U	X

Posn	11	12	13	14	15	16	17	18	19
Msg	P	R	T	F	Z	R	O	S	T
Crib	B	E	R	I	C	H	T	E	N

Now the codebreaker can see that none of the letters in the crib map to themselves in the message, meaning that this could be a potential fit.

• • • • • • • • • • • • • • • • •

'Then write a program for the Bombe,
MENU to what success is!'

The next step for the codebreaker would be to construct a 'Menu' from the crib, and it is the menu that would then be passed on to the Wrens operating the Bombes.

In order to construct a menu, the codebreaker would look for 'loops' of letters in the crib, where mappings of letters can be joined together at different points in the crib. The more loops there were in the resulting menu the better.

A simple loop can be seen in the above set of mappings: 'C' maps to 'P' at position '3', 'P' to 'B' at '11', 'B' to 'Z' at position '8' and then 'Z' back to 'C' at '15'. This would be written out in a grid form by the codebreaker as follows:

```
     3
 C ——— P
15|     |11
 Z ——— B
     8
```

The chance that any given menu might be successful depended on how reliable the crib was (does the guessed at text actually appear in the Enigma message?) and also on how compact the menu itself was, i.e. how many letters of the message the menu spans.

The construction of a menu relies on the wheels of the Enigma all being in the same relative position throughout the loop. However, at some point the turnover ring will activate and move the middle wheel on one letter, ruining the integrity of the menu.

The codebreakers knew that this would happen once every 26 letters, so the longer the letter-span in the menu, the more chance there would be that a turnover may have triggered.

Our simple example above spans 13 letters of the message – positions 3 to 15 – and so there is a 50/50 chance that a turnover may have taken place during this sequence.

The codebreakers would often create two menus from the same crib to reduce the risk of a turnover.

• • • • • • • • • • • • • • • •

'The operators load the drums,
and wire-up per the Menu'

The menus provided the maps that allowed the Bombe operators to connect the different sets of drums. Remember, each set of three Bombe drums is replicating an Enigma machine.

Our simple menu has been constructed around four letters and so four drum-sets would be loaded up on the Bombe.

The Bombes did not take the Enigma wheel ring settings into account, so each drum was wired as if the ring had been set to the 'Z' position. This meant that the Wrens would have to set the start positions of the drums based on the menu, with each drum-set being connected to the Bombe offset by the relative number of the letter in the crib.

So, in our example the drums in drum-set one would be set to 'C', not because it is a 'C' to 'P' mapping, but because that mapping was in the third position of the crib and 'C' is the third letter on the drum.

The drums in set two would be set to position 'K' (for 11), drum-set three to position 'H' (for 8) and finally drum-set four would be set to position 'O' (for 15).

Around the back of the Bombe the Wrens would be faced with a mass of cables. These cables were used to connect the drum-sets together. In our example the cables would be plugged so that our four drum-sets were all connected.

The more complicated menus would have several loops of letters, which could give rise to what the codebreakers called 'junction points'. A special set of connector cables at the back of the Bombe called 'commons' and labelled C1, C2 etc on the Bombe would be used to link these junctions.

Menu junctions and the special Cn common connection cables allowed a voltage to be applied to any of the 26 wires – not just the primary one being tested – and it was this that allowed the codebreakers to make an attack on the Enigma's plug-board.

A good menu would have lots of loops since this would reduce the chances of the circuit completing and thus reduce the chances of a false stop.

Menus would be labelled based on the number of letters and the number of loops in the menu. So, our first example menu would have been labelled as a '4 and 1' menu since it has 4 letters and just the one loop.

Consider our example Enigma message and crib once again. A more complex '7 and 4' menu could be constructed as follows:

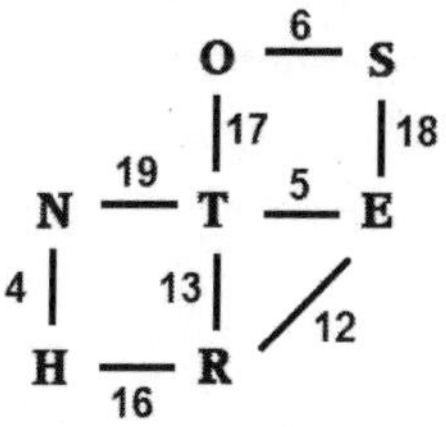

O 6 S
17 18
N 19 T 5 E
4 13 12
H 16 R

. . . .

'Sometimes they have to clean the wires,
watch closely what the Wrens do!'

Looking at the back of each individual drum you would see an array of electric contacts, and it is these that the Wrens had to carefully check when loading the Bombe.

These drum contacts would touch electrical connectors on the face of the Bombe as the drum spins around, and it was vital that the connections were good and that they precisely lined up, and that shorts did not occur midway through a Bombe run.

Great care also had to be taken to keep the cables at the back from getting tangled. The Wrens had to make sure all the electrical connections on the cables were sound and that pins did not get bent as cables were plugged and unplugged.

Settings had to be done quickly and one hundred percent accurately. Electric shocks were not uncommon!

. . . .

'We're waiting for the Bombe to stop,
a potential rotor setting'

Once the Bombe had been loaded it would be switched on and the first drums in each connected set of three would begin to spin, testing all 26 letters in about one second. Once all 26 letters had been tested on the first drum in each set, the second drum would click round one letter, and so on.

As the connected drum-sets rotated, they would be simultaneously testing the paired letters in the menu to see if they could be consistently enciphered by an Enigma machine with its wheels in the same starting position.

Note that the Bombe would not just be testing the actual letters defined in the menu, but in our second example would be testing any set of seven different letters that satisfy the configuration defined in the menu in the 17,576 possible wheel settings.

If a starting position of the wheels is a good one, then electric current would flow around the loop of connected drum-sets eventually coming out at the place where it started causing the Bombe to suddenly stop. If the current came out somewhere other than the place it started, then the Bombe would move on to test the next starting position.

Remember though that the menu relies on the fact that the wheels are in the same relative configuration for the loop, and if at some point the Enigma ring has kicked-in and turned the middle wheel, then the integrity of the menu and crib is ruined.

....

'We were heading for disaster but
Gordon Welchman made it faster'

The problem with Turing's original design for the Bombe was that it was not processing all the possible settings fast enough and also that it produced too many false 'stops' since it was not always possible to create a multi-loop menu.

Gordon Welchman came up with an idea for improving things, which was also built on the fact that an Enigma was reciprocal, i.e. if 'A' maps to 'Z' then 'Z' will map to 'A' and so on for any mapped letters. This fact would also apply to any false outputs, and crucially Welchman realised that if 'A' did map to 'Z' then any other 'A' mapping could be instantly ruled out. Thus, as soon as any single connection became 'live', then the Bombe could rule out 25 others immediately.

This modification became known as Welchman's 'diagonal' and proved to be a straightforward modification of adding a new cross-over-board to the back of each Bombe.

....

'Readings taken from the Bombe,
and then passed on for checking!'

On each Bombe 'stop' the potential settings had to be checked. It did not always follow that the 'stop' had found the correct settings.

The plug-board was the Enigma's biggest challenge, presenting the codebreakers with a vast number of potential settings, many more than the problem of the wheel settings, over hundred and fifty million million more!

There was also the question of the ring settings on the wheels, which needed to be resolved too if all the day's messages were to be read, and not just the one that had given up the crib.

The Bombe did not have a plug-board but crucially did allow the operator to choose a cross-plugging for one selected letter. This letter was selected by a series of switches on the side of the Bombe.

A special checking machine was used to confirm the Bombe results and to also work out the ring settings.

When a Bombe came to a stop, the three indicator drums on the right-hand side of the Bombe were read. These showed the operator what the start position of the Enigma wheels would have been, and this information was passed on to the Wrens operating special checking machines.

The checking machines looked like mini-Bombes, with their own single set of coloured drums.

Although the Bombe had proposed a single plug-board cross-plugging, the checking machines allowed the remaining nine plug-board settings to be established fairly easily.

The checking machine would be loaded up with the drums positioned as per the Bombe 'stop', and the Wren operating the checking machine would then manually turn the drums to the different menu positions and check the results.

....

'Now hoping for a "Job Up!" shout'

If the Bombe result all checked out, then there would be a cry of 'Job up!' and the Bombe would be stripped down and made ready for its next run.

The Bombe Song

•••••••••••••••••

'Our TYPEX beats Enigma's style'

The British had determined that Enigma was not secure enough for military use during the 1930s, and instead had developed their own mechanical enciphering machine which was called the 'Typex'.

A Typex machine could be adapted to work just like an Enigma and so was used to convert Enigma messages back into German once the Enigma settings had been established.

The Typex machine did not have a lamp-board, but instead printed out the deciphered text on a thin strip of paper.

These strips of printout were then cut and pasted onto regular sheets of paper before being passed on to the relevant intelligence department for assessment.

Missing Dilly

THE GIRLS ARE BUSY at work in the cottage as usual, battling Enigma but missing Dilly. Spirits are lifted when they hear that Dilly has been awarded the Order of St Michael and St George for chivalry. But then Betty appears with terrible news that shatters the girls.

....

'Oh it's just not the same, now that Dilly's gone'

It was Christmas 1941 when the Enigma Research Section in the cottage officially became ISK, and by this time everybody could see that Dilly had worked himself to his absolute limit. He was very ill and was really suffering. From this point forward he would continue his work from home with just the occasional visit to Bletchley.

In February 1942 Peter Twinn was told that he was to regard himself as being in charge of Dilly's ISK section. Dilly was fine with this appointment since he had worked with Twinn before and held him in high regard.

It was during one of Dilly's visits to Bletchley in February when a new Abwher machine network was discovered, which Mavis quickly broke into using Dilly's now established methods. This new network was named 'GGG' after one of the Abwher's call signs and involved German spying in the Mediterranean area.

But it was back at Courns Wood where Dilly worked on establishing a network of his own, a network of key contacts at MI5, at the Admiralty and in SIS. Dilly was determined to ensure that the intelligence being recovered by his ISK section found its way to the people that needed it, and that it was used effectively. He was also equally determined to ensure that his ISK team received all the information that they needed to run the section efficiently.

Messages were often passed on between the different German intelligence networks using different enciphering methods, and Dilly knew that the sharing of intelligence and of broken messages could provide a vital crib or some other crucial clue in another section's battle to solve their particular problem.

The ISK section was top secret, with everything being done under the cover of Strachey's ISOS section. The fact that there were actually two separate Abwher sections in operation at Bletchley was only known by a select few.

The Abwher intelligence became even more important during 1942 as Allied focus turned from a largely defensive one of survival, to one now involving invasions and landings of their own. Plans were being drawn up for an Allied invasion of North Africa, which was to be codenamed Operation Torch, and it was critical that commanders knew whether German High Command believed the false intelligence being sent back to Germany by the double agents. Abwher provided the confirmation that the Allied commanders needed; the Germans believed that the Allied fleet was heading for one of Malta, Crete or Sicily, and not for the north of Africa.

Admiral Godfrey made a point of visiting Dilly at Courns Wood as often as he could to keep Dilly informed as to how deceptions were being planned as a result of the intelligence received from ISK and Abwher, and to keep him updated on the planning for Torch which was being scheduled for the autumn.

Peter Twinn and Mavis visited Dilly regularly, and on recovering from her illness Margaret was based permanently at Courns Wood working on a problem not connected with Abwher. Mavis suspected that they were working on Russian codes, since Dilly had been heavily involved in these codes back in the 1920s.

Margaret drove Dilly back to Bletchley for visits as often as his illness would allow. As Dilly's condition grew worse, he stayed in his study working on various code breaking problems with Margaret.

. . . .

'It's cancer, it's spread,
and poor Dilly hasn't long'

As Dilly's conditioned worsened he had to be admitted to University College Hospital in London.

Mavis went to visit him there and found him and his elder brother Eddie in fits of laughter as they read the book 'The Art of Dying' together, trying to decide on what Dilly's last words might be.

. . . .

'He's been honoured by the King, awarded CMG!'

Dilly left hospital and returned home to spend his final days at Courns Wood, where Olive nursed him devotedly.

Just before his death he received notice that he was to be appointed as a Companion of the Order of St. Michael and St. George for services to his country.

Dilly insisted on getting dressed to meet the emissary sent from Buckingham Palace, and he sat shivering in front of a large log fire as he waited for the visitors to arrive. His body had wasted away, and his clothes hung loosely around him, but he stoically made it through the ceremony.

The Visit

JEAN GOES TO SEE DILLY at his home and finds herself there as he passes away. She sings sadly.

This is another imagined scene as there were no visitors from the cottage when Dilly died.

....

'There's his last breath, our Dilly has gone'

Dilly's younger brother Ronnie was at Courns Wood for Dilly's final days. Ronnie was a devout Catholic priest and spent much of his time praying for his brother. Dilly's son Oliver was also there, having been given compassionate leave to be with his father.

Dilly died at home on 27th February 1943 aged 58. His last words were 'Is that Ronnie outside in the corridor bothering God about me?'.

Naphill Wood

MAVIS HANGS DILLY'S MEDAL on the wall of The Cottage and sings about Naphill Wood. The song ends with the girls gathered around Dilly's grave in amongst his precious trees.

....

'Dilly has sent us his medal'

Dilly died just a few weeks after receiving his CMG medal, but in this time he was able to write a final letter to his girls at the cottage and send them the award saying that it was the team that had earned it. He touchingly referred to the 'traditions of the cottage' and thanked them for their 'unswerving loyalty'. But Dilly being Dilly, even in this final letter he went on to stress again his belief that it should be viewed as impossible to separate code-breaking work from the resulting intelligence.

In an old naval tradition, the letter was written in green ink on blue paper.

....

'And yours was here among the trees,
the trees of Naphill Wood'

When Dilly and Olive were first married, they moved in together with Frank Birch and his wife Vera at Number 14 Edith Grove in Chelsea, London.

But Olive quickly tired of life in London and longed for a move back to the countryside. So, in 1921 they sold some Great Western Railway shares which had been left to Dilly by his mother, and purchased Courns Wood, a lovely country house which sat in 40 acres of Chiltern woodland just a few miles from High Wycombe.

Dilly did his best to enter into the spirit of village life, and he and Olive joined in with some of the various local activities, though there was no way that Dilly could ever see himself becoming a country gentleman.

Dilly was a good tennis player and could regularly hit an un-returnable topspin forehand or backhand shot at the local tennis club parties. At bridge he and his partner usually won, since with only 52 cards Dilly could quickly calculate all the probabilities. But he did not much care for socialising with the locals and began to keep a notebook of verses he wrote about all his neighbours, some not very complimentary! His heart lay back at Cambridge with the Professors, Dons and Fellows.

So, Dilly found solace in the woodlands around Courns Wood, and during his time there planted several acres of trees himself.

As well as planting, Dilly would also cut and saw wood, building log cabins and tree houses for his boys. He also made a wooden cart with a large wheel which Christopher and Oliver would stand on as their dad pushed them along.

Olive would marvel at how creative her husband was out in the woods, and yet at the same time how he would struggle to put up a shelf that would last in the house!

....

'I remember last spring,
you asked me come stay'

Dilly invited Mavis to visit Courns Wood one weekend during his last spring as he wanted her to see the glorious cherry blossom which was in bloom out in front of the house.

By now Dilly was too weak to do any cutting or sawing in the woods, so he and Mavis spent time chatting as they shook pine seeds into tins ready to be scattered in the woods. Mavis later wrote that she learned so much about the Chiltern Woodlands that weekend, and that Dilly was still so passionate about his trees.

....

'So rest in peace our dearest friend,
for ever here you'll lay'

Dilly was laid to rest in his precious woods.

Dilly's Message

THIS IS ANOTHER IMAGINED SCENE showing a celebration and commemoration service for Dilly. When the vicar begins the prayers it all falls silent, and Dilly's ghost appears and addresses the audience.

Dilly begins his song under the Endless Hours melody. It then picks up pace as he explains how the service being portrayed on stage would never have happened due to everyone having to sign the Official Secrets Act. This leads into lots of short fun verses as he lists many of the different jobs that the women at Bletchley did, and the song finishes with all the ladies in charge of the singing.

....

'We eight thousand are the Bletchley gold!'

By January 1945 there were more than ten thousand five hundred people employed at Bletchley Park and three quarters of these were women.

Most old photographs from this time show the ladies hard at work in the huts, or the Wrens operating the Bombe machines and Colossus computers.

But there were lots of other jobs that the women did which are less well known, and some were very dangerous indeed.

Dilly's Girls

• • • • • • • • • • • • • • • •

'Dispatch riders, staff car drivers,
all weather road survivors!'

As you wander around Bletchley Park, around the back of the mansion you will find the garages, and in one of the garages there is an old 1943 Norton wartime motorcycle on display.

Up on the wall behind it there is a huge picture showing a row of lady dispatch riders all sat on their motorcycles ready to set out on another journey with the precious intelligence in their satchels.

Most of the intercepted messages that arrived at the Park during the war were delivered by dispatch rider, and most of these dispatch riders were women. More than four hundred riders would enter and then leave the Park every single day, always carrying vital messages and other top-secret documents with them.

These ladies would often have to ride hundreds of miles on a single trip, and these journeys were continually being made, 24 hours a day, seven days a week.

This was a dirty and very dangerous job.

All had to learn how to maintain their motorcycles, and to be able to patch tyres and fix chains while out on the road.

They would be riding at high speeds of up to 70 miles per hour, in all weathers, at all times of day and through the night. They would have to traverse dark country lanes in the dead of night with very little lighting allowed on the bike.

Sometimes they would be quite literally riding through a town, dodging German bombs as they fell all around them during a bombing raid.

Many of these ladies received medals for their bravery, but sadly more than one hundred of these riders lost their lives during the war.

This was such a critical role in the Bletchley story that has more often than not been forgotten.

Two Years

THE WHOLE CAST SING this song which is a tribute to everyone who worked at Bletchley and emphasises Bletchley's legacy, which historians have often said was to cut at least two years from the war.

....

'At least two years,
that's what historians will say'

Almost every article or news report on the activities of the codebreakers at Bletchley Park during the war will put forward the theory that at least two years were shaved off the duration of World War Two as a direct result of their code breaking successes.

The importance of the Battle of the Atlantic cannot be overstated, and there can be no doubt that the breaking of Dolphin and Shark Enigma had a massive impact on events at sea. Those convoys from the United States were quietly literally Britain's lifeline, and if the German U-Boats had been left with free reign to reap terror on the allied shipping that lifeline would have been cut.

This would not have just cut-off vital supplies of food, fuel and armaments, but would have also dramatically slowed the deployment of US troops to British soil, delaying any attempt to land Allied soldiers in France.

A delay to D-Day and the invasion of mainland Europe would have allowed Nazi Germany to further strengthen its defences along the coastline, making any attempt to land much harder, maybe even impossible, and certainly making it far more costly in lives.

Not only that, but such a delay would have resulted in hundreds more V2 rockets and other bombing raids being launched against Britain, and of course more Allied bombing raids over Europe, causing more mass destruction and the loss of potentially hundreds of thousands more lives.

Even with Shark broken and the Allies now having the ability to track U-Boats as a result, without the Abwher Enigma success there would have been limited ways of knowing if German High Command believed the false intelligence being past back by the double agents now controlled by the British, which clearly would have an impact on the planning and success of any invasion.

Also, if D-Day had been delayed, how would this have changed the impact of the Russian advance from the east? With no second front in the west one can only wonder how different the post-war map of Europe might have looked.

Bletchley or no Bletchley the United States would have entered the war when the Japanese attacked Pearl Harbor, and the Americans would no doubt have still ended the war with Japan by the dropping of the atomic bomb.

Maybe the atomic bomb might have then ended up being deployed over Europe, and even more terrifyingly, how close might Hitler have come to developing his own nuclear weapon?

No one can know for sure, of course, but it does seem probable that the Second World War would have ended one way or another during 1945 or early 1946. But without Ultra the cost in lives would most certainly have been massively higher.

I recall reading somewhere that seven million deaths resulted from each year of fighting in Europe. So maybe the contribution of Bletchley Park should be measured in lives saved, and this figure may well translate to about two years of actual fighting.

Finale!

SPIRITS ARE LIFTED AGAIN as we end our show with a rip-roaring rendition of the 'Bletchleyette Boogie' which is sung by the cottage team!

....

'Working that text here at Station X,
these girls are ready to strive'

The cottage ladies given their own verses in Dilly's poem 'Swollen Heads', which was written as a tribute to his team after the battle of Matapan, were: Claire, Jane, Nancy, Mavis, Margaret, Phyllida, Hilda, Jean, Mrs Balance and Elizabeth.

PART FOUR

Dilly's Girls

EPILOGUE

Epilogue

THE SATURDAY MATINEE HAD FINISHED, and the Sondheim Theatre was steadily emptying as all that afternoon's guests made their way down the stairs and out into the chilly December early evening air.

The Sondheim stands proudly on the corner of Shaftesbury Avenue and Wardour Street, and as the theatre emptied the crowd grew ever larger out on the street in what was the usual post-show electrically charged atmosphere of people laughing, chatting, and some even singing some of the songs that they had just been enjoying. This was a scene being repeated across London's West End and one that is so familiar to anyone who has a love of musical theatre.

This year had marked 85 years since the beginning of the Second World War and there had been so many anniversary tributes during the year across all forms of the media. But there had been one in particular that had caught the country's imagination.

Once the veil of secrecy around the activities at Bletchley Park during the war had begun to be lifted through the latter years of the last century, more and more details and stories from Bletchley had surfaced. Just a few years ago that final end-of-war musical which had been put on by the codebreakers in the Bletchley Assembly Hall had been rediscovered.

Frank's lyrics and Joanna's music had been found and published, and the most incredible turn of events had seen these old codebreaker's efforts adopted by the world's most famous musical producer.

The words 'Dilly's Girls' now shone out in bright lights above the theatre's main entrance, and pictures of Dilly, Mavis, Margaret, Jean and many of the other girls from the cottage, looked out onto the excited crowds from the building's windows.

Down on the street a spritely old lady gazed up at the words in lights above the doors from her wheelchair.

'Are you alright, Flo?' A man standing behind the chair leant forward and adjusted the blanket covering the old lady. 'You're not too cold, are you? Did you enjoy the show?'

The old lady did not reply. She was lost deep in thought and memories as she gazed at the lights which seemed to sparkle and dance in the cold winter air.

'Did you enjoy the show, Flo?' the carer repeated.

'Oh yes, dear, sorry, dear, yes, very much. It was wonderful, truly wonderful.'

The old lady shivered and reached up to pull her coat more snugly around her neck. Suddenly a cold panic swept through her and she began to desperately pat her coat with her hands and started to look down around her on the pavement.

'What's wrong, Flo? What's the matter now?'

'It's my pin, dear. It is my badge. I seem to have lost my badge.'

'Oh, Flo, we told you not to wear it today, didn't we?' The carer began to hunt around on the floor and in the folds of the chair. 'It will be here somewhere. Don't worry'.

The old lady suddenly felt a gloved hand touch hers and looked up to see a young girl, maybe 14 or 15 years of age, standing by her chair.

'I saw you drop this.' The girl smiled. 'I hope it's not broken.'

Flo looked up at the young lady smiling back at her. The girl had the prettiest face, with pronounced rosy cheeks and lovely short cut, wavy dark hair. It was uncanny. The girl reminded Flo so much of . . .

'Ah there you go, Flo,' the carer offered, 'I knew it wouldn't be far away.'

Flo did not answer; she was still transfixed by the young lady who was holding her hand, smiling at her.

'Your badge,' the girl continued, 'I hope it's OK. I know what it is and what it must mean to you.'

'Oh, the pin. Thank you, my dear.' Flo looked down to the girl's other hand which was held out toward her. In the middle of the woolly glove she could see her circular golden badge with the blue stone at the centre. 'Really? You know what this is?'

'Oh yes.' The girl smiled back. 'It means you were at Bletchley during the war, weren't you? It is such an honour to meet you. Did you enjoy the show? I thought it was marvellous!'

'Yes, yes I did, thank you, dear.' Flo's voice was shaking a little, and she found herself gripping the girl's hand tightly. 'Tell me, how do you know about Bletchley?'

The girl knelt down next to the wheelchair, leant in toward Flo, and whispered, 'Don't tell anyone I have told you this, but my dad works at GCHQ. He has so many books about Bletchley and I have read them all. We have visited Bletchley Park so many times. It is like my second home.

Flo meets a new friend.

I have helped out there too during the school holidays, in the gift shop. Everyone there is so friendly. I love history, but maths is my passion. I'm hoping to become a codebreaker too one day, after I've been to university.'

'Oh, my dear, that's wonderful.'

'May I ask,' the girl continued, 'did you know Dilly and the girls?'

Flo could feel tears welling up in her eyes. 'Yes, yes I did. He really was the loveliest and most brilliant man. We all adored him.'

'You were one of Dilly's Girls?'

Flo smiled. 'I was, dear, we were so lucky to have worked with Dilly in the cottage.'

The girl instinctively threw her arms around Flo and hugged her.

Flo held the girl tightly for several moments and then the girl stood back up.

'I had best go, Mum and Dad will be wondering where I have got to.' She smiled. 'But meeting you has really made my day.'

'Oh, and mine too,' Flo replied, 'it was lovely to meet you too.'

'And I'm so glad I found your pin for you.'

The girl held her hand out once more toward Flo.

Flo looked at the golden pin in the upturned hand and reached out with both her hands, but instead of taking the badge she folded the girl's fingers back around it.

'Keep it.' Flo smiled. 'And wear it for me.'

'Flo, are you sure?' her carer interjected. 'That's your special badge.'

'I can't possibly,' the girl began.

'No, please take it. I have no family of my own to give it to, and I think meeting you here today was meant to be.' Flo smiled. 'Just promise me that you'll follow your dream.'

'I will, but can I write to you perhaps?'

'Oh, that would be lovely,' Flo replied.

'Here–' the carer reached out with a card– 'this is our address. It's a care home, so just send any letters there addressed to Flo and we will make sure she gets them.'

'Thank you, I will. Are you completely sure, Flo?'

'Yes dear,' Flo answered, 'but you haven't told me your name yet.'

'I'm Mavis.' The girl smiled back. 'And I have a big sister Margaret.

Dad has always told us that we were named after the two most famous ladies at Bletchley.'

'I somehow knew it!' Flo laughed.

'Right, we must be going now Flo.' Her carer had released the brake on the chair and was beginning to manoeuvre it around. 'Say goodbye to Mavis.'

'Goodbye, my dear.'

'Goodbye, Flo, and thank you so much.'

'No, thank you!' Flo replied, waving her hand above her head as she disappeared into the West End crowd.

Mavis stood watching Flo being pushed away until she could see her no more. She felt a hand on her shoulder and looked around to see her father.

'Here you are, we were wondering where you had got to. Who was that you were talking to?' he asked.

'That was Flo, Dad,' Mavis answered, 'she was one of Dilly's Girls!'

Acknowledgements

THE INSPIRATION FOR MY Bletchley journey was one of my sons, who is an exceptional mathematician and who also shined as a talented actor, director, and producer of so many wonderful productions while he was at university studying mathematics. One of his university productions was 'Breaking the Code', which is a play about Alan Turing. Allowing his dad to help by making an Enigma machine for his production was the catalyst that sparked my interest in the wonderful story of Bletchley Park. Wanting my prop to be as accurate as possible triggered the most enjoyable period of research and reading.

Then there is the Park itself. The Bletchley Park Trust is a registered charity and runs Bletchley Park as an unfunded museum that relies on revenue generated from visitors to the park, donors and other supporters. It is the most inspiring day out, for all the family, where you will find yourself quite literally walking in the footsteps of the World War Two codebreakers as you visit the mansion, huts and blocks. The Park boasts the most impressive collection of displays, presentations and of course original buildings and artefacts from the war years, and a very informative website. But perhaps most importantly of all it also has the most wonderful group of loyal, friendly, helpful and very knowledgeable support staff, who have in my experience always been happy to chat and answer questions. It is my sincere wish to pass on any profits that might be generated by sales of this book to the trust, so that I might in some small way help to maintain this national treasure.

Acknowledgements

Thanks must go to Louise Ridley, whose article I chanced upon when first searching for information about Dilly on the Internet. It was here I first encountered Jean's story.

Thank you to my wonderful cousin Helen and my dear friend and work colleague Elaine who have both read my 'songs' and have given me so much helpful and encouraging feedback.

The words of William Blake were my inspiration for the title of the song that rounds off the first act of my fictional codebreakers's production. Blake's poem was put to music by Hubert Parry to lift the spirits of the British people during the First World War and of course includes those most famous words 'our green and pleasant land', which so perfectly reflect what the British people were fighting for during both world wars. Part of the hymn Jerusalem is also sung by the cast at the opening of the church scene.

Enigma – The wooden prop that led to this book.

I had great fun imagining the melodies for all my 'songs' in the show, but the 'Bletchleyette Boogie' in the finale has been based on the Chuck Berry song 'Roll Over Beethoven'. Written by Berry in the 1950s this rock 'n roll classic has been covered by so many bands over the years and a US military swing version just seemed to me to be the perfect way to end my musical.

Thanks also to Ruth, Jay, and everyone at UK Book Publishing for their help with my project.

Finally, a massive thank you to my other exceptional and hugely talented son for sharing with me his inside knowledge of the workings of a theatre and for also taking the time to proofread my book and provide me with such invaluable input.

Illustrations

ALTHOUGH I HAVE hand drawn all the illustrations featured in this book, some are copies of photographs I have found on the Internet.

I sincerely hope that I have not caused any offence or breached any copyright by basing some of my drawings on these pictures.

References

I MUST ALSO GIVE a massive thanks to the authors of the following books about Bletchley Park.

I have thoroughly enjoyed reading each and every one of them. Every one has been read more than once and some so many times now that my copies have become dog-eared and well worn.

These books provided me with such a comprehensive source of historical material and facts, with so many including quotes and pieces written by the actual Bletchley codebreakers themselves.

Mavis Batey	Dilly, The man who broke Enigmas
Michael Smith	The Secrets of Station X, How Bletchley Park helped win the War
Michael Smith	The Debs of Bletchley Park
F.H. Hinsley & Alan Stripp	Code Breakers, The inside story of Bletchley Park
Penelope Fitzgerald	The Knox Brothers
Mair and Gethin Russell-Jones	My Secret Life in Hut Six, One woman's experiences at Bletchley Park
Tessa Dunlop	The Bletchley Girls
Dermot Turing	Bletchley Park, Demystifying the Bombe

References

Frank Birch, Dilly Knox & G.P. Mackeson — Alice in I.D.25, A codebreaking parody of Alice's Adventures in Wonderland

Sinclair McKay — The Secret Life of Bletchley Park

Sinclair McKay — The Lost World of Bletchley Park, An illustrated history of the wartime codebreaking centre

William Blake — The hymn Jerusalem. Blake's poem was put to music by Hubert Parry to lift the spirits of the British people during the First World War and includes those most famous words 'Our green and pleasant land' which so perfectly sum up everything being fought for during both world wars.